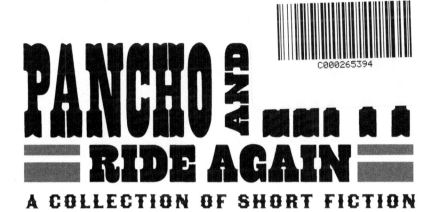

PANCHO AND LEFTY RIDE AGAIN

A COLLECTION OF SHORT FICTION

IRISHTOWN PRESS

Cónal Creedon is an award-winning novelist, playwright and documentary filmmaker.

www.conalcreedon.com

PANCHO AND LEFTY RIDE AGAIN
A COLLECTION OF SHORT FICTION

Cónal Creedon

IRISHTOWN PRESS

Published in 2021 by Irishtown Press
irishtownpress@gmail.com

© Cónal Creedon 2021

The moral right of the author has been asserted.
A catalogue record for this book is available from the British Library.

ISBN 978-0-9557644-9-3 (paperback)
ISBN 978-1-7399180-1-9 (hardcover)
ISBN 978-1-7399180-0-2 (digital)

www.corkcitylibraries.ie
One City
One Book
We are Cork.   Waterstones

Launch of *Pancho and Lefty Ride Out*. Murphy's Brewery, Cork, November 1995.
Photo: Michael MacSweeney.

I dedicate *Pancho And Lefty Ride Again* to all those who stood fast and held the invisible frontline during the darkest days of the pandemic. Those everyday people who stood up to the mark when faced with the challenges of this extraordinary time. Those who maintained a sense of calm in a time a global panic; those who held their heads when all around were losing theirs – baking bread and stockpiling toilet paper; those who became our surrogate friends, family and confidants during those extreme socially distant, anxiety-ridden months of the first Covid lockdown – the bus drivers, the supermarket staff, the coffee shop baristas, the taxi drivers and paramedics. I dedicate this book to all those men and women who maintained a sense of normality and kept this ball of dirt we call earth spinning at a time when life as we knew it had shuddered to an unprecedented and uncompromising halt.

I am very grateful to John Foley and Lisa Sheridan of Bite Design – who have been encouraging and instrumental in the bringing together of this publication. And thank you Nancy Hawkes and Aonghus Meaney for being there when the call went out – your patience and diligence is above and beyond the call of duty.

My special appreciation to those who have been a constant source of support for my endeavours – Liz Hayes, Arnolda Stankaitiene, Jill Hodge, Tony McGrath, Rachel McGovern, Siobhan O'Neill, Shirley Fehily, Birgette Jobs, John Breen, Ken Corr, Darren Hennessy, Sue Walsh, Martin Lynch and Mary McCarthy – I am blessed with so many friends, family and neighbours who continue to offer me unconditional encouragement, far too many to mention you all here by name.

And finally, to Fiona with love: fearless in the face of adversity, calm in the eye of the storm and always fun when belly laughs are thin on the ground.

Pancho And Lefty Ride Again
Acclaim and Reviews

AWARDED
ONE CITY
ONE BOOK
WWW.CORKCITYLIBRARIES.IE
CORK 2022
Waterstones

Pancho And Lefty Ride Again by Cónal Creedon – is one of six finalists in the prestigious Next Generation Book Award 2022 (USA). Next Generation Book Awards USA is the largest international awards program for independent publishers worldwide.

Recognition for Cónal Creedon's short stories
· George A. Birmingham Awards
· Francis MacManus Awards
· One Voice Awards, BBC 4
· Life Extra Awards
· P.J. O'Connor Awards [adaptation]

Fans of The Quirky Cork Radio soap, *Under The Goldie Fish* by Cónal Creedon – whose gist, according to this paper's radio critic, would make Gabriel García Márquez turn puce in a pique of jealousy – will find much to enjoy in this collection of short stories.
Tom Widger – SUNDAY TRIBUNE

Real life hops off the pages of this book which is contemporary Cork.

If you are looking for a Christmas flavour in the stories of Cónal Creedon's latest book, you will find it. But like everything else that comes from the fevered imagination which gave radio listeners the zany *Under The Goldie Fish* – it will not be what you expect. The Father Christmas in Creedon's wonderfully off-beat *Pancho And Lefty Ride Out* calls himself Santy boy in the flattest Cork accent you've ever heard. You can hear the Cork accent in many of the other stories, [all] penned in an old Volvo parked outside his No. 1 Launderette on Coburg Street, only dropping his pen to dash inside and look after his customers. Cónal describes his world of ten-spots, touts and backhanders with vivid realism which proves that observations of life on Coburg Street are as valid as observations on East 52nd.

Clodagh Finn – THE EVENING ECHO

Pancho And Lefty Ride Out successfully follows the tenet to write about what you know: in his detail of location, Creedon is to Cork what Stephen King is to Bangor, Maine. Permeating these stories is both a great love of the city and a keen awareness of the way in which its fate and that of its people within it are inextricably entwined: if its citizens take on occasional camouflage, the city itself at times seems to breathe and feel. Creedon's characters are often surprised by joy in the middle of depression, boredom and hopelessness: the drunken Nero snatches a fiddle tune out of an alcoholic stupor; middle-aged Benny joins the Rave scene; old men become heroes again for a day; the deeply depressed Pluto finds himself as reluctant assistant in the rescue of a drowning pigeon; the cleaner at an art gallery emerges as the most sensitive critic of them all; and Santa Claus turns out to be a Corkman, and a disreputable looking one at that. In particular, Creedon's visions of childhood are charming without being sentimental.

Sharon Barnes – Books – IN DUBLIN MAGAZINE

Meanwhile Cónal Creedon – for it is he – has blasted into the Gutenberg Galaxy with this publication of short fiction. Not stories by and large, but definitely fiction. Creedon is building a world between the real one and Goldie Fish, where characters are constantly testing frontiers and checking loyalties. He plays around too: in *Every Picture*

Tells A Story it takes a while inside the small art gallery before we realise that the title is literal; similarly in *Penny For Your Thoughts*.

Dialogue and dialect are strong like Mrs Crowley's tea, but the sweetness is all comic. The final story delivers a rooftop Santa to bring back all belief – it's a delight.

Mary Finn (Books Ed) – THE RTÉ GUIDE

Pancho And Lefty Ride Out, is a collection of short fiction by Cónal Creedon, who has become well known over the past few years for his surreal radio drama *Under The Goldie Fish*. Over 200 episodes of the soap have been broadcast and it has been widely praised. These stories are set in Cork and as the title suggests they are as whacky and off-beat as the soap Creedon has penned. They are written in a racy colloquial style and focus on the ordinary lives of Cork people. The characters are uniquely Cork, down to their faithfully reproduced accents [– Have ya got one that will blow the head offa me] but the situations they find themselves in are universal. You will laugh, cry and be moved in the company of Pluto, Nero, Brenda the Brasser and the tragic Paudie. *After The Ball* is a very accomplished story, stark and moving. The one Christmas story in the book, *Come Out Now, Hacker Hanley!* is about a child's encounter with Santa and, the author assures, is completely true. Creedon was born and raised in the centre of Cork City and laments its demise with eloquence.

Frank O'Donovan – THE SOUTHERN STAR

The book is good. Its slice-of-life focus and camcorder psychology display a rare honesty of intention. Amidst other adventures the main protagonist/perpetrator surveys the loss of his wife/best friend/mistress/adoptive family quietly through the bottom of a glass of homebrew. This is a Corkman at home in his world; a desperate heroic character riddled with Dostoyevskian self-delusion/self-analysis. Say no more boy.

Brendan Lucey (Books Ed) – THE LIST

Fans of Cónal Creedon's daily drama series on RTÉ won't be disappointed by his first published work. They may be surprised, however, for the collection reveals much more than just a talent for irreverence. Some pieces are sad, others thought-provoking, all show a gift for observation and an awareness of the nuances of speech. *Pancho And Lefty Ride Out*, shows his diverse talent – his sense of humour, his compassion and his great gift for observation.

Tina Neylon (Books Ed) – THE IRISH EXAMINER

Consistently layered with meaning, each well-crafted story gives pause for reflection, making this a book to be savoured and reread. The collection presents a motley crew of beguiling, sometimes funny, sometimes tragic characters all set in a world which is swiftly passing. The impact of the characters are visceral and charged. Some of the stories will bring you to tears. A golden thread of humour weaves its way throughout the book too and many of the stories are quite frankly hilarious. There are multi-faceted meanings in his zesty prose as his characters drink, dance, go shopping, hide under duvets in grubby bedsits, nurse broken hearts, and grapple to stay afloat in a constantly changing world.

Aisling Meath – THE EVENING ECHO

Finished it the other night. Thoroughly enjoyed it. If Cork ever suffered a severe earthquake they could reconstruct the city and its denizens from the writings of Mr Conal Creedon.

Danny Morrison – WEST BELFAST FESTIVAL

Conal Creedon is an Award Winning novelist, his writing taps into the power, passion and glory of the Second City's streets and neighbourhoods.

Donal O'Donaghue (Books Ed) – RTÉ GUIDE

What can you say about Cónal? Documentarian, playwright, film-maker, He's such a gifted writer, so evocative and lyrical, and he's Cork to the core. Thoroughly recommended.

John Breen/Donal O'Keeffe – ECHO LIVE

Anthologies

Cónal's short fiction has featured in numerous literary journals and has been widely anthologised including: [incomplete list]

- *Crisis and Comeback: Cork In The Eighties,* The Collins Press. Cork, Ireland
- *81 Sprüche Zur Enthärtung Unserer Welt* – Berlin, Germany
- *Cork Review* – Cork, Ireland
- *Beijing – Millennium Edition.* Beijing, China
- *Painted Bride Quarterly* – USA
- *Volume* – CWPC – Cork, Ireland
- *Atlantic Currents* – USA
- *Cork Literary Review. vol. XIV* – Cork, Ireland
- *Cork Literary Review. vol. XVI* – Cork, Ireland
- *An Éire of Senses – Irish Contemporary Art World Expo* – Shanghai, China
- *CORK Europa Erlesen* – Berlin, Germany
- *The Elysian: Creative Responses* – Cork, Ireland
- *Southword. vol. 3 – No. 2* – Cork, Ireland
- *Kunappi: Post-Colonial Writing* – University of Leeds, UK
- *Quarryman* – UCC, Cork, Ireland
- *Mother Tongue in a Foreign Land* – Shanghai, China
- *Cornerstone* – UCC, Cork, Ireland
- *Shanghai Writers' Association Magazine* – Shanghai, China
- *Motley 5* – UCC, Cork, Ireland
- *Eine Kulinarische Reise durch die Irische Literatur* – Berlin, Germany
- *Studi Irelandesi, Journal of Irish Studies* – Florence University Press, Italy

CONTENTS

* *Come Out Now, Hacker Hanley!* is autobiographical.
The events and characters in Come Out Now, Hacker Hanley! are true and accurate
in every detail, to the best of my recollection.

Cónal Creedon with Finbarr the dog, Devonshire Street, 1994. Photo: Gerard McCarthy.

The Accidental Author

New to social media, I found myself hanging out on a platform with a gang of virtual friends. We were talking about this and that and nothing at all. Someone mentioned *Pancho And Lefty Ride Out*.

Now, that was a blast from the past. My first book, a collection of short fiction published by The Collins Press over a quarter of a century ago. Someone else asked if I would send on a copy. So I searched the house high up and low down and, odd as it may sound, no book was found. Here's the thing: I'm a pathological book-giver-away-er, and as my condition suggests, I have an overpowering compulsion to give away books that I hold most dear. And so, my copy of *Pancho And Lefty* had long gone the way of so many of my favourites.

Surfing the virtual world, from time to time I have come upon little snippets of chatter about Pancho And Lefty. And every now and then, I get an enquiry about its availability. I was intrigued by the interest my little book seemed to generate. So I put out a call around my virtual village looking for a copy with a view to publishing a short print run to mark the twenty-fifth anniversary of the first edition.

What can I say about the kindness of people that has not been said before? First out of the traps offering his own personal copy was John Breen of Waterstone's, followed almost immediately by a copy from Shirley Fehily – next my niece Ellen Fayer – within a week I had accumulated a neat little stack on my bookshelf courtesy of family, friends and the kindness of strangers. My enquiry seemed to have stirred up a wazzies' nest of interest. Photos of *Pancho And Lefty* began to appear on social media from the eight corners of the globe. Paraphernalia and memorabilia connected with the book began popping up online, including a stack of photographs taken back in the day. My friend from that time Lillian Smith unearthed a 25-year-old invitation to the book launch at Murphy's brewery. Then from nowhere, Eddie and Emma of Frameworks sent me a ten-minute film clip featuring the madness that unfolded on the night of the launch – filmed back in the days when a camera was the size of a filing cabinet.

It was the maddest book launch. Then again, back in the last century before health and safety had been invented, book launches and art exhibitions tended to be rowdy and bawdy affairs. Typically, occasions of attempted drunkenness, yahooing, yodelling, followed by a bop in Zoës, chips, cheese and garlic sauce in 7's and then back to a decrepit bedsit in some semi-derelict house in the heart of flatland 'til dawn. The launch of *Pancho And Lefty* was one of those memorable nights the details of which I can't seem to remember. But I seem to recollect that Murphy's brewery placed an embargo on book launches soon after that.

Anyway, there I was for the first time in quarter of a century with a dog-eared copy of *Pancho And Lefty Ride Out* in my hands. So tactile, so evocative, everything about it seemed to tell a story; the touch of it, the look of it, the scent of it. But then in a startling moment of clarity, it occurred to me that the online chatter surrounding that little 98-paged, short run, slim volume was not about the book. No. The curiosity it aroused had nothing whatsoever to do with the book, but rather the interest was all about what the book represented: a time, a place, a state of mind. And just like that, I was catapulted right back to the closing decades of the last century.

It was a time before email, internet or personal computers. A time before CD, DVD, iTunes, Spotify or YouTube. A time when the C60 cassette and a Sony Walkman was all you needed to be wired for sound. A time before the invention of the smartphone, when the most intelligent device in my house was the toaster. Put it this way, it was so long ago, that way back then salad came in tins, olive oil was sold in pharmacies and used for dropping into your ear and bottled water was the biggest joke in town. Jesus, and it seems like only yesterday.

Christmas 1985. George Michael. Don't get me started on George Michael. There he was on the telly, frolicking around in the snow, surrounded by a bevy of beauties. Himself and Andrew Ridgeley, the two of them, one as bad as the other, in their designer-cut, over-sized, overcoats, blond highlights and bouffant hair, with more money than sense. They were somewhere in the Swiss Alps by a log fire, sipping eggnog, port or brandy – on a fucking skiing holiday, if you don't mind. And we over here in Cork perished with the cold, buying Christmas presents in the pound shop and queueing for a living on the streets for the dole.

— *Last Christmas I gave you my heart* – me hole!

By the mid-1980s, Ireland had been battered by a gale-force recession, and Cork was in the eye of the storm. Now, let's be clear here, I don't hold George Michael responsible for the economic crash, but it was a time of finger-pointing and *what-about-ery*. By 1985, half the town was unemployed, the other half redundant. Verolme dockyard had slung its hook and abandoned ship. Our beautiful English Market had burnt down twice, and the plans were to put the space to more profitable use as a multi-storey car park. The Monahan Road Motown of Ford and Dunlop had padlocked their gates, never to open again. The dockers clocked out and shouted last call at the Donkey's Ears – and a string of early-morning houses stacked their kegs by the quay wall for the last time. This port town was going down and going down hard. Cork sank.

A whole generation of school-leavers and graduates clawed over each other to get a seat on the next plane, boat, train or Slattery's bus leaving town. They were striking out to start a new life in the squats, kips and bedsits of Brixton, Berlin, Boston and The Bronx. My story was slightly different; living in Newfoundland, Canada since 1979, I found myself swimming against the tide – when I returned home to Ireland during the darkest days of the recession.

I was seventeen years old when I first set foot on Canadian soil. Emigrating in the midst of formative years seemed to imprint a stylised vision of home in my brain. Home for me became like a George Michael video: all happiness and light; a magical place, where the sun always shone, and smiles were shared with everyone you'd meet and greet. It was like living in a musical with the sing-song sound of people talking and nuggets of gold the size of your fist to be plucked up off the street. But memory is an unreliable witness, and without internet or drone footage to offer corroborating evidence, the mind can play games. So when word reached me that my mother had been fighting a long, hard battle with no cure on the horizon. I came home and stayed – say no more.

I remember walking across Patrick's Bridge that first morning and something had changed. The ornate lamps along the parapet were damaged, mantels desecrated. That's when I noticed the string of shops and pubs along Merchants Quay all battered and boarded like a mouthful of broken teeth. The glass facade of Mangan's iconic clock shattered. Jesus, downtown was like a warzone. Flagship shops had taken the brunt of a full economic broadside. The premises of long-dead Merchant Princes – The Queen's Old Castle, Egan's, Burtons and The Munster Arcade were decrepit and decayed; doors locked, windows blocked and abandoned. The Savoy, The Pavilion, The Palace – these Victorian music halls and art deco cinemas, once bustling and full of life were now hollow and empty shells. The Cork of my youth that had been indelibly etched in my brain had fallen into terminal decay – and like Oisín's return from Tír na nÓg, I had dismounted from my white steed and was destined to stay.

The city was destitute. The citizenry strapped, trapped in poverty – not only young school-leavers, this was generational depravation. Whole families – fathers, sons, mothers, daughters – were all unemployed. And it is a sad state of affairs when there's no work for a once proud working class.

AnCO was the only game in town. Initially established to train apprentices for the trades, as the recession advanced the trades receded, and AnCO became less discerning; less about offering realistic employment or career opportunities, and all about keeping the new poor, the redundant aspiring middle classes, failed business owners, nurses, teachers and university graduates off the dole.

My abiding memory of that time was walking the streets with empty pockets looking for diversion. It was a time when turning a bob was a full-time job. And yes – it was a time of bleak bedsit land, damp and draughty flats, skip-scavenging to feed open fires, strumming guitars for entertainment, queues stretching around the block on White Street. Everyone pulling a stroke just to get by. It was a time of whispered passwords through sliding hatches; a time of ten-spots, touts and backhanders; a time when draconian licensing laws saw nightly police raids on semi-legal nightclubs and drinking dens. The frustration could be neatly summed up by Yosser Hughes when he uttered the immortal words, – *Gi's a job. I can do that …*

But don't get me wrong, there was fun to be had back then – but it's a different sort of fun when you've nothing to lose. It's a different kind of tension when law-abiding folk are forced to straddle the black economy. It's a different type of reality when people lose hope. It became a time of subversive activity, and the hard line of legality became blurred at the edges.

Recession and mass unemployment has a tendency to galvanise a population into collective thought, word and deed. Life choices became politically charged – and an angry young population went in search of a banner to stand beneath. I would never consider myself a hard-line activist, but night-time public marches through the streets of Cork became the new going out. We were marching for peace and marching for war; marching for hunger and marching for hunger strikes; marching for equality and marching for inequality. But above all we were marching for jobs and in retrospect, we the disenfranchised were marching for any campaign that was denied a voice at the table in this new Ireland. Every gathering seemed to reach a point where the frontline came face to face with the thin blue line of law and order – and so the chasm between *the haves* and *the have-nots*, between *the us* and *the them* became more entrenched and polarised. We were the redundant generation that had been cast on the scrap heap, and maybe some of us were unsure of the cause we were rallying towards, but yet we seemed to find ourselves on the same side of the line as the marginalised voices of inequality, shouting for parity of gender and sexuality, for civil rights and an end to apartheid. It was an era that gave rise to Cork's own Pat the Picket, now sadly departed. And in keeping with the black humour of the time, it was respectfully agreed by those who attended his funeral service that Pat's first action in the afterlife would be to mount a picket at the Pearly Gates.

It was a time of positive action when something as simple as a photocopier in the right hands was considered seditious, a time when resources shared among people doing it for themselves gave rise to iconic keystones of the city, such as Quay Co-op, the Cork Artists' Collective, Triskel. A time when pubs such as Loafers, The Phoenix and The Spailpín stood for something and by their very existence and tolerance they became resources in themselves.

Having done my time in Canada, I turned my back on the verdant faraway hills of the Great White North, found myself in Cork and decided to stick around. I picked up odd jobs here and there, dabbling in everything from the fringes of pirate radio, to trimming the grass around the headstones at the Quaker Graveyard. Eventually, I got on an AnCO Start Your Own Business course, a new government initiative to kick-start the economy by enticing people off the live register. The plan was to encourage entrepreneurial spirit with a small cash lump sum paid into the hand, then after that you were on your own, expected to make your way without further government assistance.

I opened my launderette at 1, Devonshire Street in 1986. At the counter of that steam-filled, hot and sweaty, damp and condensation-dripping little shop I met the most interesting spectrum of humanity. Ordinary, everyday people from all walks of life, people who had time to stop and talk, people who had time to think: it became a meeting place for poets, writers, musicians and actors; a meeting place of minds and for those who valued and validated creative expression. My little launderette became a magnet for gatherings, for a while it

Cónal Creedon outside No. 1 Launderette, Devonshire Street, Cork, 1989. Photo: Barry Fitzgerald.

doubled as a neighbourhood micro home brewery, and I would guess it is one of the few launderettes in the world to be raided by the boys in blue during one particularly boisterous poetry reading – our cultural soirée was summarily shut down unceremoniously with threats of arrests. To be totally honest, at times running that launderette was like going to war, but my launderette was my education. And when the Backwater Artists moved into a warren of old warehouses at the bottom of my street, maybe twenty or so of them, a world of creativity opened up before me like Aladdin's Cave. The Backwater Artists represented the generation who, just like me, dug their heels in and stayed.

Ever since I opened the launderette I had been writing frenetically, filling copybook after copybook, putting word after word down on paper, but to no end and with no grand plan. Not so much stories, but observational semi-autobiographical scribbles. Short lyrical vignettes: not poetry as such, but abstractions that seemed to instinctively form a narrative of sorts. Publication was the furthest thing from my mind. I'm not sure any of it was publishable in any commercial sense. But it didn't matter. I was writing for writing's sake and loving it.

Up to that point, I had been too shy or too coy to claim ownership or authorship of my words. I was in the habit of having my hand-written manuscripts typed at the Cork Secretarial College around the corner on Patrick's Hill. I would tell a white lie and say that I was dropping off a story that had been written by a *friend*. Over time, the staff and students at the college twigged that my imaginary writerly *friend* was actually me. And so it was there in that secretarial college on Patrick's Hill that I found my first readers. Securing an impartial readership, albeit a student in a typing pool, was a big step for me. It paved the way for my first third-party reviews: comments scribbled by the typist on the return envelope, something as simple as, – *I liked this one*. Or – *It was too sad, small Paudie should not have died in the end.*

With my audience of one firmly consolidated and a handful of hand-written reviews under my belt, I submitted to literary festivals. To my surprise the work received recognition from a number of literary awards.

UNDER THE GOLDIE FISH
"Dolphin of the airwaves"
RTE RADIO CORK • 729MW / 89FM

"The gist of *Under The Goldie Fish* would make Gabriel García Márquez turn puce in a pique of jealousy."
Tom Widger, The Sunday Tribune

"They were discussing what should go into the Irish Millennium Time-Capsule. If they are looking for something to represent Ireland, how about Cónal Creedon's *Under the Goldie Fish*? It's so off the wall, that it shouldn't ring true, but the most frightening fact is that it does ..."
Eilís O'Hanlon, Sunday Independent

My story *Come Out Now, Hacker Hanley!* was adapted for radio as part of the P.J. O'Connor Awards and produced by RTÉ 1. This opened a window of opportunity to write for radio, and following a frantic week devising a pilot, I was commissioned to write a ten-episode series. *Under The Goldie Fish* was conceived as a surreal exploration of my neighbourhood and the lives of those who lived in a spaghetti bowl of streets and lanes beneath the golden fish weather vane of Shandon steeple.

Under The Goldie Fish took off at a gallop and quickly established a hardcore loyal audience who tuned in to this mad, bizarre, daily pseudo-soap with storylines as farfetched as alien abduction, time travel and a Cork caped crusader Captain Crubeen could be relied upon to always save the day. The original ten-week series grew legs and ran and ran – extended to a four-year production from 1994 to 1998, eight series and clocking up over 400 episodes – cited by *The Irish Times* radio critics as Best Radio Programme for 1996 and 1998.

Under The Goldie Fish stands out as a most fantastical, exciting, off-the-wall creative time. It was a seat-of-our-pants production line, at times still editing within minutes of broadcast. It reflected a world where real-life events and people sometimes unfolded as fiction over the airwaves. Surrounded by every actor in the city and working with producer Aidan Stanley and sound engineer Denis Herlihy in his recording studio located in Knapp's Square, just around the corner from my launderette, fun factor became the order of the day. It was during those intense years that I learned that true creativity could only be achieved when fear of ridicule is abandoned.

I moved from scribbling at the counter of my launderette to the relative comfort and privacy of writing in my old clapped-out Volvo parked on the street outside. Without strategy, plan or ambition – I became an accidental author.

And so, for the first time in a quarter of a century, I found myself with that dog-eared copy of *Pancho And Lefty Ride Out* in my hand. This tactile connection to a very specific time in my past seemed to stir up emotions. I became consumed by memories and personal experiences; some happy, some sad, some downright heart breaking – some far too personal to reveal here and others so private that my mind is reticent to revisit them at all – and in that split second a vortex of images of decades past flashed in full living colour across my cranium.

Maybe it was the curse of a generation lost to emigration, but Cork seemed smaller more intimate back then. I remember a chance meeting with Sean Dunne on Academy Street sent me around the corner to Con Collins' bookshop on Carey's Lane. At the time, Sean was the books editor with The Irish Examiner and having come across some of my stories he suggested a publication might be in order. – *Tell Con who sent you,* was his personal reference, seal and bond. Con accepted my bundle of scripts for consideration. On my return to the bookshop a week or two later, Con had a note from the then unknown to me Tom McCarthy, the poet. Tom had adjudicated the work, and his words of affirmation in broad strokes of penmanship across the A4 clearly stated, – *These stories need to be published.* And so, the publication of my first book was set in progress. Nancy Hawkes worked with The Collins Press at the time and in the intervening years she has gone on to new heights in the world of publishing. It was fortuitous for me that I met Nancy, because so began our free-wheeling friendship that has spanned over a quarter of a century and continues to grow in strength and depth.

Now, maybe I should make it clear that I'm not in the habit of reading my own books. But as I stood there that day with this 25-year time capsule in my hand, I succumbed to the overpowering desire to bend back the spine and flutter through the pages.

Aware that this little book had originally been written longhand, it struck me that by today's technological standards, the transfer of text from biro-marked page to printer's block offered limited opportunity for correction. It had been published in the pre-digital world, a time when computerised word processing was still in its infancy. So, at first glance, I saw the flaws. The work needed a cold editorial eye and a well-honed scalpel – but all that aside, my eyes couldn't resist the urge to read on.

What surprised me most of all was how personally revealing the writing was. The narratives explored and characters exposed seemed to present pure autobiography thinly veiled as fiction. It dawned on

Outside Backwater Art Studio, Pine Street. ART TRAIL 1997.
Back: Julie Forrester, Catherine Hehir, Irene Murphy, Cónal Creedon. Front: John Adams,
Finbarr the Dog, Suzy O'Mullane, Maurice Desmond, Nickie Dowd. Photo: Fiona O'Toole.

me that maybe my initial obsessional struggle with the page may have
been an ad hoc self-therapy of sorts. It then became apparent that these
seminal extracts and unfinished fictions were in fact, unbeknownst to
me at the time, works-in-progress of future published texts.

The two stories with Limbo in the title are clearly early drafts of
what eventually became my novel *Passion Play*. An amalgamation of
He Ain't Heavy and *The Entomologist* seemed to dovetail together as
an early draft of my stage play *The Cure*. *Same Old Tune*, presents a
serious non-comedic exploration of my comic character Nero, who
featured large in *Under The Goldie Fish*. *Arthur, The Exhibitionist And*

Nigel Rolfe, is clearly a lament for the demise of the short-lived Boot Boy era of my teens, later explored in more detail in *Passion Play* – the narrative also presents a record of the development of Triskel Arts Centre, from a single-roomed basement on Bridge Street to the Arts Centre it became on Tobin Street via a brief stop-off as a pop-up on Fitton Street, I was surprised to find that I had name-checked Robbie McDonald. Though not blatantly obvious, *Every Picture Tells A Story*, is most certainly inspired by aspects of the Cork Art Now exhibition hosted by the Crawford Gallery during the late-1980s – and is a veiled homage to artist James Scanlon who had given me a painting that still to this day hangs in my front room, simply signed Scan '94. Even the inclusion of a number of references to pigeons offered insight into a theme I would revisit in my work many years later – in my documentary *The Boys of Fair Hill*, my Irish Times column *Video Paradiso* and of course most significantly in my novel *Begotten Not Made* in the character Dowcha Boy. And yet, with all this fiction-in-progress I was most perturbed by the sheer amount of personal soul-searching and autobiography laid bare, invisible to the unsuspecting eye, but jumping out at me from each and every page. *Penny For Your Thoughts* is probably the most flawed piece in the collection and yet for me it stands as one of the more revealing and interesting.

It occurred to me that re-reading *Pancho And Lefty Ride Out*, was far more than a fuchsia-tinted journey of nostalgia. This little book presented a serious reassessment of my own personal past, and I was surprised by what I found. I decided there and then to let sleeping dogs lie. I thought it best to rebury the time capsule that is *Pancho And Lefty Ride Out*. Fortunately, over the decades, most of the stories in *Pancho And Lefty Ride Out* had been re-edited, republished and transferred to digital format for inclusion in various anthologies. Others had been re-imagined and adapted as radio plays, stage plays and monologues.

And so, for those of you who may have a passing interest in reading *Pancho And Lefty Ride Out*, I have decided to collect together the digitally remastered versions with additional bonus tracks to mark the twenty-fifth anniversary of its publication. I hope you enjoy.

George Michael? Ah, me and George made our peace a long time ago. He was just another lad like me, trying to make his way in bleak times. He was living the dream, giving those of us who had lost all hope some idea of what a dream might be – Dowcha, George! As I say, it took time, but in time I learned to – *Listen Without Prejudice.*

The launderette? Well, suffice to say my obsession gradually became my occupation, and after a dozen years or so washing clothes, I set the spin cycle one last time – then shut my launderette down – or more to the point, one day I just didn't open the door. For many years it remained there silent, undisturbed and intact like Miss Havisham's wedding table.

And the rest, as they say, is fiction …

PANCHO AND LEFTY RIDE AGAIN

RIDE AGAIN

A COLLECTION OF SHORT FICTION

And The Big Fish Drowned

Finny raised the hammer and crashed it down on Macker's head. Blood pulsed in spurts across Macker's face and gathered in pools of red mucus before dripping down onto the gutter. Macker lay there stretched out lifeless.

— Never again, Finny roared. – D'ya hear me! Never a-fuckin-gain …

But the damage was done, and the lesson learned was too little too late.

The door of The Zodiac opened. Drinkers poured onto the street. They swarmed like ants, a squirming mass around a core of rotten fruit. Above the chaotic racket, Finny could hear Jacinta Healy. She was whispering something like,

— Jesus, what have you done, Finny? What have you done?

Or maybe she wasn't whispering. Maybe she was screaming. Maybe she was crying out loud. Or maybe she was saying nothing at all. Maybe it was just the jumble of noise in Finny's head. But Jacinta was there. He could see her standing over beyond, in the half light of the door, her hand to her mouth, the glint of silver streams running down her cheeks.

Pacing like a caged wild animal, Finny turned to the crowd and raised the hammer above his head. Then a glimmer of reality returned to his frenzied face. He looked to the ground. It was as if in that split of a second, he suddenly realised what he had done. His best friend Macker lay there motionless, feeling no pain. Finny lowered the hammer to his side, turned his eyes towards the orange streetlamp and howled.

There followed a deathly silence, and like the Red Sea of old, the crowd parted. They turned and looked the other way as Finny walked past. In the distance, the yellow and cream glow from The China Garden shone out like a beacon. Quickening his pace, Finny vanished into the dank darkness.

It's said there's no life without light, well, in this part of town there was no light without life. Even the dullest streetlamp had a cluster of people. They chatted, they sang, they shouted, they fought, they made love and then they went home.

Nothing special about MacSwiney Street, the kind of place you had no business stopping, unless you had a good reason to stop. It was a world of its own and it had rules. There was no law on MacSwiney Street, but they lived by a code. The code was clear:

Big fish eat small fish and small fish are bait.

It was as simple as that.

With the sound of the sirens in the distance, they stepped back from the corpse and faded into the night. Some slithered back to their bar stools in The Zodiac and dipped their snouts to the trough. And when the boys in blue arrived nosing around and asking questions, no one saw nothing. Because the first thing you learned on MacSwiney Street was to say nothing to nobody about nothing, and then say nothing at all.

Finny was cold and sweating by the time he reached the flats at the top of Castle Street. He passed down behind the hackney stand, through the gap in the chicken wire and over the wall into the schoolyard. In the corner of the bicycle shed he lay down on the bench, blood-dripping hammer by his side. He fumbled in his pocket, found a topper and lit it. His heart pounded out a regular beat to the rhythm of each rush of blood through his veins. His stomach was in a knot, his brain twisted in pain.

— Bastard deserved it, he thought to himself.

He inhaled the blue smoke through his nose as it billowed from his jaw-hung mouth. By the time he had stubbed out another, his breathing had found a regular pace. A feeling of calm returned to his tormented mind and his thoughts became less frantic and more rational.

He had overreacted. He knew he had overreacted. But Macker had stepped over the line, and it wasn't the first time.

It was always the same: Macker would throw back a few pints, skin-up a joint or two and it would begin with a bit of slagging. But it always got out of hand, especially when Jacinta Healy was around.

Finny was no pushover, not the sort you'd want to mess with. But Macker would push it right up to the limit, right up to the point where Finny would be just about to snap. Then Macker would just laugh, like it was all just a big joke. Everyone knew it was only a matter of time before he pushed it too far. And that evening in The Zodiac? Well, enough was enough. And even when Macker tried to make things right with a laugh, it was too little and too late.

Finny struggled to make some sense of what had happened. It was like a rage that had been festering beneath the surface just erupted and blinded him. Macker just didn't know when to stop, he kept pushing and pushing. Finny spotted the hammer on the shelf behind the counter, and just like that, – Snap! He reached for it and lowered it full force right down on Macker's head. Splitting his skull in two.

Finny raised his Doc Martens up onto the bench and lay back, sucking on his cigarette. He exhaled a stream of blue-grey that just hung there suspended in mid-air the full length of the shed like a veil billowing in a gentle breeze.

This shed was their world. Their universe. They grew up in this shed. It was here on this broken bench it all began. Finny smiled as memories seemed to appear out of the darkness. He sees himself and Macker smoking their first cigarette. Macker is coughing and spluttering, saying his mam would fuckin' murder him if she ever caught him smoking. Then the late nights drinking flagons of cider and getting the gawks. He remembers their first nodge, a ten-spot. They chipped in and bought it down the Pot Black Pool Hall. It was one of those long, lazy summer days balmin' out on the roof. Macker rolling his first three-skinner and making a total balls of it. There they were on the roof of the shed, naked to the navel, basking in the baking sun. The two of them laughing like they didn't have a care in the world. They didn't have a care in the world.

It was around that time Jacinta Healy came into their life. She turned up at the shed one night and just walked in out of the darkness. She said she wanted some cider and asked Finny for a smoke of his cigarette, and just like that, she just fitted right in. Finny, Macker and Jacinta, that's how it was.

Maybe things did change slightly, but not for the better, not for the worse. It was just something different, that's all. And maybe at that time something different was exactly what was called for, because change for change's sake can be a good thing. Up until that night it had always been just the two of them, Finny and Macker. They lived in each other's shadow. Jacinta arriving like she did, when she did, was a godsend. She was a breath of fresh air. She was what she was and two became three.

Finny remembers Macker's first kiss – it strikes him as odd that he remembers Macker's first kiss, but that's how it is. There they were, the three of them, Jacinta Healy sitting between Macker and himself. Finny handed her the cider, she took a mouthful and just like that she turned towards Macker and they started. The two of them, tongue wrapped around tongue. She then turned towards Finny and pushed her lips to his.

— Gowan, said Macker. – It feels magic …

Maybe Finny was caught off-guard, maybe he felt awkward, or maybe he was just taken by surprise; whatever the reason, he gave Jacinta a peck on the cheek then moved to the far end of the shed with the cider.

And that was the thing about Macker, Jacinta and Finny. It was never about ownership. It was never about envy or jealousy. It was never about boyfriend or girlfriend. It was the three of them against the world. Whatever they had, they shared.

— Come on, Finny luv, don't be like that, she'd whisper.

— Come over here to us.

But Finny was happier with his lips around the neck of a cider bottle than his tongue wrapped around Jacinta Healy's tongue; the very thought of it made him shudder. So, Finny would make his excuses and stay.

Macker and Jacinta seemed to need that physical connection. It was only a matter of time before shifting and snogging became fumbling with bra straps, flesh on flesh, getting it on and getting it off, grunting and grinding his thighs into hers. Or Jacinta's face buried in Macker's groin, and he thrown back on the bench praying to the Almighty.

– Oh, God! Oh, God! Oh fuckin', Jesus!

He'd close his eyes and sigh in a release of ecstatic pleasure, then lighting a cigarette he'd say something like,

– Finny, you need to try this, man. You really do! he'd say. – Fuckin' amazin'! Do Finny next, Jacinta. Go on, do Finny …

And Macker was right. Jacinta's lips wound around did feel amazing, and in and out, and in and out, and in and out of her mouth. It was absolutely amazing. But something about it just didn't feel right. Maybe at fourteen years of age Finny was just not ready. Maybe he was too immature. Maybe he was plain scared. Or maybe Finny was happiest when it was just him and Macker, the two of them wrestling and running through the high grass at the back of the school, puppy dogs at play – or those warm summer days on the roof of the shed stripped to the waist, in the sun, smoking weed and laughing.

~

Finny pulled his hoodie tight around his rakish adolescent frame. He was cold. He was lonely. It was strange sitting there in the shed alone with just the glow of his cigarette for company. No laugh. No Macker. Finny was heartbroken.

He had seen this day coming. Drinking cider, smoking three skinners, throwing shapes and acting the bollocks was all fine and dandy. It was all about hanging out just having a laugh, and everything was hunky-dory. From the outside it might have looked as if the arrival of Jacinta Healy was the beginning of the end, she did cause a subtle reshuffling of the pack. But Finny knew Jacinta was a positive influence that held them together. No, Jacinta had been a force for good. Finny knew that Jacinta had been a force for good, he could pin-point the moment that everything changed and went bad to the very first day they started dealing ten-spots.

It all began innocently enough. They sold a bit so they could smoke a bit. It was as simple as that. But dealing dope and turning cash put a new spin on everything, and before long it was all about the money. It was like everything, including their friendship, came with a price tag. Finny and Macker were born into poverty, but maybe that's why money became Macker's God. It was never enough. He wanted more. More money and all the things that money could buy – but what he craved most was power and respect.

– Big fish eat small fish and small fish were only bait, he'd say.

And when friendship is counted in pounds, shillings and pence, the sum total never tallies. Someone always has a finger in the till. In fairness to Jacinta Healy, she stood as a buffer between them. But when Macker began to see himself as top dog, well, their friendship could only take so much, and something had to give. Yes, Finny had seen this day coming, things were going off the rails, even a blind man could see it would all end in tears. But killing Macker was never part of the plan.

– Jesus Christ Al-fuckin-mighty, Finny whispered.

It crossed his mind that if Macker was dead, he was in trouble. But if Macker was alive, he was in big trouble. So, there and then, in the shed that night, he made up his mind he had to go, had to get the fuck out of this god-forsaken port town.

Finny pushed himself up off the bench, walked out of the shed, flicked his cigarette across the yard and threw the hammer as far as he could over the roof into the long grass. He slid back over the wall, out through the gap in the chicken wire, around by the side of the hackney stand and headed down past the flats, up the hill and home.

Finny was on the train to Dublin to catch the boat to England the next morning.

～

Macker didn't die that night. He spent the next six months on the flat of his back. It was touch and go for a while. But eventually, he was on his feet again. The scar down the side of his head only added to his swagger. In the years that followed, Macker grew into the biggest fish in the small pool that is Leeside. He did time in his early twenties for something stupid, his defence in court pleaded that he had anger issues due to his deprived upbringing and regular beatings at the hand of his father. Macker was in and out the revolving door of Butlin's by the Lee, and back on the streets in six months. And so, the myth was born. Macker became the hardman of crime. It was a myth he encouraged, a myth that struck fear into anyone who challenged it.

Macker's reputation grew arms and legs: a break-in on the northside, an armed robbery downtown, a shooting on the southside, but Macker was never found. And so, the story grew. A hardman taking credit for crimes he had no hand, act or part in – striking fear into the hearts of low-life. As always, the myth was larger than the man. Macker was a liar and a lout. He sold drugs to kids through kids. He drank too much, and with no self-respect, he had less respect for anyone else. He abused all those around him, especially those close to him.

Jacinta Healy was still with him. He married her about a year after he got out of hospital. Three months later, she had his child. A boy. Junior they called him. Maybe his bones were on the mend, but Macker was broken. He never really got over the loss of Finny and the friendship they shared. He'd be the first to tell you that Finny was a fucker, and often swore that he would have him killed on sight. But Finny had disappeared without trace, and the memory of him became mixed up in a storm of emotion, pain, fury and revenge. Macker missed Finny. Deep inside, his body and heart hurt. Jacinta Healy did the best she could to pick up the pieces. The birth of their son Junior gave Macker something to live for, but in the years that followed, Macker gradually grew into the scum he became. He screwed around, messed around, hung around. Hanging around with hangers-on. That was Macker. He lived in a world of ten-spots, touts, backhanders and back-stabbers. Surrounded by a bunch of no-minds, his organisation went from strength to strength on the back of hangers-on and free-loaders. His was a world where fear was law. Macker put the fear of God into anyone who as much as looked sideways at him.

Money came easy in the drugs game. Buying in bulk through the Molloys, a well-connected Dublin-based gutter-family. Macker sold on to the street through a string of runners. Simple. No banks. No tax. No paperwork. No problem. And if ever there was a problem, someone would get their head burst open – problem solved. Macker lived by a simple code and might was always right.

— Big fish eat small fish and small fish are only bait, he'd say.
And when a small fish became ambitious, showed initiative or stepped out of line? Well, that was the end of the line. Ambition always ended in a heap down some back alley. That would be a first and final warning. Sometimes there would be no warning at all.

~

When Macker's body was pulled from the river there was no question in anyone's mind. It was a hit by the Molloys. No one in this town was big enough or stupid enough to take on Macker. He must have stretched his elbows just that little bit too far and poked Joe Molloy's ribs, and that's something you really don't want to do. Macker was dead. It all added up.

Macker had dealt with the Molloys for over twenty years, buying third-rate shit in bulk and selling down the line, everything from hash to heroin. Smack was never a very big runner in Cork, but Macker had it on his menu. A point of prestige, showing the Molloys that in Cork, he – Macker – was the go-to man, the only game in town. The Molloys knew where to buy, how to buy. They had the hardware and people to bring the stuff in. There lay Macker's dependence on the Molloys. In the greater world of the underworld, Macker was only a small cog in the Molloys' well-oiled wheel.

But the 90s brought change. E, disco biscuits, yokes, call it what you like – ecstasy arrived, and everything changed. E hit the scene and Macker supplied it. He dealt directly with England, quality gear, no middlemen, no Molloys. E was small. A hundred tabs would fit in a fag box. Profit high. Risks low. No middlemen. No Molloys. E was big.

Macker was ambitious. But one man's gain was another man's loss. Joe Molloy was that other man, and he wouldn't take loss sitting down.

Molloy's blood was up. Macker's was spilt. The Drug Squad sighed a sigh of relief when Macker's body was hauled out of the river.

— Misadventure, they said.

But everybody knew it had the mark of the Molloys all over it.

~

Gi'me, Gi'me, Gi'me!
A man after midnight.

The jukebox thumped it out. ABBA were back and so was Finny. He was back for Macker's funeral, back for the funeral of his boyhood friend, back for the funeral of a friend he would have halved his heart for, back to pay his last respects to the friend he would have died for, back to pay his respects to the friend he would have killed.

Twenty-three years had passed since that night he levelled Macker outside this very pub. He hesitated in the doorway; it took time to get the measure of what was once home.

Tomcat and stale drink, the smell from the toilets soiled the air. Finny rubbed his nose. Not a lot had changed. The sound system and big screen were new. The extension with the pool table and jukebox, that was different. But The Zodiac was still the same. The same smells, same heads, same dump. Finny paused in the doorway before stepping into the bar, followed closely by Trevor.

Trevor was young, a stylish chav, dressed in a black polo-neck, maybe it was Armani, maybe it wasn't, but his light-blue jacket looked the part with the black trousers, gold chain and matching Rolex. Trevor looked sharp. Finny's eyes darted around the bar. He was looking for a familiar face. But a couple of decades had passed, it was a case of same heads but different faces.

A hand of friendship reached through the crowd. It was Jacinta Healy, Macker's widow.

— Finny?

She reached out across the painful years.

— Jesus, Jacinta! We flew over when we heard the news.

— I knew you'd come, she said. – It's been a long time …

— Too long …

Their hands clasped, and in an emotional few seconds the pain of a lifetime's separation was bridged. There was an ease between them, like they found comfort in each other's company. A couple of decades had passed since those nights in the shed with Macker supping cider, but it seemed like only yesterday. She offered him a drink. He accepted a mineral water. She commented on how well he looked. He stood there dripping designers, tanned and trim on the right side of bling.

— You're lookin' well, Finny, she said.

Maybe it was grief, or maybe she was just weary of it all, but the years had taken their toll on Jacinta. She looked rough. So Finny skipped the false flattery and sympathised.

— It was all such a long time ago, he said. – I don't know where to even begin. I suppose I should begin at the end and tell you that I'm sorry for your loss.

— Thanks, she whispered and held his hand tighter. – I knew you'd come, that's enough.

— Don't know where to start about what happened outside the door of this place all those years ago. I've been through those few minutes of madness a thousand times, he said. – I loved him you know …

There was sincerity in his voice. Jacinta was consoled.

— I know you did, she said. – You two were like brothers. Tell you the truth, I don't miss him, she said. – I loved him too, but I don't miss him. No, I don't miss him at all …

Her eyes were cold.

A hand from a hanger-on stretched through the crowd and reached towards Jacinta, followed by the hollow words,

— I'm sorry for your troubles. Macker was a great man.

Jacinta nodded and shook hands with the hanger-on until he released his grip, parted and walked away.

— Ye had a son? Finny continued.

— We did, she said. – Junior …

— Junior?

— Junior, after Macker, she smiled. – That's him over there.

She pointed to the pack of young bucks by the pool table.

— Is he a good lad?

— He's good to his mother, Jacinta smiled.

— Good. That's all that counts, he said.

Finny stepped aside and Trevor leaned forward to offer his condolences. But before he could reach out his hand or utter a word, Jacinta's eyes flashed fury.

— I know you, she said. - I've seen you before.

Jacinta studied Trevor.

— We may have …

Trevor was about to answer, but she cut him off mid-sentence.

— There's no, we may have, about it, she snapped. - I know you! I do. I recognise you. You work for the fuckin' Molloys. You supplied Macker.

Finny moved between Jacinta and Trevor and attempted to calm the situation.

— You got it wrong, Jacinta, he said.

But Jacinta was no fool. She knew what she knew.

— He's one of the Molloys, one of those fuckers that murdered my husband.

— No, Jacinta, I'm tellin' ya …

— Finny, he's one of the fuckers that murdered Macker!

— Jacinta, ya got it wrong …

Finny firmly held her arm.

— Come outside, Jacinta, he whispered. - You're upset. I can explain.

Finny guided her towards the door.

— Explain? she shouted. - Explain what that fuck is he doing here. He's one of the Molloys!

— Trevor is with me, he said forcefully but quietly.

Finny led her out of the pub.

Outside, MacSwiney Street was still on the wrong side of town, every second building was boarded and battered like a mouthful of broken teeth. Finny placed his hands on Jacinta's shoulders. She leaned there against his waiting car in a daze.

— Trevor is with me, he said it again.

Then Finny told her how it was. He spoke of Macker in a way that no living soul had ever spoken. He knew details of Jacinta's life as if he had been there for every tear drop. He spoke about her son Junior, her hopes and dreams for him and her life's disappointments.

— Macker had to fight for everything, she snapped.

— I'm not gonna say nothing bad about Macker, he said. – Not tonight. Not any night. It's all too little, too late …

— We never wanted for nothing, she said. – Macker was a good provider …

— And who's gonna provide for you now that he's gone? he said.

Finny spoke the truth, and for a woman who had heard a lifetime of lies, she knew the truth when she heard it.

— It was no bed of roses for me either, he whispered.

Finny told her of the early, lonely days in London, living in kips, mixing muck for a living. Pissing his wages against the cracked tiles of some pub between Cricklewood and Kilburn. And then in Brixton everything changed. It was there he met the dark lads.

— The dark lads and the Irish have a lot in common, you know. Clawed my way up from the pubs and backstreets of Brixton dealing ten-spots of skunk. But that was a long time ago …

— What about this fucker and the Molloys? she pointed to Trevor.

— You're not listening to me, Jacinta, he said. – The Molloys are fuck-all. They're only small fish. The Molloys are my messenger boys. Who do you think supplies the fuckin' Molloys …

Finny then laid it out straight, that Trevor had always been Finny's man, not the Molloys', and had been dealing with Macker for years. Finny explained that Macker never knew that Trevor was Finny's front man.

— Macker was a fuckin' dreamer, he said. – And if he wanted to put it about that he was dealing with a big Dublin gang, who gives a shit. But the Molloys are fuck-all. As far as Macker was concerned, he was dealing directly with Trevor, this young kid who had a finger on the pulse in London.

And then looking deeply into her eyes Finny told it as it was,

— Macker didn't know he was buying from me. Fuck sake, he didn't know if I was dead or alive and he didn't care. Think about it, Jacinta! Just think about it! And as far as the story that Macker was murdered by the Molloys? Well, that's nothing but a load of bollocks, he said. – And you know it, Jacinta. Macker was a waste of space. No disrespect to him. But you know it, Jacinta. Fuck's sake, Macker a hardman criminal mastermind? Me hole! Macker was a fuckin' eejit, and he's laughing all the way to the gates of hell.

Macker probably fell over the quay wall in a drunken haze, and good riddance. And you know that better than anyone, Jacinta. He was a fuckin' drunk.

— Don't you say that …

Jacinta saw glory in death, and Macker's myth was the only pride she had to cling onto.

— Look, I'm sorry, Jacinta. But the truth's the truth. The Molloys are small fish and Macker was only bait …

— You can't step back here tonight after all these years and stir up shite about Macker!

— Ah for Christ's sakes, Jacinta! You're not listening to me. Me and Macker were like that!

He raised his two fingers, clinched together.

— Like that, he said it again. – I loved Macker, girl.

— Fuck you, Finny! she hissed.

Finny clicked his fingers and pointed to the car.

— Trevor, I'm done here, he said, and stood back.

Jacinta raised her arm to strike a blow at Finny's head. Trevor's hand shot out and held her wrist. His grip was strong and uncompromising. Trevor opened the door of the car. Finny sat into the back seat.

— Take yer hand offa me, ya fucker!

Jacinta looked daggers.

— We came to offer our condolences. And now …

— Fuck her! Finny shouted from the car. – Fuck this kip of a town! Get in the car, Trevor.

Finny was close to tears.

— Mrs McCarthy? Trevor whispered and gently squeezed her
wrist.

Jacinta had been called many things over the years, everything from
Macker's wife to Macker's aul' doll, but never Mrs McCarthy. She was
flattered, it brought a confused smile to her face.

— Please, Mrs McCarthy, said Trevor. – Please accept this …

He slipped her an envelope. Inside, a wad of cash, maybe ten grand
sterling.

— It's from Finbarr, he whispered.
— Finbarr? she laughed as she made the connection. – Finny?
— That's right, said Trevor. – Finbarr wants you to have this. You'll
  have expenses over the coming few weeks …
— Finbarr? For fuck's sake! Is that what he calls himself? Fin-
  fuckin-barr!

Her laugh was loud and shrill like the wailing of a banshee. But she
was no fool, she knew that everything had changed now that Macker
was gone. She knew that ten grand was ten grand. She knew Trevor
had something to say – a message to deliver. So she calmed down and
listened. In very short and precise sentences, Trevor made it clear that
Macker's link in the chain would have to be filled.

— … and now that Macker is gone, Mrs McCarthy, I want to
  continue dealing with your son Junior.
— Junior? Drugs? No fuckin' way! she said. – Who the fuck do
  you think you are coming here with your wad of cash and sayin'
  that my son …

She was making noises and saying that she was having none of it, but
she sounded like she could be convinced otherwise.

— Look, if Junior doesn't fill the gap left by Macker, someone
  else will. Junior is dealing already, and you know it. It's in his
  blood. Let him join the big league, he said. – Let Junior step
  into Macker's shoes. He's well capable of filling them …
— And what about the Molloys? I'll have another corpse on me
  hands!

Jacinta needed reassuring.

— The Molloys? Did you not hear a word? The Molloys are fuck-all! Finbarr would eat 'em for breakfast. Finbarr feeds the Molloys. Can you not see what's happening here? Finbarr is the fuckin' big fish. Is now, was then and ever shall be the big fish!

Jacinta stood there confused, her eyes filled with tears.

— Just think about what I said about Junior, Mrs McCarthy, he said. – Finbarr insisted, that I clear it with you before I talk to Junior. I'll be in contact.

Trevor slipped slickly into the back seat of the car next to Finny.

— Drive on! he gave the order.

Trevor cradled Finny and rubbed his fingers affectionally through his receding hairline. Finny's cheeks were streaming.

Jacinta thumped the roof of the car.

— You're a bastard, Finny. Macker always said it, yer nothing but a fuckin' fucked-up homo.

As the limo drove off, she grabbed at him through the window. Trevor fended off her feeble attempt. Finny cried like a baby, unashamedly.

— Don't worry, love. It'll all be alright, whispered Trevor.

Trevor caressed Finny and kissed him comfortingly on the forehead.

Orange streetlights flashed overhead. Finny watched through watery eyes, as MacSwiney Street became more and more removed from him. Jacinta faded in the distance, with her the emotional hold of memories of youth. The ghost of Macker had been laid to rest.

Finny struggled to hold back the tears. He pointed to a narrow, dimly lit street and said,

— … that's where the hackney stand was, and down around the side the hole in the chicken wire that led to the school yard …

Finny's eyes welled up, his thoughts were of Macker.

— Trevor? Did I ever tell you about the time me and Macker broke into Tommy's Bar? Jez, that was some night. We were walkin' home along, just up that street there, and …

Finny was off on a, *me an' Macker* story.

Trevor smiled. He had heard the stories a thousand times before. He had heard them from Macker, he had heard them from Finny. He had heard all about the bicycle shed and the gap in the chicken wire behind the hackney stand. He had heard of the late nights drinking cider, and long, hot summer days balmin' out on the roof smoking three skinners.

Over the years, Trevor had been the only living link between Finny and Macker. Each time Trevor returned to London, Finny would be excited and waiting to hear about home. But most of all Finny would want to hear every detail, every single word spoken by Macker. Trevor had heard both of them call each other every name under the sun, but always with a strange deep affection and undying respect. He knew that his lover Finny always had a special place for Macker deep in his innermost soul, and though Macker would never admit it, their lost love was a two-way street.

Finny had not seen Macker since that night all those years ago when he left him stretched out on the street outside The Zodiac, but the separation only served to deepen the intensity and detail of their shared memories and feelings. Trevor was jealous of Finny's love for Macker. It didn't matter that more than twenty years had passed, when Finny walked away from The Zodiac all those years ago he left with a Macker-shaped void in his heart. Trevor knew it was a void that he could never fill – not as long as Macker lived.

Trevor was jealous of something he would never have, something he would never understand. This jealousy was a problem for Trevor. And a problem was a problem – financial or emotional, it didn't matter. In Trevor's world there was only one way to solve a problem. And so, Macker's body ended up dumped in the river.

Trevor looked to the future, to the humming drone of Finny chuntering on about, *me an' Macker* and the rose-tinted past. But old school was for old fools, Trevor was sick of glorified tales of pints and flagons of cider. Dealing ten-spots to school kids was sweet shop stuff. The world had changed, and smack was the future. And for Trevor, the future was far more interesting than the past. He imagined his dealings in Cork now that Macker was out of the way. He looked forward to his new partnership with Macker's son Junior. He knew Junior. He knew him well. He had thrown him a few bags of yokes over the years. Junior knew the score, working with Junior could be fun and nice eye-candy too.

The limo purred as it cushioned them from the hacked surface and depravation of the Southside. Finny, occasionally turning to glimpse out the back windscreen, rambled on, reliving legends and creating myths. Trevor, eyes front, smiled as the crest of the Mercedes guided them through the damp, smoky mist that always hung on MacSwiney Street – up past the flats, down by the park, behind the schoolyard and up the hill to the airport, homeward. Trevor smiled. The ghost of Macker had been laid to rest, problem solved.

But Finny was not one to be messed with. Maybe it was the flash of the streetlight on Trevor's face, and in that glimpse of a second Finny recognised the glaze of ambition in Trevor's eyes. Ambition could be a dangerous thing and Trevor wouldn't want to be getting ideas that might be too big for him.

And it crossed Finny's mind that after all these years the ghost of Macker had finally been laid to rest. Maybe it was time for a homecoming. He looked forward to his future dealings with Macker's son, Junior – he was the head off his da, and twice as cute. And so, the big fish drowned. And Trevor? Small fish are only bait …

Limbo Junction

Did you ever wake up with *Waterloo Sunset* running around your head?

> *Dwang diddy dwang!*
> *Diddy dwang!*
> *Diddy dwang!*
> *Diddy dwang!*
> *Diddy dwang!*
> *Bab ba ba ba ba*
> *Ba ba ba ba ba ba*
> *Ba ba ba ba ba*
> *Ba ba ba ba*

You know how it goes? Well, that's how it was.

~

Ding-Dong

Spring was late, two and a half years late, to be precise. But the light was beginning to shine through.

Ding-Dong

There it goes again. It was for one of the other flats. Nobody ever calls for me.

Ding-Dong

Jesus! Will someone answer the fuckin' door. People were forever ringing the wrong bell. My bell. You see, this house has eight flats, sometimes seven and a studio. That depends on Herman, our resident German. When he's flush, he usually takes Number 6 as a studio. A studio, if you don't mind. A flat is a flat is a flat. A fuckin' studio. Some people. Really? They'd drive you to fuckin' drink …

I mean, it gets to the point where the rest of us, including Willie the Rent, call Number 6, The Studio. A bloody joke, that's what it is.

I'm the ground-floor flat and, by some incredible technical feat of electrical wiring, I'm the top doorbell. Strange. Actually, now that I think of it, this house has only seven or sometimes eight flats, but we have twelve doorbells, and not one of them has a name tag except of course Number 6. Number 6 has the word Studio, in Germanic artistic scrawl, stuffed in behind the yellowing plastic I.D. holder. Is it any wonder I don't get many visitors?

Ding-Dong

— Jesus! Will someone answer the bloody door?

I buried my head deeper down between the gritty sheet and grubby cover. Deep down into the darkness, a winter darkness. Somebody famous once said that the light at the end of a tunnel was probably the light from an oncoming train, that's how I was feeling. But I was beginning to sense a new beginning, or was it the beginning of a new end?

The Land of the Midnight Sun, that's what it was like. Two years of sunshine followed by two years of total darkness. And darkness is strange, it's so passive. It's just the lack of light. Darkness doesn't do, it just is. At least the sun has to shine, but darkness sits there doing nothing, just being dark all the time. It had been a long, dark winter and there was some class of a lunatic outside my door, ringing my fuckin' bell.

Ding-Dong

— Ah, for fuck's sake!

The duvet cushioned me from the ringing of bells, the laughing, the footsteps on the ceiling, the insanity beyond my door in the dim hallway and the sinister madness outside the front door. The door that leads out onto Waterloo Terrace that looks out across the schizophrenic estuary of the city. It was dark down there in the duvet, my knees curled up to my chin. It was musty, damp and airless, but it was safe ...

Ding-Dong
Answerthefuckingdoorwillyaanswerthefuckingdoor!

Depression? Call it what you like, but I was safe. This was my second stint down under the duvet. I remember the first time; it seems like a lifetime ago. Then again, maybe it was a lifetime ago. And if not a lifetime ago it was certainly a different life, because I have changed.

～

She was young, I was younger. She was French, from Montpellier. I was travelling north on my Eurorail ticket. North to Germany and then south to Italy but my money ran out in Amsterdam. That's where I first clapped eyes on Yvette. She was sweet, sophisticated, sensual and working in a shit-hole juice bar just off Damrak. I can't remember the name of the place, in fact there's a lot about Amsterdam I can't remember, but I remember Yvette. She was tall, slim and firm. She stood there behind the counter, the bulb of her bum perched on the cooler for comfort, cigarette hanging from her lips. She was talking to her workmate, a taller girl, a taller black girl, from Africa or Germany or someplace. In fact, it was the Afro-German I first noticed, hard not to notice a six-foot-two black woman with a flame-red skinhead. She was wearing a pale blue halter-neck, sort of a boob tube thing, that barely held it all together. She had shorts so short that they just about covered the V of her legs. And her well-formed legs ran all the way from counter to floor.

I think I was in love, real love. Now that I think about it, there was no think about it. I was in love, and no more about it. I just wanted to go to bed with this exotic vision, not that I wanted to make love or anything. Making love was the furthest thing from my mind. I stood there, five-foot-ten, a twenty-year-old virgin entranced, mesmerised, immersed in love.

She leaned over, her crotch caressing the counter-mounted bottle-opener. Well, maybe it wasn't caressing the bottle-opener, but it just seemed that way to me.

Me make love? No way! I wanted to marry this girl. I wanted to take her away from all this. I wanted to save her from herself, save her from all the leering eyes. I wanted to …

I wanna hold your ha-ha-ha-haaaaa-aa-nd,
I want to hold your hand.

The Beatles zapped crystal clear from the hi-tech CD jukebox.

Her lips puckered not three inches from my forehead.

    — Vot do you vant?

She pointed to the menu on the wall behind her. My eyes scanned a list of fruit drinks and smoothies.

    — Pawpaw, I said.

I wasn't too sure what a pawpaw was, but I knew it was a fruit and it sounded hip, and it couldn't be much different from an apple or an orange. She glanced at the shelf.

    — No pawpaw, she said.

She raised her hands in the air. Up went her arms, they in turn raised her shoulders and up went her halter-neck top. Down dropped her melon-like bust line, revealing a sleek chocolatey-brown board-like stomach, untarnished except for a wrinkle of a navel. God, I really, really, really, really loved that girl.

    — Mango?

I sucked my stomach in.

    — No mango!

She didn't raise her hands.

    — Papaya?

I knew I was making an impression.

    — Papaya? No papaya.

This time she didn't even look at the shelf.

    — Melons!

I spouted, the next exotic fruit that came to my mind.

    — Listen sunshine, don't fuck me around! What do you want?

Actually, now that I think about it, maybe she wasn't African or German. She sounded more north of England, Newcastle or someplace like that.

    — Whatever ya have, says I, trying to be agreeable.

She presented a menu and walked off, her shorts riding higher and higher into the crease of her buttocks.

    — Ah yes, menu. Now let me see … Holy St Finbarr!

They had everything, red Lebanese, Moroccan black, blonde, green, every colour hash under the sun. They had weed, grass, tops, Thai sticks, heads, big flowery heads.

Now, my drug experience up to then had been fairly limited. I might have had a puff or two of some class of grass, or something like that, but really, the whole dope scene was something that had just totally passed me by. Call it peer pressure, call it what you like, but I didn't want to walk out of that café without making a purchase. I looked down the counter. The black girl was talking to the as-yet-unknown-to-me Yvette. She threw her eyes to heaven and pointed Yvette in my direction. Yvette swayed up the counter, I grinned hopelessly at her black friend.

– Bonjour, she said and didn't smile.
– How's she cuttin'? says I.
– So, you see anything you like? she hissed in that inimitable French way.
– Yer friend! says I, and left a – Yahoo! out of me.
– Pardonnez?

She stood there looking confused. I looked at the menu. I may as well have been looking into a hole in the ground.

– So eh, what's the difference? says I.
– Well, obviously, ze price, she says.

Then she proceeded to explain the relative merits of the different colours, scents, textures of hashes and grasses on the menu.

– Zis one will bring you up. Zis one down. Zis one smooth easy. Zis one very happy.
– Have ya got one that will blow the head offa me?

Looking back on it, I suppose that was a stupid question.

– How you mean?
– Like, which one is the best?
– Zere is no best. Zere is no better. It is all excellent.
– Look-it, I explained. – I want to do some real brain damage.

I knew that sort of talk would impress her. Let her know I could hold me drugs as good as the next man, like.

– Oh, she said, and she produced a ready rolled joint. – I suggest you smoke zis, a leetle only, yes?

Her maternal instincts had surfaced, and handing over a handful of guilders, I winked and smiled at her tall black friend.

— And a cup of coffee! A good strong one. Dowcha, gurl-ya!
I sat down, lit my joint and waited for my coffee.

Ra-ra-Rasputin

It got louder and louder and louder,

Ra-ra-Rasputin

I sat there for what seemed like seconds or hours, I'll never know.
Everything was so clear and cloudy at the same time. It was hell. It was
heaven. It was Boney M.

Ra-ra-Rasputin
lover of the Russian Queen.

And it got louder and louder. Then just like that, everything made
sense. The why of life. The answer to the unaskable question. Suddenly
it came to me that it does matter if that tree falls in the woods. I sensed
my spirit, my life force, my soul. I could see my soul, it was there on
the back of my hands, pink and white dots beavering away, all over my
body. It was fascinating. Turning to the palms of my hands, I watched
my soul filter away back between the gaps of my fingers, back behind
the hairline of my wrist. My skin tone changed from red to purple
and the veins, buried deep inside my hands, rose to the surface from
blue to black. The skin gave way to a trembling pulse of raw, fleshy,
sinewed, foul meat that dripped, molten lard-like from my cupped
palm to table. I held my festering hand over the ashtray and sat there
in horror, watching the fluid flesh drip. Attempting to scream for help,
all I could manage was,

Ra-ra-Rasputin

I couldn't move my hands or my head or avert my eyes from the
unfolding surlifeism as my left hand painlessly, gorily dripped into
the dirty ashtray.

Ra-ra-Rasputin

And then something moved inside me, like a squirming alien deep
inside my guts and the most uncontrollable rumbling from down in
my bowel. I somehow managed to make my way to the toilet. I sat
there in the cubicle for an eternity, watching the portaflek paint on
the back of the door play cowboys and Indians as the world fell out of
my bottom.

Knock-Knock

— 'Ello, 'ello, everything is alright in zere?

It was Yvette. She was at the toilet door asking me if everything was alright. I didn't know if everything was alright, but I was feeling mighty fine.

— Everything is wonderful, says I.

I sat there staring at the toilet door, as this epic western unfolded before my eyes. For once the Indians seemed to have the upper hand, but that was probably due to the fact that they were securely stationed inside the circled wagons. The cowboys were riding around and around in circles outside, a whoopin' and a hollerin', shooting into the air and generally acting the bollocks. The Indians just crouched there behind the wagons taking pot-shots, picking off the cowboys one by one. And then, just when it seemed that the cowboys were well and truly licked, there came a faint sound of a bugle. It seemed to come from the door latch. I concentrated on the minute dots expecting to see a company of the 7th Cavalry charging, blue steel flashing, to the rescue. But no, not at all. Not a blue coat in sight, nor red coat, now that I think of it. It was a host of saviours. This gallant band of light cavalry charging to destroy, or to their own destruction, was an elite corps made up of the heroes of all the displaced nations of the world riding to the sound of the guns. They rode in an orderly fashion to the rhythm of their triumphant war harps. I'm sure it was something from the Ó Riada Mass or maybe something by Micheál Ó Súilleabháin. Anyway, who cares, it was glorious just to sit there watching as the losers of the world charge to the rescue of the Indians, who were actually well on top of the situation anyway. They were all there, all those who had fought the good fight and lost. Asians, South Americans, Aboriginals of all casts, even the Dalai Lama was in there with his regiment. And out in front was a squadron of men and women under a green flag emblazoned with a golden harp, the Irish, led by James Connolly on the left flank and Countess Markievicz on the right, screamin' for blood. For once, I felt sorry for the cowboys, but then again, it was so refreshing to see history revised and written by those on the receiving end of it.

Knock-Knock

— 'Ello? 'Ello?

It's Yvette in the distance. Everything is blurry. I don't know who won the battle, it could be still raging there on the back of that toilet door in that café off Damrak for all I know. But whatever about that battle, I think I know who won the war.

How I left that cubicle is a mystery to me. On my feet or on the flat of my back, I'll never know. All I knew was that I woke up next morning in the arms of Yvette, feeling airy and free and no longer a virgin. And that was how I met my wife, the beautiful Yvette.

Those were days of dreams and ideals, a future of a happy-ever-after and poetry. The sun shone down where on we walked. That was before the darkness set in for the first time. It was a time when all in the world was beautiful, young and good.

∽

Ding-Dong

— Jesus! Somebody get the shaggin' door! I screamed into the mattress.

Thump-Thump

Thump-Thump

Banging on the ceiling.

— Pluto!

A muffled scream through the floorboards.

— Will ya answer yer fuckin' door!

It was Brenda the Brasser up in Number 3. Now, I don't know for sure if Brenda was really a brasser or not. I couldn't swear on my mother's soul to it, but everybody called her a brasser.

Strange thing, a name. Everybody calls me Pluto. I even call meself Pluto but it's not my real name. Paul O'Toole, that's my name. Always has been, always will be just plain and simple Paulie. Well, that was until they started calling me Pluto. Don't ask me why but it was a name that stuck.

Ding-Dong
Ding-Dong
My bell again.
Thud-Thud
Thud-Thud
On the ceiling.
— Pluto! The fuckin' door!
Another muffled scream.
— It's not for me, Brenda. Answer it yerself! I roared.
Tap-Tap
Tap-Tap
I can't believe this. The phantom caller was at me shaggin' window.
I pulled my head up from under the heavily scented covers, a pot
pourri of fish heads and socks.
Tap-Tap
Tap-Tap
— Wrong bell! I roared. – Ring another bell!
And then, silence. Thank Christ. Peace at last. I pulled the covers
around my ears, right hand reaching out for a cigarette. I fumbled it
from packet to mouth and then …
Click
… of my Bic. I drew in deep and the cleansing, life-giving smoke
stretched my lungs. My right hand replaced the lighter on the
upturned orange box, fingers finding the switch on my clock radio.
Tick
— And bringing you to the news at eight and *What It Says In The
Papers*, here is the duet from the Pearl Fishers.
It was John Creedon on Radio 1. I lay back, sucking my cigarette,
smoke bellowing from my mouth, flicking the ash into my coffee mug.
Well, it wasn't so much a coffee mug as an ash tray. It looked like a
coffee mug. You know, mug shaped with a handle and traces of soured
coffee, but it hadn't been a coffee mug in about two, two and a half
weeks. Since then, it stood, coagulating coffee at the base, next to my
clock radio, an ashtray, an almost full ashtray.

Ding-Dong
— Fuck off!
Thud-Thud
— Pluto, the fuckin' door!
Tap-Tap
Tap-Tap
— Ah, Jaysus, this is ridiculous!
So I threw on my overcoat and slipped into my untied boots. I placed my hand on the handle of the door that led to the bulbless hall, the hall that led to the front door, the door of the bells.
Knock-Knock
Knock-Knock
— Is there no peace in this world?
I jerked open the door.
— What! What do you want!
I was on the offensive. There, in the darkened hall, stood Herman, overalls daubed in layers of coloured paint, canvas overalls better than any canvas I had seen up in his bloody studio.
— What, Herman? What do you want?
— Is your doorbell, ja?
He stood there up to his neck in continental arrogance.
— Look, why don't you open the door, you're nearest it, I snapped.
— Is your bell, ja?
But there was no budge out of Herman.
— Look! I explained. – Just 'cos it's my doorbell, don't mean 'tis my visitor. It's probably for you, Brenda or the Monk.
— Ja! Ze Monk! Could be for ze Monk? Herman reassessed his position.
Jimmy, or the Monk, as we called him, lived up in Number 4, a Neanderthal in his late forties. He had spent half his working life on the roads and building sites of England. A tough life for a tough man but at the delicate age of forty-five he returned home, unable to keep up with the rat race of the building line. He first came to live in our house about two years ago and ever since he has been in the process of refurbishing his imaginary cottage out in Carrignavar, Carrigaline,

Carrigadrohid. Well, 'twas Carrig a-something. He had a habit of collecting bits of broken furniture, cracked toilet bowls and non-reflective mirrors from skips around the town.

— For the cottage, he'd say.

Everybody knew there was no cottage. He was a hoarder. A hoarder flogging the odd few bits and pieces in the second-hand shop down on George's Quay. But the pile in the hallway got higher and higher. Anything the Monk did never bothered me. I had enough insanity behind my door than to be worrying about the madness in the hallway.

~

Ding-Dong

— Christ's sake, Pluto! Answer yer bell!

It was Brenda the Brasser.

— It's okay, Brenda. I'm here in the shaggin' hall.

I stood there in my boots and overcoat getting the last blast of nicotine into my lungs.

Ding-Dong

— Will ya get it, Pluto?

— Jesus! I'm getting it! I'm getting it! Don't get yer knickers in a twist!

I looked up; she was like a mushroom-induced vision. Brenda the Brasser stood there at the turn of the stairs in her pink fluffy slip and flip-flops, pink satin viscose-mix dressing gown, her peroxide beehive down around her ears and, like me, she strained to get a final hit of nicotine from a well-burned butt.

— Ah, how are you this morning, Brenda? Herman smiled.

— I'd be a lot better if he'd answer his fucking doorbell!

She pointed at me.

— I was just telling Herman that it might be my doorbell but it's not my visitor, I explained again.

— I don't give a fuck who the visitor is for, answer the fuckin' door! she snapped. – And what's more, what about all that rubbish in the hall?

Brenda always had a problem about the hall, I suppose it affected her clientele.

— Well, it's not mine, I said. – That plastic bag there is mine but the rest, I looked at Herman. – Well, eh, I don't know.

— Don't look at me, Herman protested. – Okay! Okay! Zis big chunk of wood here is mine. I make sculpture in the back yard, yes? But all this things here, phaaa!

Herman threw his arms towards the bulbless light fitting.

— I'm sure most of that stuff is the Monk's, I added.

Enough said. Brenda had too much going on in her own mind than to be getting involved in the tangled mess that contorted and distorted between the Monk's ears.

> *Ding-Dong*
> *Ding-Dong*

— I comin'! I comin'!

Herman shuffled towards the hall door.

I stood there in anticipation. Because at this point, I was interested to see who was at the door. Probably the Monk and he'd locked himself out or something. Brenda was also interested, her head bent to her waist and turned sideways in an effort to catch a glimpse of the visitor from her obstructed view at the turn of the stairs. I swayed from heel to toe with an, – I told you so, arrogance, sucking my cigarette. Nothing but an overcoat and old pair of boots to conceal my nakedness.

The front door opened, a dazzling brightness of morning sun silhouetting Herman.

— Eh, is me dad there? a small voice asked.

— Your father? Herman echoed. – Who is your father?

— Paul O'Toole, she said. – His name is Paul O'Toole …

— No, little girl. There is no Paul O'Toole living in zis house, Herman said.

— Is that you Veronica? I pushed past Herman.

— Oh Dad! I'm glad, I wasn't sure if this was the right house!

— Jesus, Veronica girl! I buttoned my overcoat. – Come in, come in! What brings you up here this time of the morning?

This was an awkward one. Veronica isn't really my daughter at all, but Mags, her mother, was my ex-girlfriend, or more like my ex-ex-girlfriend, because I was out with another girl since or, should I say, while I was going out with Mags. I know, I know. It confuses me too, but what can I say. Hey, that's life. You see, when I first met Mags, I was coming from Limbo. I had reached the point where I had stopped struggling with the loss of my wife, the beautiful Yvette.

When Yvette walked out of my life it was goodbye to naivety and hello to cynicism. I realised that the prince didn't necessarily marry the princess and I suppose sometimes the princess might have to kiss a few frogs before she meets her prince. And I was content to be a frog for a while, that's when Mags and the others came into my life. I really didn't care. And as for this, – they all lived happily ever after, well fuck that for a game of darts.

So, I had no Yvette. I had no future. That was when I first found myself deep down under the duvet, deep down in the darkness. Two years there, two anguished years of drink, disillusion and delusion. I fell down a lot and woke up in the most unusual places. Two years of head space, two years of insanity, out of body, out of mind, out of head. It was my Limbo, and Limbo does exist. It's the absence of supreme love due to ignorance rather than any misdeeds. That's Limbo.

Not such a bad place. It's a place of total objectivity. It's a place where you are free. Free to float around in your ignorance. It's a place of self-assessment. But it doesn't last forever, it only seems like that. Like drowning, when you stop struggling you just float gently back to the surface, and all is hunky-dory.

And, as I say, that's when I first met Mags. She was an unmarried mother, and I was a wifeless husband. She was a Leftie. A bleeding-heart liberal, with right wing tendencies. She was Left of Labour and Right of Fianna Fáil. You know the type. But sometimes she was so far Left she was Right. I suppose if I were in my right mind, I wouldn't have touched her with a 10-foot barge pole. But my mind was far from right. I had just been blasted headfirst, without a helmet, through the barriers of a broken marriage in holy Catholic Ireland. Yep! I thought Mags and her little girl Veronica were the best choice during a bad time. They moved into my place, and I moved into their life. It was good while it lasted. I'm not bitter or anything but,

— Fuck her and anyone who looks like her, is all I can say.

~

I looked down. There stood Veronica with a face more beautiful than her mother's.

— Eh, come in, Veronica love.

— Thanks, Dad.

She was always a mannerly child.

Brenda the Brasser vanished back up the stairs, in a pink flash of Lurex while Herman still hovered around my door saddle.

— Do ya mind, Herman, I'd like a word with me daughter.

— Oh, by all means, by all means. Do carry on as if I'm not here, he said.

And there was not a budge out of him.

— In private, I said, and gently slammed the door in his face.

There I was in my overcoat and boots standing in the middle of my kip of a flat, with a young girl who insisted on calling me Dad. Veronica stood there wide-eyed. Odd really, she was the first stranger, and when I say stranger, I mean person living outside our house, to cross my threshold and, having my hovel viewed with a new set of eyes certainly opened my eyes and nose. There was a stench of rot about the place, a total mess, like a bomb had hit it.

— Jesus, Veronica girl, good to see ya. How's yer mam and everybody, eh? Here la', excuse me manners, eh, take a seat. Take a seat.

And, like *Norwegian Wood*, she looked around and, you guessed it, no seat. So I lifted the coffee mug-cum-ashtray and clock radio from the orange box.

— There la', I pointed.

— Thanks, Dad.

She was never one for small talk, but she had a message to deliver.

— Eh, Dad?

— Yes, Veronica girl?

— It's Eddie's Confirmation today and Josephine asked me to come up and remind ya.

Now, this is where it gets confusing. Josephine, like Mags, was an ex-girlfriend. In fact, Josephine is the ex-girlfriend I had been out with since Mags. And Eddie, he's Josephine's son. What can I say, I'll never be sure about him. They all said I was his father, but really, I'll never know.

— I suppose I should be getting back and giving Mam a hand.

Veronica stood up to leave. She was never one to hang around. Herman could take a leaf from her book.

— Well, if ya gotta go, ya gotta go!

I made it easy for her.

— So, will we see ya later?

She wanted confirmation on the Confirmation.

— Oh, chalk it down, Veronica girl. But eh, where exactly is the Confirmation?

— Eh? The North Chapel! she said, with a not amused look on her face.

It was as if I was supposed to know these things.

— And, eh, time? I tempted fate.

— Eleven o'clock, she said, and she made to leave.

— Eh, Veronica girl?

— Yes, Dad?

— Eh, what date is it today?

She looked at me as if I was some class of an imbecile.

— It's the 23rd of April, is that good enough for ya?

She looked through me and turned to walk away. I followed her to the hall door. I mentioned that I'd have to collect my dole first. But promised that I'd meet her up at the Confirmation, after I signed on.

— Look! she snapped. – Be there early, be there late, or don't be there at all! Do you think I give a shit! I'm only the messenger.

She stood there brazen-faced. Not a girl to mince words. A dark horse, our Veronica.

— Ah, no, no, I giggled nervously. – I'll be there, I guarantee ya.

But I don't think my guarantees counted for much, not with Veronica anyway.

— So, eh? See ya later so, Veron!

— See ya, Dad!

She raised her hand in a dismissive wave and walked away. I stood there and watched Veronica saunter out of Waterloo Terrace and down into the filth of the city, a woman before her time.

After The Ball

Down our street change comes slowly, so slow it's undetectable. Undetectable like aging, yet inevitable. Some things never change. As usual there's Richie standing at the far side of my shop counter, snatching a free read of the death notices in the evening paper before heading home for his tea.

Traffic is thick, spluttering heavy metals that make their way up to the first-floor windows and stick like tar. Through my shop window I see frustrated faces, facing home, but no move in the traffic.

— Busy out there? says I, in the hope of conversation.

— Nothing new about that, he mutters. – This street was ass to
   nose with ox in Viking times …

Outside, I notice a driver abandon the gridlock. Hazards flashing, he leaves his car and makes a beeline for the shop. The doorbell announces his entry. His eyes scour the cigarette shelf.

Fags! A pack of them there! he points.

It crosses my mind that here's a man who has been battling with cigarettes and I'm witnessing his most recent breakout.

— Shockin' out there, says I, being sociable.

— Shockin'? Dia-fuckin'-bolical!

— This street is always diabolical, says Richie, and he lowers the
   paper.

— Bloody bottleneck!

He struggles to get a cigarette from packet to mouth, while ranting on about two lanes coming into three, or something like that. I take his money, say thanks and send him on his way.

Traffic has moved a couple of feet up the street. Horns honk. Fists flake the air. The cigarette smoker slips into his car apologetically, drives that couple of feet and stops, still going nowhere, just ticking over.

It crosses my mind that maybe this street was ass to nose with ox in Viking times, but it wasn't always that way. So I turn to Richie, and say,

    — Would you believe that we played eight-a-side soccer up and down that street without interference from the traffic, and that wasn't the Dark Ages?

    — Well, ya wouldn't play pickie out there now, says he.

And with a flick of his wrists, he's trawling through the small ads.

I make my way towards the window and look out on the insanity of it all. Maybe it's the curse of middle age, but for some reason through the car exhaust and dusky haze, I'm transported to another time.

The stretch of city street between the old bakery and the gate next to the bookies was our stadium. And with every goal, foul or near miss, the roar of the crowd echoing inside our heads would erupt,

    Oooooaugh!

To the sound of the Kop, North Bank or Stretford End.

And that's where you'd find us, every day after school, the downtown dirty faces funting a ball up and down the street, shouting, roaring and red-faced.

It's about a quarter past four, coal smoke fills the air, sky dark, street dimly lit. The clock is ticking and it's getting late. I stand up from the kerb threatening to go home and say,

    — Someone call over to Georgie's house and get the ball …

    - There's no way his mam will give out the ball without Georgie.

    — Well, someone call over to the house and get Georgie.

    — Hang on! I think I sees him!

    — There he is!

    — That's him!

And there's Georgie, turning the corner of Brewery Lane, ball under his arm, and trailing behind him, his kid brother Small Paudie.

    — Hoi, Georgie!

    — Come on!

Photo: Mirrorpix/Reach Licensing

— Kick the ball!

Georgie hears us, but he's still out of range. He walks out onto the street and raises his finger in the air as if judging the wind direction. In one slick swoop the ball slips from under his arm onto his outstretched left hand. His pace quickening to a trot, ball drops and without missing a beat he gives it a lash. Like a rocket it vanishes into the darkness way above the streetlamp.

— On the head!

— Lay it on!

— Chip it in!

A quick tap around, the teams picked, and the game is on …

There was an uneven number of us out that evening, so Georgie's brother Small Paudie was once again selected to be the floater. And as a floater, Small Paudie's job was to even the odds. So, in the event of a goal, he had to endure the indignity of changing sides to play for the losing team. It was pathetic to see him, night after night, turn around and play for the losing side while his ex-teammates jumped and howled to the roar of the crowd. What a way to start life? Always on the losing side, always the reject. That was Small Paudie, a born loser.

Looking back on it now, Small Paudie was just that little bit too young and too small to be of any use to any team. He was a hopeless soccer player. He was a hindrance. So each night he would spend the whole game running his little heart out without as much as a smell of the ball. Except when it went wide and ended up miles off down the street, Small Paudie was always the one who'd run after it. Anything, anything for a touch of the ball.

… it's coming towards the Angelus, the score 14-all. The women of the street are calling for us to come in for our tea. It's time to call it a night.

Up goes the shout.

— Next goal wins!
The rule is on. The ball is out.
The pressure is off.
All men forward.
Both sides playing attacking defence.
And after twenty-eight goals rip-roaring and rattling the back of the onion sack,
the next goal is the only goal that counts.
A quick break.
A clatter of sparks from quarter-irons.
Roaring.
Backward running.
Shirt-tugging.
Shoving.
A rocket sends the pigskin squealing two inches wide of the post.
The Stretford End on their toes …

Oooouagh!

Ball is out.
A long clearance sends it high and to the left.
Draws the midfield to the wing.
Opens a gap in the hole.
Georgie makes a break along the side.
Plays the ball off the high footpath.
He weaves inside the parked Morris Minor.
He beats one!
Beats two!
He shoots!
Keeper is sent full stretch to keep it out of the net.
Keeper lofts it down to the halfway line.
It's intercepted and sent back in.

Picked up by Georgie.
Georgie's on the ball, the world is at his feet
and he's thundering down the wing.
Small Paudie at the far post.

— Georgie! Pass the ball! Georgie! Pass the ball Georgie! To me!

Georgie sees his kid brother waving frantically and calling for the ball. Maybe it's because Small Paudie has two left feet or maybe it's because Georgie is a glory hunter, whatever the reason, in that split of a second Georgie decides to go it alone. He takes a crack.

Ball screws off his boot, clips the footpath, spins in the air and bounces out wide. Keeper leaves it off. The Kop, in full voice,

Georgie Worst, Super Spa.
He walks like a woman,
And he wears a bra!

From nowhere comes Small Paudie, his little legs like pistons, knees pumping under short pants. His right foot reaches out awkwardly, left shin drawing blood as it scrapes along the road. Ball connects with Paudie's ankle. It rebounds off the kerb and bounces …

Small Paudie tumbles over, flat on his face. Sprawled out there on the road, he looks on as the ball bounces, spins and bounces again. Keeper is caught flat-footed. He can do nothing but watch as the ball bounces just beyond his reach and into the goal.

Goal! Goal! Goal!

The word, – Goal, echoes across the street, from gate to gate and all around the stadium. The Kop in all its glory is on fire,

Give him a ball – and a yard of grass,
He'll set you up with a perfect pass.
Give him a ball – and a yard of grass,
Paudie'll leave you – On yer ass!

Small Paudie's eyes are bulging in his head. And stretched out, there in the middle of the street he raises his arms above his head in a V for victory.

Small Paudie is on his feet. He makes a dash inside the keeper, picks up the ball and waves his right hand to the invisible crowd behind the goal. He hears them call out his name. They are chanting,

Nice one, Paudie! Nice one, son!

Nice one Paudie! Let's have another one!

He jumps in the air, shaking his little clenched fist. This is Small Paudie's night, his moment of glory. Not only has he scored the winning goal, but the game is over. Full-time whistle. Small Paudie can't be sent to the losing team. In one of those magical moment of footballing history – Small Paudie has won the game.

Georgie runs up behind his baby brother and rubs his feather-like hair with a father-like pride ...

— Dowcha, Paudie boy!

Small Paudie is peaking. He will remember this goal for the rest of his living days, but right now all he wants to do is get home and tell his dad.

— Dowcha, Paudie boy! Georgie says it again.

— Sorted, Georgie! Sorted!

Small Paudie gives a thumbs-up and he's off on a lap of honour.

Three foot-two eyes of blue,
Paudie Buckley's after you,
and we love him,
we love him, we do ...

～

It came out of nowhere. To the sound of screeching brakes and the smell of burning rubber. We turned. We just stood there unable to move. Hopelessly helpless. Unable to do anything but look on horrified as two tons of rubber and steel just chewed up Small Paudie, splattering concrete and tarmac with blood, crushing schoolboy skull and bones to asphalt ...

Georgie cradled his baby brother's mangled body until the ambulance men prised the little corpse from his arms. And kneeling there in the middle of the street, Georgie wept. Georgie was never the same after that. Nothing was ever the same after that.

I have vague memories of neighbours on the street with prayers and tears. It was the first time I heard the words, *closed casket funeral*, I wasn't too sure what it meant. All I knew was that I never saw Small Paudie again. Paudie the floater was gone.

Georgie's family moved out of our street soon after that, others followed. Of all the boys who played ball that evening only one remains living on my street. And maybe I don't remember some of their names, but I have lived with each and every one of their dirty faces etched indelibly on my brain.

It was a day I remember vividly. It was the day we lost the game. It was the day street soccer became a thing of the past, the day that Small Paudie died.

$\sim$

It's dusky outside. Traffic has moved a few more feet up the street. Richie folds the newspaper as neat as he can and places it back under the bundle on the counter. It's almost six o'clock. He's heading home to catch the news on the telly.

— I was just reading there, says he. – The Council are talking about pedestrianising this street.

— This street? says I.

— Says it here in the paper, that they want to attract families back to live in the inner city, he says.

And as Richie spouts some gobbledegook about inner city rejuvenation it crosses my mind that the people who live here never called it the inner city, it was always just plain downtown. And one thing I learned over the years is that when you hear the words inner city bouncing about, the crushing ball of development is never far behind.

— … it'd be nice, wouldn't it? he says. – It' d be nice to have the place pedestrianised …

I'm tempted to say that this street was pedestrianised long before there was traffic on it, but I just don't have the heart to get into all that. So I just say,

— Yer right, Richie. It'd be lovely. A few flowerpots and benches, that sort of thing …

Richie shoves his lunchbox inside his coat and heads off into the dark, home to his gas coal-effect fire and telly. I watch him cross the street, weave in and out through the traffic and pass over beyond the lane where Georgie and Small Paudie used to live. Somehow I know, pedestrianisation or no, football will never be played on our street again. The families are gone, never to return. They have moved on to the corporation reservations on the northside, out of the heart of the city.

I remember the day Small Paudie died. It was the day street soccer became a thing of the past. It was the day the traffic won the game and the heart of a city stopped beating.

Co Mayo: On the road to Westport Arts Festival with Backwater Artists (*After The Ball* by Cónal Creedon – Award Winner). L–R: Éilis Ní Fhaoláin, Cónal Creedon, Kevin Holland, Geraldine Creedon, Chris Samuels. Photo: Brendan O'Connor.

Every Picture Tells A Story

I suppose my happiest days were when I was finding myself, lost in the mind of my creator.

∿

— Veeronni-ccaaa! Veeronni-ccaaa! she'd scream.
The gallery would shake.
— Maaam! Are ya lookin' for me? Maaam! Where are ya? Maaam?
The gallery would quake.
— I'm up in de top gallery, Veronica girl! Veeronni-ccaaa? Can ya hear me? Veeronni-ccaaa, I'm up here!
And from the sculpture gallery, two flights down,
— Wha'? Maaam! You lookin' for me, Mam? Where are ya? Maaam?

∿

Mary had been cleaning these halls for as long as anyone could remember, and now she was handing on the baton and in the process of training in her teenage daughter Veronica.

Mary was part of the gallery. Her wit and sharp turn of phrase were legendary. But by those of us who had recently arrived and were new to this world and didn't have the years behind us to build up a relationship with Mary, the first thing that struck us was her wild sense of colour and contrasting textures. With her hair tucked up under a chequered head scarf, and a Gaudí yellow, acrylic polo-neck peeping out under her blue-red floral nylon dust coat, her white sports socks over her brown tights and fluffy slippers. She was a walking installation. Cigarette hanging from her lip and buckets and brushes and mops dangling and jangling from her arms, Mary would manoeuvre around the gallery, dusting, sweeping and mopping.

Dusting a frame, she'd notice her own reflection in the glass. Seeing her face surrounded by the frame, she'd stop, pucker her lips, adjust her head scarf and move along.

The clip-clop clatter of Veronica's teenage, black patent, sling-back platforms announced her arrival across the well-worn teak-block flooring.

— Do ya want me, Mam?

Mary looked up.

— Jesus, Veronica, where were ya? I was looking for ya all morning. Did ya check de top toilets?

Mary pointed her mop handle to the ceiling, in the direction of the upstairs toilet.

— Ah, Mam! Dem toilets don't need cleaning.

Veronica knew that Mary knew that the toilets in this gallery were as classy as the Metropole and as sterile as the operating theatre in the Bons. But Mary knew there was a job to be done, and there's no point doing a job unless you do it right, and her job now was to keep Veronica focused of every detail, even the things people don't notice, it was a vital part of her training.

— Go up and clean 'em, anyway and make sure everything's there, like!

— And don't use the lift! Take the stairs!

Veronica clattered off in a huff, dragging her mop behind her.

I remained silent. Mary continued her dusting, unaware that I was observing her every move. Strange, really, that in all the years Mary had spent in and around the gallery, she seemed totally oblivious to the art that surrounded her. Gallery or gutter, it didn't matter, cleaning was cleaning. She spent as much time on the skirting boards as she did on the frames. A surface was a surface, and everything deserved equal attention.

And yet, despite herself, in her own instinctive way, over the years Mary had become familiar and comfortable with contemporary art. She knew her art. She knew artists. Some she liked. Some she didn't care for at all. After all, she had seen it all: from the classical landscapes and portraits to the ultra-modern Coke tin sculptures, or sand, glass and feather installations.

She smiles when she remembers her first week working in the gallery. That naked man rolling around the gallery floor, with nothing but a string of toilet paper wrapped around his head and chest and a turkey leg hanging from his neck protecting his modesty.

    — Performance? she muttered, as she munched her tea-soaked fig rolls. – Dat young fella's making a show of himself!

She later admitted that when she walked in and found him there stretched out naked on the floor,

    — Jesus, Mary and Joseph, she whispered. – I didn't know whether to call an ambulance or the cops.

Over twenty years pottering around this old building she had learned to curb the honesty of her naivety. But Mary had seen it all. She knew her art. She knew what she liked.

J-Cloth flying, she had completed the full circuit of the gallery and was heading in my direction to collect her mop and brush before moving on to the stairs. She looked at me. I felt her gaze was deeper than her own reflection in the glass. I became self-conscious. She stopped, stepped back two steps, stared and sighed. She then walked right up to me until her nose almost touched the glass. Reading the signature on my lower right corner she whispered the name of my creator,

    — Han '95.

And stepping back again, she panned the whole gallery, the blending of colours, the formation of composition, the intensity, the softness. She leaned forward again, forensically studying the detail until the magic was broken by the clip-clop clatter …

    — Finished de toilets, Mam.

Veronica was back, the moment lost.

    — Good girl.

Veronica smiled with the embarrassment of pride.

Mary pointed at me with the mop. I tensed up; my paint stiffened as I drew back from my mounting in an effort to hold my composition.

    — Isn't dat dotey?

— It is, Mam. But what is it?

Veronica couldn't make head nor tail of me.

— It doesn't matter what it is …

Mary drew close to Veronica and went on to explain the unimportance of how a rainbow gets up in the sky, or what makes the sunshine, or where the moon goes by day, or who made the world.

> — Dey're all creations, she said. – And, like all creation, it's a mystery.
>
> You either like it or you don't. And I like dis.
>
> — It's beautiful, alright, Veronica nodded.

She stepped back to take in the whole picture.

> — Girls!

I was enjoying the attention, until the curator walked in,

> — Girls! he repeated with a tone of authority and clapped his hands to get their attention. – Must get the lead out! Have ye finished the stairs yet?
>
> — Just starting now, Mr Peterson.

Mary kept her head down.

> — Well, must get a move on! Big opening tonight! Big night! Big wigs! Opinion leaders down from Dublin, he says and mentions *The Irish Times*.

Mr Peterson was buzzing, but Mary was used to his ways. He always flustered and fussed on opening day.

> — On our way now, Mr Peterson. But we were just saying, like, isn't dis painting dotey, Mr Peterson?

She pointed her mop in my direction.

> — Dotey? he repeated with a dismissive laugh. – I'm not sure that dotey manages to capture its significance, he laughed again. – I can see it now, under the artist's statement in the catalogue described as dotey.
>
> — Catalogue? Mary echoed.
>
> — … this is probably one of the most prestigious pieces of the decade, he pointed towards me. – Dotey?

And he laughed again. But Mary was not one to be brow-beaten by unchallenged superiority or entitled sarcasm.

— And I'm sure you'll be telling me the cost of it? she said. – Worth
every penny of it too, no doubt. But I still think it's dotey ...
Mr Peterson was too busy to stop. He headed towards the door issuing
orders to his personal assistant, who was hanging on his every word
and coat tails and repeating out loud his checklist for the evening.
Once again, he made some statement about important people coming
down from Dublin and *The Irish Times*.

Mary topped her cigarette into her mop bucket and headed off
in the direction of the stairs, giving a swipe of her duster to the No
Smoking sign as she trundled off. Mr Peterson sniffed and held his
breath. He placed his hand on my frame to make sure I hadn't been
tipped off-centre. He turned and walked out. The gallery was lifeless.

~

The gallery was alive. The atmosphere was electrified by a spiralling
sense of anticipation. Like Gulliver, I towered over those gathered
and yet I was smaller, a 24x40 acrylic on paper. I looked at them,
they looked at each other. Flashes from Nikon and Pentax announced
the glitterati. It was the usual who's who big night out in small-town
Ireland. All in all, it was the makings of a mighty show. They had
gathered for the art yet spent very little time viewing us. This was the
big event in the social calendar. Red dots were flying, left and right of
me. I was one of the privileged ones, on loan from a private collection
with an NFS tag in place.

Arts students circled the wine table like vultures.

— It's your turn.

— I can't go again.

— Look, I got the last lot.

— They'll fuck me out if I stroll up and pick up six glasses of plonk!
He was under pressure.

— Just chill and act casual. There's a rake a' gargle there. Just act
like you own the place.

— Jesus, alright, but they're on to us, and if I get shagged out.

— Look, just get four glasses, two each ...
He struck off, through the furs and silks where all that glittered was

gold. He was as inconspicuous as any gangly eighteen-year-old with a mohawk and a hacked biker jacket could be in such a situation. These were his formative years; he had flown the nest and had set out on the adventure that is life. He returned hands full and smiling, a little boy in a young man's frame.

The movers and the shakers were holding court. Grey-haired suits, all ponytails and sunglasses, they nodded, winked, waved, shook hands and generally rubbed shoulders. Cheque books carried, catalogues rolled and pointed and slapped against thighs. They liked what they saw.

∼

Clink – Clink – Clink
The sound of a clinking wine glass calls order.
– Ladies and Gentlemen, ahem!
Mr Peterson stepped forward.

An uneasy dash to the wine table for a re-fill, this could take some time. Freeloaders to the rear. The speeches began. The show was officially opened by the holy trinity of the art world, an academic politician with a high media profile. With a few witty anecdotes, we were all praised, including our creator. And following the acknowledgment of his genius, he took his bow with humility.

– And now, I'd like to declare this exhibition open. Thank you!
A hearty round of applause, and so it began. They mingled, raised a glass or two and laughed. This was a good opening.

From the corner of my frame I noticed my creator, he was uneasy, cornered by a self-proclaimed art expert.

– You'd be mad not to accept, argued the expert. – One of your paintings in my collection would be a feather in your cap. Your name up there with the best of them. Cash into the hand, no gallery fees. What they don't know won't bother 'em. Look-it, knock a hundred quid off catalogue price, cash into the hand. No gallery fees. Do we have a deal? Shake on it and you'll have a wad of cash in your arse pocket on your way home.

    — I appreciate your generous offer. But really all sales must go through the gallery.

The creator was backed into the corner by the expert's continued pushing.

    — What are ya afraid of, you're a fool, man! I'm here standing in front of you, cash in hand.

    — Look! I'm not a horse trader. I can't be cutting side deals at my own exhibition. If you'd like to call to my studio sometime, I have work there …

The creator stepped back.

    — Ah go on outa that, it's my last offer. Take it or leave it.

When the expert made the hackneyed haggling manoeuvre, the false walk away, a look of relief came over the creator's face.

    — Mr Hanlon? a timid voice.

The creator turned. An elegant lady faced him, no furs, no silks, but elegant from her shoulder-length hair held back with a bow, to her slender ankles.

    — Mr Hanlon? she repeated.

I nearly jumped off my backing board with the shock. It was Mary, Mary the cleaner, looking very chic, totally colour coordinated in a navy A-line classic and matching petite pumps.

    — Don't mind your Mr Hanlon. Han's the name, everybody calls me Han.

The creator recognised genuine interest.

    — I've no invitation, she said. - I'm not sure if I'm supposed to be here at all. I'm the cleaner here in the gallery. And I see a lot of art coming and going out of this place, most of it, I could take it or leave it. But I was in town doing a bit of late night shopping and I felt I just had to drop in and tell you how much I liked your paintings. Been in and out of this room all week, looking at the exhibition being hung up on the walls and …

She stopped abruptly, clearly embarrassed, when it occurred to her that maybe she was talking too much.

— I know you, said the creator. – You've been here for years, since I was a student. You're Mary, aren't you?

— That's right, she smiled. – Mary Harrington.

— Well, I'm delighted you like the show.

— Like it? I love it, it's lovely. In fact, that one there, she pointed at me. – I was only saying to my daughter this morning that it's dotey. But this one here, she cast her eyes towards the painting that had caused the creator such grief with the expert. – This one's very cute too.

— Do you really think so?

— Ah, well now, not that I'd know a lot about art, she explained.

The creator beamed pride.

— Right! said the expert, and he stepped between them. – I'll throw another fifty quid at it. But that's my final offer!

The creator whipped a pen from his pocket and printed N.F.S. in broad bold, capitals on the white tag beneath the painting.

— Not For Sale, says he.

And placing Mary's arm under his oxter, he guided her towards the wine table, leaving the expert standing there.

— Would you like a glass of wine, Mrs Harrington? Have you seen the rest of the …

He led her towards the wine table. Mr Peterson cleared his throat, sniffed and smiled uneasily. Mary and the creator strolled around the room in conversation, in unison, they chatted and laughed, good belly laughs, as if totally unaware of the floorshow that surrounded them. He spoke his dreams and ideas, she spoke her observations, simple but no less in-depth, accurate and valid. Slightly uncomfortable in their surroundings, they found comfort in each other's company and safety in a sea of insanity.

The wine ran out, the opening closed, and for the following fortnight we just hung around. We were observed and analysed; it was nice. And there was something reassuring about observing Mary and Veronica, their humours and unpredictable routine.

It was like rummage day at the Charity Shop.

Two weeks had passed, the exhibition closed. Paper, twine, bubble-wrap, Scotch tape and artwork strewn across the gallery floor. We were manhandled down from the wall. I was propped up against a sculpture plinth as my fellow paintings were wrapped, stacked and made ready to be handed over to their new owners. Mary and Veronica were busy, going at full tilt keeping on top of the endless stream of litter and clutter.

— Closings are as crazy as openings, she said.

By mid-afternoon, the gallery was cleared. Mary had the floor brushed and mopped.

— … and I'll give that a good polish tomorrow when it's dry, she said to herself as if justifying the fact that she was going home early.

The sound of Mr Peterson clearing his throat caught her by surprise. He had the knack of appearing out of nowhere, behind her when she neither expected nor needed him.

— The floor is still damp from the mopping, Mr Peterson, she said. – So, I'll have to come back tomorrow to polish it.

It sounded like a weak excuse for knocking off early.

— I'm glad I caught you before you left, he said. – This was handed in at the desk for you.

Mr Peterson handed her the parcel.

— For me?

— It was dropped off by the artist Han …

— For me? she said it again.

The shape of the package left her in no doubt, and the tell-tale sensation of bubble-wrap beneath the wrapping paper only confirmed what Mary instinctively knew. She had seen enough paintings in her lifetime, she knew exactly was it was. Mr Peterson smiled and cleared his throat again, he stood there in expectation, waiting for her to unwrap the painting. But Mary had made a decision there and then that it would not be revealed until she got it home safely to her front

room. Once again, Mr Peterson cleared his throat, as if to say,
   — Well?
But this was one artwork that would not be having a gallery preview.

Mary walked off with a little skip to her step, her treasure clutched tightly in her outstretched hands – the clip-clop clatter of Veronica's shoes trailing behind. The attendants winked, nodded and smiled as Mary passed the front desk. Eager to get home, she didn't stop for the usual chat.

And so, the exhibition ended. Next day I was delivered back to my private collector and placed in a room of my peers, a Louis le Brocquy, a Brian Bourke, a Mick Mulcahy. I should be honoured. I have been elevated to this position of distinction. But for some strange reason, I seem to have lost my dream quality and my inspirational power. I have become a name, in this room of names. I am classified and judged by a language of strict terminology, the language of experts, a language of academics, a language not mine. Life is lifeless. My existence is measured only by the reflected prestige I give my owner.

My creation was my death. I hang here in suspended animation, lifeless. In my lucid moments I dream, how nice just to spend a day over Mary Harrington's fireplace, being chatted to and loved. But when I feel dark, and sometimes I get very dark, I just wish I had never been created. Before a brush was put to paper, that was the time of my potential, before I was hung out to dry. I lived in the mind of my creator, it was a time of eternity, where all was one and yet none. It was a time of colour and freedom and expression. In that eternity before creation, the possibilities were endless. I could have been expressed as anything, the mystery, the excitement, the unrealised and potential expectation. We built pyramids and viewed the world through the tinted lens of spotless stained glass.

Arthur, The Exhibitionist And Nigel Rolfe*

Coming out of my teens, crossing Patrick's Bridge, in a time when Boot Boys Ruled – OK. Twenty-four-inch parallels and Crombie, hair cropped tightly, snake-eyed, my style was slow and calculating. Evenly paced, air hissed from my punctured AirWair.

    – Hoi, Arto! Arto! Over here!

It was Hacker, Macker and Slasher, red silk linings from Crombies flashing, they were weaving in and out between bumper-to-bumper, Saturday afternoon downtown traffic.

    – Hoi, Arto, check it out!

Hacker pointed in the direction of 5a Bridge Street. I could make out the words, Triskel Arts Centre and Exhibition.

    – Dere's a fella' over dere! On his knees. Naked!

Slasher looked shocked.

    – Naked?

    – That's right, said Macker. – A fish tied 'round his fuckin' neck!

    – You're takin' de piss, lads?

I smiled, they did not. This was something I had to see for myself. So I crossed the street to check it out.

    – A bunch a' fuckin' steamers!

Hacker warned, and we went our separate ways.

    It was voyeuristic. It was masochistic. It was sadistic. There he was, the exhibitionist, on his knees and naked. And just like Macker said, he had a fish tied around his neck.

    – Somebody pick him up for Christ's sake! my mind screamed.

This poor misfortunate needed help. But no one moved to lend a hand. They just stood there, sipping wine, mute and pensive, looking on. I didn't understand. I was shocked and puzzled. I questioned. Maybe I understood.

— Jesus, I'm outa here! I thought to myself and roared, – Steamers! I took the stairs two at a time and back out onto the normality of Bridge Street in the rain. Soon after that, me and the lads grew up, signed on and went our own ways.

～

Ten years squatting in a kip in London, I was home for Christmas, looking for a job.

— Hoi, Arto! Over here, Arto!

It was Hacker. A decade down, but we picked up exactly where we'd left off. It was like I had never left. Gone were the Crombies and parallels, but things were the same.

— Of course I'm not workin', I'm an artist.

— You? An artist? You couldn't draw a straight line.

— That's what makes me an artist, says he.

— Gowan outa that.

… and locking onto his neck, I ran him at the *Echo* boy outside Roches, sending Echoes flying and earrings jangling as Hacker's biker jacket crumpled up over his neatly shaven head. Things never change.

Hacker said he'd like to introduce me to the arts, and that evening he brought me to the opening of an exhibition. We guzzled free wine, eye-balled the ladies, more drink and on to Zoës for a bop. An opening addict, that's what I became. What more would you want of a Tuesday night. Free drink, culture and Zoës for a bop. What can I say? Gabba, Gabba, Hey! It was party time in Artsville, and I was home to stay.

～

— Slasher? I hesitated. – Slasher?

I wasn't sure. It must have been twelve years. He was twisted on Liberty Street. Unrecognisable.

— Arto! he smiled.

I helped him to his feet. We hugged and talked about the old days. He hadn't seen the lads for years. I told him I was meeting Hacker.

Boot Boys Rule OK! Image © Robin Dale, courtesy of Mary Evans Picture Library.

He wasn't interested. I may have mentioned something about an exhibition opening. If I did, it was a mistake, because somewhere in the jumble of garbled talk the words free drink slipped out. Slasher swayed there uninvited and invited himself.

So I carried him down Tobin Street towards the new Triskel Arts Centre. Slasher was locked. He was cursing, swearing and lashing out at anything that moved. He was crying tears of nostalgia, tears of joy.

He was a mess. How would I explain this to Robbie, the curator. This was a slow-motion social car crash, and I was in the driver's seat with the pedal to the metal. But what could I do? I knew I had no business bringing Slasher to the exhibition, not in the condition he was in. Not ever. But what could I say? I knew what I was doing was wrong. But when have I ever done the right thing, if given a free choice.

Long story short: me and Slasher both got fucked out on our ear. Put it this way: it was a memorable night, best forgotten.

~

Time flies, things change, and people move on. I've moved to the suburbs of Artsville and the manic nights of lowering free wine and smoking joints 'til dawn have moved to a different part of town. I've moved on. Don't get me wrong, I'm not knocking the wine guzzlers, a few glasses of free wine is a cheap education. Because eventually this freeloader took his eyes off the drinks table and looked at the walls. Over time it became less about alcohol and more about the art, and learning without instruction is the greatest form of education of all. For a lad like me, just to be in the environment of a gallery, comfortable in that space, learning to trust that my opinion is valid – well, that's education. This was a life experience I would never find between the covers of a book. The realisation that there's a private dimension to all public spaces was priceless. Some will argue that priceless and penniless amount to the same thing but finding myself accepted in that strange and foreign world at that time of my life was a good enough reason to be there. My education was all about exposure to this alternative world.

Exposure? When I think back to that day on Bridge Street, the naked man and fish routine, and how it impacted my life. I questioned the medium, the method, the artist, the art. I questioned myself, my being, my perception, my sexuality. Ah yes, my sexuality. I fell in love that day. There I was, a teenager, my first time experiencing nudity and though I didn't realise it at the time and I didn't understand it at the time, but I fell in love. It was my first flirtation and I fell head over heels in love with art.

I heard last week that Slasher was arrested for urinating in a public place. He was arrested on the South Mall for pissing against the door of the Imperial Hotel. A public place? It made me question how public the South Mall actually is, then again, some public spaces are more private than others. Only a very elite section of the public has any business being down the South Mall. But anyway, Slasher was arrested. I could stand up in any court of law in the land and plead his case. I would swear on a stack of bibles that Slasher was an artist. And just because he didn't have a fish tied around his neck, didn't make him any less an artist. He was an artist. He was a piss-artist, but he was certainly no exhibitionist. I would make the case that one man's exhibitionism is another man's exhibition – but I'm not sure that would stand up in court.

the performance artist described in this story is inspired by the work of Alastair MacLennan

Same Old Tune

Nero retched. Her hand reached roughly down inside his throat. Her talon-like nails pierced his throbbing heart. She dragged it pulsating, up past his oesophagus and out through his mouth, blood drenched aorta dangling. She threw it to the floor, stamped on it, spat on it and kicked it across the tiles. He watched as her aerobically taut buttocks swayed across the airport concourse towards the departures lounge. Nero stood there, helpless and heart-broken, afraid to turn and walk away. The minutes flashed by on the departure screen. His eyes begged her not to go. But 14:37 became 14:38 and Flight 205 was gone. He went home, turned on the telly, poured himself a bottle of Scotch and threw himself down on the couch.

Nobody really knew where he picked up the name Nero, but it was a name that stuck. A likeable sort of chap, a musician, a quiet and easy-going type, a bit of a dreamer. But Nero was like a buffalo in a bubble car, he just didn't fit in. And so, he spent his life on the outside looking in. Maybe it was because his father abandoned his mother, he had been classed as illegitimate since cradle days and society had abandoned Nero. Maybe it was this. Maybe it was that. Maybe it was the other. Who knows. Who cares.

Helena? She was French. She was young. She was younger than Nero. She was sensitive. She was sensual. She stood out from the crowd, and maybe that was the instant attraction that drew Helena and Nero together – two outsiders looking in. The subtle difference was that Helena stood out because she was exceptional – but Nero stood out because he was not exceptional.

Helena was a quiet sort of girl who kept herself to herself. She seemed so self-contained probably because her grasp of the English language was at best shaky – further complicated by the chaotic logic of the high falsetto sing-song sound of the Cork accent and the way it peters out the closer it gets to a question mark or full stop.

Nero's accent was particularly thick and sweet like cream. But they understood each other. They loved each other. And having arrived in Ireland, still messed-up by a fucked-up relationship with a junked-up artist in Berlin, Helena fell into Nero's arms, charmed by Nero's ways, his kindness, his devotion. She was his Helena. He played the fiddle for her. They loved each other, forever.

With Helena in his life, Nero's horizons were broadened. He no longer had the futile urgency to fit into the restrictive confines of Irish ways. Nero quickly and easily adapted to the more genteel continental lifestyle. Croissants for breakfast did not challenge him, as long as they came with sausages, rashers, black and white pudding, eggs and lashings of tea. Nero became comfortable with the notion of stretching his social habits out of the shadows of damp, dark and woody public house alcoves. Before he knew it, he was supping pints in the open air as good as any European. And fuck the neighbours, he took to wearing shorts from June to September. Nero was reborn, a rebirth without original sin, and the stain of illegitimacy had been wiped clean from the slate forever. With Helena leaning on his arm, it somehow balanced the chip on his shoulder. Nero was alive and tingling to his fingertips, and for the first time in a long time he was knocking sparks off the fiddle, playing tunes like he had never played before. Music became his language of love. He was inspired to compose a tune for her – *The Humours of Helena,* he called it. He played it over and over again, and she danced there naked in the kitchen overflowing with the joys of life and love.

But when the black cloud came over Helena there was nothing he could do to brighten her life. She was at war with herself, and in such a conflict there would be no winner. She packed her bag and left. It cut him to the bone when she walked out of his life. She had to go. Weighed down by her own internal pain, she had to get out from under the burden of Nero's emotions.

A quiet and easy-going chap.

A likeable sort of guy.

A musician.

A dreamer.

Abandoned.

Again.

Nero took to drinking. He was always drunk, but he claimed he was sober half of the time. Life as he knew it crumbled around him. He didn't lose his job, he just stopped going to work. In time his music played second fiddle to the bottle.

And so the days became weeks, and the weeks became years, and life and time became confused, and the past was another place.

❧

The couch was soft and warm. Nero just sat there watching the telly supping cheap supermarket whiskey. When the whiskey ran out his taste buds became less discerning, and eventually he was drinking anything that came in a bottle, can or plastic container. They say he drank to forget, but anyone who knew the score will know that he drank to remember and wallow in the pain of self-pity and the past. Life as he knew it became a serpentine cycle of drink-fuelled disillusion ...

> As he sipped, he slipped
> from steamed to stoned.
> And slightly cynically,
> he supped some more.

> AND

> As she slaved, she sensed
> her self-esteem slip.
> Her seduction sublime,
> some steamed man's whore.

To be fair he didn't spend all his time on the couch. He managed to sign-on once a week. He got it together to make homebrew and, somewhere along the line, he got married to Mary.

Nero and Mary had a daughter, Josephine. He'd be the first to admit that he had been a bad husband and though he seldom left the couch he knew he had been an absent father.

Nero slumped there on the couch, soft and warm, in pain. He

looked on through a haze as the events of his lifetime flashed by in front of his eyes. In his sober moments, usually first thing every morning before a drop had time to wet his lips and dull reality, his mind would cast haunting images of his drunkenness. He'd reach out for a drink, because drink was the only thing that would make it all go away. The memories of the past hurt as much as the pain of the present.

Like that time he woke up, face down in the hall, the dog licking the back of his neck. Chips from his batter burger supper caked into his forehead, peas soaking into the camouflaging carpet. His trousers down around his knees, the front door open and his keys still in the lock, he could hear Mary whispering,

— Shhhhhh! Don't be waking your dad ...

The child tip-toed around him getting ready for school and the dog wolfed back the batter burger and started lapping up the peas.

And then there was the time Josephine got pregnant. It hurt him when he realised that he was the last to know. She even went to the priest for advice before coming to her own father. And then the priest came to Nero. Nero was on his best behaviour. Mary had organised a clean shirt for him, and she cleared away the sheets of newspaper that always lay around him protecting the couch and carpet where Nero sat. Mary was sick to death of brushing up cigarette butts and cleaning the trail of mess. Nero sat there in his clean shirt, the telly off, waiting and sober.

Whispers in the hall announced Father Cleary's arrival. The whispering stopped, the door into the front room opened. There stood Father Cleary flanked by Mary and Josephine.

— Ah, hello, Father, he said. – Welcome. Welcome. Come in ...

Nero stretched out his hand and made an effort to get to his feet.

— Stay where you are, Nero, Father Cleary smiled.

Nero slumped back down onto the couch.

— Take a seat, take a seat!

Nero pointed to the chair opposite. Father Cleary pulled up the chair. Nero was doing his best to hold it together, he struggled with the clarity that sobriety brings. But he managed to show hospitality –

whatever you might say about Nero, even at his most self-destructive, he was always gentle and mannerly.

— Will you have a drink, Father?

Father Cleary was caught off-guard.

— Eh, maybe a small one, so …

Nero needed no more encouragement, he poured two mugs directly from the bottle.

— You'll try a drop? The best dis side of Texas!

Nero's eyes sparkled, he had been dying of thirst and waiting for a drink since he woke up. It was now almost noon.

Five mugs later, Nero was only finding his stride. Father Cleary was poleaxed, speaking in tongues, shouting,

— Fuck the pope!

And,

— Why in the name of Christ did I ever join the fuckin' priesthood! I spends me whole time thinking about getting me hole! I'm not cut out for this celibacy lark at all, at all …

A gibbering mess, Father Cleary was carried to a waiting taxi. He called around the next day to collect his car and have that chat with Nero. But Nero was asleep.

Or that time Mary wanted the room painted for Josephine's wedding. Nero promised he'd organise it. But the wedding drew close, and Mary gave up on him ever getting up off the couch. Sean McAuliffe from next door volunteered for the job. Arriving to paint the room, Sean found Nero asleep on the couch. So he covered the furniture with dust sheets, including the couch with Nero stretched out and snoring. Nero slept through the whole job.

Nero woke in the early hours of that morning to find the room a different colour, all the furniture had been moved, none of the usual photos or plants where they should have been.

— How de hell did I get here? he wondered.

In his drink-sozzled haze, Nero assumed he was in the wrong house. He must have somehow strayed into a neighbour's front room, too drunk to remember. It baffled him as to how or why he was there in his string vest, underpants and slippers – and no keys. He decided it best to get back home before he was missed – or worse, before someone found him in the wrong house. So, snap decision, he decided he'd climb over the wall into his own back yard, the quickest way home, and no one need know.

Mary woke up to the sound of Sean McAuliffe banging on the front door, it was almost three in the morning.

– Mary! Mary! Call the guards! Christ's sake! Call the guards! He's coming to kill me!

Seemingly, Sean had spotted Nero climbing over his back wall. He thought that maybe he had stolen Nero's thunder by painting the room. Or maybe Nero had heard the whisperings doing the rounds of the neighbourhood about the carry-on between Sean and Mary. In a panic, it crossed Sean's mind that Nero was on the warpath coming to do him in, why else would he be climbing into his yard in the middle of the night like a lunatic Ninja.

And bless him, Nero was wrestled to the ground by two young guards. His face ground to the dirt and wearing only a string vest and underpants. Nero was pleading his innocence, saying was just trying to do the right thing – to get home before he was missed.

His memories would have been funny if they weren't so sad. Living with failure was his cross in life. And so he had one more drink.

II

Nero raised the zapper in his right hand and flicked the channel to telesales. Mary ran from the room, in tears. Newspapers crunching, he leaned over the side of the chair and poured another mugful. He needed a drink. Balancing the mug on his left knee, he sat back and closed his eyes.

The door crashed open. His peace shattered. It was Josephine.

– Who in the name of Christ do you think you are! she roared. Nero opened his eyes.

– A maggot, dat's what you are! A waster! A useless waste of space! She was close to tears.

– Hoi! Nero mumbled. – Don't speak to your father in that tone!

— Father? Father? You? You were never a father to me. A fuckin'
    excuse for a human being, that's what you are. Everyone tip-
    toeing around you. Well I'm not fuckin' tip-toeing around you
    no more.
If Nero was unsure where all this hostility was coming from, Josephine
soon set him right.
— Mammy just came in here, trying to break the news to you
    gently so as not to upset you. And what do ya do? What do ya
    do? You change the channel and pour another drink!
— What *could* I do!
Nero defended the indefensible.
— You could have said something. Shown a bit of feeling! Sadness,
    anger, horror, anything! You, you, you maggot! Even a maggot
    has more feelings than ya!
— It isn't my fault she got cancer! he snapped.
— You're useless! Fuckin' useless! Always have been. Always will
    be …
Josephine's index finger stretched to within an inch of his face.
— I hate you. I'm sick of hearing about what a nice guy you were
    before drink got a hold of ya! I'm sick of hearing about how
    good a musician you were! And most of all, I'm sick to fuckin'
    death of you!
Nero puckered his lips and raised an eyebrow.
— There was no one wanted for nothing in this house, he pleaded.
    – I was always there for ye!
His eyes begged sympathy.
— Don't make me laugh! Josephine snarled. – You were never
    there for us, because you were always here! Here stretched out,
    too drunk to get up out of the couch and be anywhere else. You
    were never there for me! You were never there for Mammy! You
    care about no one. Not even yourself. You're nothing. A fuckin'
    maggot of a man …
She stormed out. The door slammed behind her.
    Nero stretched his eyelids and struggled to find focus. Newspapers
scattered around, rustled like autumn leaves. He felt old. Out between

his bald head and bristled chin, his eyes twinkled. He glanced down over his flabby chest, past his beer-swollen belly and onto the newspaper-strewn floor. Slowly he sensed his world.

— Hhhuruuppp!

Nero pulled himself up out of the couch and found his balance. Like a bear waking from hibernation, he stretched, clenched his eyes shut, then forced them open again. He rubbed the back of his head, smelled under his armpits, tugged at his crotch, scratched his arse. He shook himself.

— Jesus! What's dat godforsaken noise?

He put his hands to his ears. It was like the first time he realised the television was constantly on and blaring. Nero flicked the off switch and lay the zapper down. He stood there, a slob in silence.

He could hear the sound of weeping outside on the stairs. He sensed Josephine consoling her mother. Each teardrop falling, like a hammer-blow driving a six-inch nail into his heart. He stood there motionless. There's nothing like silence to help a man see.

Slowly he walked to the dresser. Reaching, he fumbled on top, his fingers disturbing over twenty years of dust. He vaguely remembered putting the fiddle case up there all those years ago. Maybe it was still there? He puffed and his lips stretched a smile of recognition as the case slipped into his hands, unsettling a black cloud of dust.

Nero carefully took the fiddle in his arms. He held it tenderly, like cradling a new-born baby. Then plucking her untuned stings, he gently brought her back to life. He stood there, in his stained string vest, barefoot on the newspapers, rubbing resin over the horse hairs, and slowly he drew the bow across the bridge. The strings tingled beneath his softened fingers. The notes vibrated through the sound box into his chest and resonated with the rhythm of his heart. He played, and slowly it all came back to him. The pain. The peace. The fighting. The backbiting. And the music flowed.

He stroked the fiddle until it seemed to glow. He closed his eyes, the melody moved through him, and the intensity grew. His natural rhythms took over. He swayed from side to side, the music filled his head. Newspapers curled and crunched underfoot as he moved, and he played. His breathing was strong and regular, his movement carried him off the newspapers, like he was stepping into the world. He was Nero. Elbows in the air, head swaying on shoulders, hips twisting. As if in a trance, the music moved him around the room.

Over and over and over again, he played the same tune. It was a tune he had composed many years ago. A time when all was young, beautiful and loving in the world. It was that tune he had composed for Helena. *The Humours of Helena* he called it.

With each refrain his movement became more forceful. With each chorus the music flowed more freely. Flowerpots, photographs, ashtrays and ornaments in the air, Nero moved with unrestrained intensity around the room. He danced there, barefoot on broken glass, dirt and cigarette butts.

He played notes, so rare, so pure. Sliding up and down the well-worn fretless fingerboard, strings turned to crimson as they sliced deep into his softened fingertips. Blood flowed across the fiddle and gathered in the palm of his hand. And he played. The bow knocked sparks off the strings, sparks that shot deep into Nero's head and chest, sparks that rekindled a fire, and the intensity grew. And he played. And somewhere between the agony and ecstasy came something he hadn't experienced in a long time – lucid thoughts flooded his mind.

His thoughts were of her. The same thoughts that had haunted his every sober moment since she walked away that day. And he played and he played. It wasn't that his life flashed before his eyes, but with each note struck, long-forgotten random images appeared before his eyes: he could see her plain as day, dancing naked there in front of him, weaving in and out of the haunting melody.

He felt no pain from his string-slit fingers, nor the cuts to his feet from the broken glass. He danced and he danced on blood-red newspapers and carpet. No pain, but his soul was in agony, an agony that had been numbed by decades of drink and depression.

The music surged up inside, as he bounced from dresser to cabinet. A flash, a shower of sparks from the wall socket as the television went crashing to the floor. Eyes clenched tightly shut, his cheeks moistened with tears. The fiddle wailed, *ag caoineadh*. Nero played *The Humours of Helena* again and again. A lament for a lifelong love, lost a lifetime ago. It had been a wasted life. His thoughts were of those who loved him, those who cared and lived in hope. Nero wept.

Josephine and Mary sat there out on the stairs, wrapped in each other's arms listening to the sound of Nero wailing to the fiddle. The crashing and trashing of furniture seemed otherworldly.

Mary was calm her mind rambled to a time before her life was wasted, back to the days of hope. Back to a time when she cared, when she loved. But now she felt no pain. Josephine turned towards the sound of the music that seeped out from the front room.

    — Isn't dat beautiful? she said.

    — Dat's my tune, Mary whispered.

    — Your tune?

    — Yes, she said, her eyes glistening. – Your father composed it for
      me when first we met. He calls it *Mary's Melody.*

    — *Mary's Melody?* So sweet.

Mary and Josephine sat there on the stairs listening.

And he played, and he played the *Humours of Helena* – strings vibrating to a melody that had been churning around inside his heart ever since she walked away, just like the pain the tune always remained the same. And he played it over and over and over again …

Benny Was A Daaancer!

– Rave? Dat's not dancin', Benny sighed. – All I want is a dance. Sur' dat's not dancin'!

Strange how a happy, crowded room can make a sad heart lonely.

Benny hadn't danced since he was single, real dancing. He'd freak out for the fast set, like Rory Gallagher, with his air guitar slung around his shoulder, right hand stretching to those difficult notes down as far as his knee. Then the slow set, three clingers, locking onto any girl who'd let him. He'd stand there rubbing his teenage hands up and down her back, up and down her tight lambswool crewneck, up and down hoping for a feel of bra strap. Real dancin'. Then in for the shift, eyes shut, tongue back the throat and suck face. Up and down went the hands. He'd stand there for half the first song, clung on, then disengage and straight back to the fast ones and air guitar of Status Quo.

∿

Thought he'd go to Sir Henry's for a late one. It had been a few years; everything had changed, and dancing wasn't dancing anymore. Like one of those *Beam Me Up Scotty* moments, it was like he didn't know what planet he was on. Where once the dance floor would have been empty and ten deep at the bar roaring for drink – now the dance floor was crammed and the bar area deserted.

Benny ordered a drink,

– Pint a' Beamish …

The bar man looked bored, leaning against the till. He seemed surprised when Benny sauntered up and called a pint.

– Beamish? he said as if double-checking Benny's order.

He then casually reached for a glass, half-filled it at his ease and stood back while it settled.

SWEAT

Sir Henry's

saturday
1st august
greg dowling
shane johnson
and donkeyman
doors 9 pm

sunday
2nd august
justin robertson
and usual possë
doors 7 pm
adm both nights£5

Benny looked across the throbbing dance floor. The place was alive. Yoked outa their skulls, eyes popping outa their heads, hands, feet and knees looping, bodies contorted. They were ecstatic.

— I'll never get the hang a' dis.

Benny was low.

Benny took a swallow and plonked his three-quarter-empty pint of Beamish on the juice bar, turned and walked out. It was a cold walk home and a colder home ahead of him now that Ellie was gone. She was gone with the kids. She was gone for good.

— So much for – *for better or for worse* ...

Benny clipped an empty beer can, sending it clattering across the road.

— 'Tis true what they say 'bout empty cans, Benny thought to himself.

He headed up the hill towards the North Infirmary, homeward.

~

His first dance, a long time ago, the Parochial Hall, one eighth of a bottle of vodka inside him, nicely steamed. Barely a boy and he was out looking for a woman. He stood there in the corner, being foolish, observing the big bucks. His courage fading,

They shoot horses, don't they?

A classic clinger crackled from the battered speakers. Benny knew it was now or never. He made his move. He eased onto the dance floor and tapped her shoulder.

— Are ya dancin'?

— What's it look like, fatso?

Benny assumed her smile was an invitation to dance, so he grabbed onto her. His first clinger. A new experience. A rite of passage. And then it happened, the most excruciating pain in the place where you don't put food. A size 10 Doc Marten lifted him off the floor: the jealous boyfriend staking his claim. Benny had a lot to learn. But in the weeks that followed he learned the steps of courtship, and Benny was a dancer.

The front door creaked open to a smell of death and decay. Benny had missed the rubbish collection again. Since Ellie walked out, he had worked his way through every cup, saucer and plate in the house. Now he was eating directly from tin or packet. Every room was a dining room. Even the toilet had two empty cereal bowls and a clatter of cups. His castle in tatters, his kingdom destroyed, Benny needed a queen.

He had been out of the dating scene for over a decade. Everything had changed. The dance hall and discotheque were relics from another age. No more fast sets, no more clingers. Curry and croquettes and sliding around the dance floor on a slurry of chicken skins – all a thing of the past. The days of sinking pints 'til closing time, eyeing up the talent and then stumbling onto the dance floor for a few clingers in the hope of a dry ride on the way home were no more, and he lamented their passing.

Ecstasy had arrived. Rave was sweeping the land. Techno was the thing. Once or twice, after the pubs closed, Benny had bumbled into a rave club looking for a late pint, but the scene just made him feel old. And with Ellie gone, it crossed his mind,

   – How in the name of Christ will I ever meet a woman if there's no clingers anymore?

And then it dawned on him.

   – I'll have to learn to Rave.

Friday. Benny was back in Sir Henry's, back among the Ravers. Ten pints into the night, his ankles loosened. Sports coat bulging under his 40-inch-waist Farah trousers, his steps clumsy. He was over-dressed and over-nourished. He looked hick, but he was Raving, raving from drink. The sounds buzzing in his head.

Techno – Techno – Techno

Benny moved cautiously under the gaze of a thousand pin-sized pupils. He swallowed his pride with a mouthful of stout and slowly began to move to the groove. Groove was in his heart, and he was there to learn. The first thing he observed was that the girls danced with the girls and the boys danced with the boys. Physical contact? No one was touching no one. No conversation. No slow ones. No snappy chat-up lines. It crossed his mind,

— Where in the name of God will the next generation come from? Benny began by throwing a few shapes, not the slickest mover on the planet, but he had picked up a few steps at the Irish college céilí when he was a young fella, and it got him moving. Benny was in motion. He was grooving. He was moving. For the first time in his life, Benny was dancing for dancing's sake, and he was loving it.

Benny the Raver. Big Daddy of the Rave Scene. They liked him. They stepped aside and gave him space. And maybe his moves were awkward, clumsy and a bit all over the place, but he earned their respect. It was a forgiving crowd – everyone loved up and everything's wonderful on ecstasy. The weeks were good to Benny. Benny, King of the Ravers, raved on. Still a king without a queen, but it didn't matter, he had a life. Benny lived for Friday nights. Benny was a Raver.

~

She was more club than chav, a little older than the rest, more mature, not so feral. Benny had noticed her moves. She held her space every week over by the fire exit. It crossed his mind that maybe he might bump into her accidentally on purpose at the juice bar some night. But still unsure of the steps of courtship in the Rave scene, Benny decided it best to keep himself to himself. So he just continued to focus on his own very personalised and unique dance steps.

Groove is in the Heart – two, three ...
Hop to the left – two, three ...
Hop to the right – two, three ...

Benny concentrated on his every move. E pumping through him, sweat bubbling from his nose, neck, knees and armpits. He was as fresh as a daisy.

Close the eyes – two, three ...
Shake the hips – two, three ...

Hands in the air – two, three …
Groove is in the Heart – two, three …
He mouthed his steps, steps practised at home to his *River of Rave* compilation cassette. His moves were well-rehearsed but rigid.
Pump it up.
Pu-Pu-Pu-Pu Pump it up.
Benny opened his eyes. There she was moving to the groove, pumping it up directly in front of him. In his heightened sense of interconnectivity, it was as if she was dancing for him and him alone. Her legs splayed, head down, hair over her face, her hands waved and weaved in and out between her knees. Bending under flexing thighs, she leaned back as far as gravity would allow, hands rolling up past her well-formed silhouetted body.
Pu, Pu, Pu, Pu, Pump it up.
She surged no more than two feet from Benny's belly. He mimicked her movement, not to perfection, but as best he could. And in a moment of ecstatic clarity, the truth became glaringly obvious.
– My Queen – two, three …
My Princess – two, three …
Hop to the right – two, three …
Must impress – two, three …
Try a new step – two, three …
Benny diverged from his well-rehearsed routine into a series of furious scissor-kicks. This was his moment. Hands above his head flying faster and faster. Ravers stopped, stepped back and stared, wondering,
— What the fuck is he on? And whatever it is, I want some.
Faster and faster into open space, eyes shut, Benny's legs flew in and out. This was it. Now was his time. His eighteen-stone bulk bounded across the floor and with a hop, skip and a most almighty jump, Benny was airborne.

Suspended there in mid-air for what seemed like an eternity, intending to hit the floor, heel to toe and into the splits, he hung there. And for that split second as time stood still, Benny was God. This was his moment, and he knew it. Suspended there in mid-air, it was like,
— This is it! This is it! This is fuckin' it!

This is fu, fu ... Uh! Uh! Uh! Uh!

It was like a vice grips crushing his ribcage. Everything went from multi-coloured to blue, to grey to black. He crashed to earth in a heap, bursting his skull wide open as it hopped from table to step to floor.

— Mind his head!

— Give him room! For Christ's sakes, give him room!

She leaned over him, unbuttoning his shirt.

— You're okay. I'm a nurse.

How many fingers do you see?

What is your name?

How many fingers do you see?

What is your name?

Benny's eyes rolled in his head.

— What is my name? he whispered.

— I think it's his heart! she said. – Call an ambulance! Now! An Ambulance!

— My name? I'm Benny, he mumbled.

His pupils turned one more time, and his eyelids gently closed. He saw Ellie and the kids. He saw the good days, the happy days. He saw what could have been, what should have been, what might have been.

— I'm Benny, he whispered. – I'm a daaancer!

And his eye lids closed to whiteness.

— Wha' did he say?

— I think he said – I'm Benny. I'm a dinosaur?

Out of time and out of place – Benny was a dinosaur ...

Rites Of Passage

— Jojo flaked the guard, full force in between the eyes. Levelled him out on the road and roared, – You've no rights to pass through here! The guard picked himself up, stepped back and scarpered. In the days of hard men, Jojo Duggan was the hardest of them all.

My dad cackled, exposing gums as tough as ivory. His eyes sparkling. His mind reliving every scrape and adventure he had shared with Jojo Duggan. I knew better than to interrupt him when he was in full flight reliving the adventures of his well-spent youth in the company of Jojo. So I sat there driving the car, hungover and late for work.

~

It was Saturday morning. Late. I was supposed to be in for ten. I had been out 'til three the night before sculling wine in the Café Lorca. My alcohol-soaked skull was rattled by an early-morning phone call. Head splitting, tongue thick and furry, small talk didn't come easy.

— Of course I'll drive ya, Dad, I said.

It's difficult to refuse a man who never said no.

— I'll be there in a minute, I reassured him.

In the horrors from drink, I needed to hang-up the phone and get a Solpadeine into me, but my dad needed to talk.

— They're falling like flies around me, he explained.

This was his fourth funeral in almost as many weeks. It was a tight schedule in what would otherwise have been a slack social events calendar.

— Listen, Dad, my head is burstin' open. Hang up the phone and I'll be down to ya as soon as I can.

— Just drop me out to Jojo Duggan's house, he said. – Jojo will drive me to the funeral. He's still driving, y'know? Eighty-five and he's still behind the wheel! A hard man is Jojo. I'd pity the doctor that'd try to cancel Jojo's driving licence on age or health grounds …

He was ready to settle in for a long chat.

— On my way! I said and hung up.

Jojo Duggan. His name echoed around our house all my life. Jojo was a man that myths were made of. He had fought in a war, but I was never really sure which war, but the enemy always seemed to be the Brits, the Blueshirts or Franco. He had been in jail, or on the run, or something. Sometimes myth-making defies detail. I had heard all the stories, blow by blow, and yet I had never actually met Jojo. I suspected that maybe my mother had barred him from our house because, myths or no myths, Jojo Duggan was a hard man, and my dad was a married man.

I dragged myself out of the bed and drove to collect my dad. He was at the door, cap on head.

— Hop in, Dad. I'm mad late.

He sat in, and it began. It was Jojo this and Jojo that.

— Do I know Jojo? I interrupted his flow.

— Of course you do! he said. – Everybody knows Jojo!

— But did I ever meet him?

— Ah, you'd have met him when you were a young lad …

And without taking a breath the stories continued.

The Solpadeine was beginning to take the edge off the damage in a cloudy sort of way, and my head was feeling no pain. I have never had respect for drunken drivers, but that morning I must have been well over the limit – fuelled with the excess of the night before. It crossed my mind that if I was stopped, I'd blame the drink. My only defence was that I wouldn't be drunk-driving if I was sober. I sat there bleary-eyed, stuck in traffic, late for work and listening to what Jojo did next. There in the passenger seat my dad was churning it out, pausing occasionally to give directions or take a breath. I had heard it all a hundred times before, but despite my best efforts, the epic of Jojo Duggan seeped in and filled my head.

Jojo was larger than life, treasured as a friend and feared as a foe.

— … and then, that I may be struck down dead in front of you, Jojo picked up the bicycle, swung it over his head, and threw it. Flying through the air it went, knocking four of the Kenmare lads. I pounced on two of them while Jojo sorted out the rest. Ran for their lives, so they did. Tough as nails.

His boyish eyes sparkled inside their well-worn lids.

— … and I'll tell you one thing I learned from my days on the road with Jojo Duggan, he said. – When yer outnumbered and the odds are stacked against you, you stand back-to-back. Stand back-to-back and stand firm against all-comers. Back-to-back against the world, that was me and Jojo.

— How long do you know Jojo, Dad?

My question filled the gap in his gobbledegook.

— For generations. Our family and the Duggan's were like one. Inseparable! Me and Jojo came to Cork together. We worked on the buses together …

Enough background information, he was off on another episode from the annals of the life and times of Jojo Duggan. As the stories flowed, I listened, and there before my eyes a picture of Jojo magically conjured up from a sea of words. He was invincible in sport and in war. Whenever there was a job to be done, he was always willing to step forward. In the troubled times he was first to fall in with the column. He was fearless, and when duty called he never hesitated to use the gun. In a time of crisis, Jojo Duggan was the man you'd need at your back.

— Jojo unharnessed the dead horse and got under the cart himself. He pulled the cart, all the way into the village. A horse of a man is Jojo!

My dad thumped the dashboard with a laugh.

— A horse of a man, he repeated.

— Do I go left or right here, Dad?

— Straight on! he roared, and the stories continued. – And the day we cycled to Innishannon. Drank two quarts. Ran in the sports. Jojo came first, I came second. More drink. Cycled to Bandon.

More drink. A dance. A spot of courtin'. Fought five townies and won. Cycled home in time for work next morning. And that was a quiet night by our standards, he smiled defiantly.

The stories smelt of embellishment, but the exaggeration always stretched plausibility to within the limits of credibility, making it next to impossible to know where facts faded to fiction.

    — Slow down! he roared. His hand stretched out. – This is it. Park behind the red Fiesta!

I pulled in.

    — Will ya come in and say hello to Jojo? he invited.

    — I won't, I said. – I'm mad late for work, Dad! Just check and make sure it's the right house before I drive off! I suggested.

My dad pulled himself out of the passenger seat and vanished in the garden gate. I changed channel on the radio, trying to find the right time. It was twenty past, I was late. But I had no mind for work. I looked to my left, and there he was back at the gate. Beaming. He gave me the thumbs-up, all clear, mission accomplished. So I started the car.

    — Hoi, wait! he shouted.

    — Jojo's comin' out to see ya. Wait a second, just a second …

His eyes pleaded with me to stay. Then he stood down from the path and stepped to one side. There behind him stood Jojo. This man of men – Jojo Duggan.

A sharp intake of breath, I refocused and readjusted my gaze. All preconceived expectations of Jojo Duggan shattered and crumbled in front of my eyes. And I stared. He was old, very old. Older than my dad. Old, crumpled and grey. His nose running, eyes red around the rims and watery. His skin about three sizes too big for him. Shoulders hunched, back bent and curved. My father stood there flanking his friend, his mouth stretched from ear to ear. His smiles were genuine smiles of pride, proud to stand shoulder to crumpled shoulder with Jojo the invincible.

Try as I might, I could see no more than my eyes would reveal. He was an old man. They were both old men, unsteady and vulnerable.

Jojo hobbled to the footpath and stepped to the road one foot at a time, then around to the driver's side of the car. I lowered the window. He reached in and I clasped his shaking hand, steadying it.

— The last time I saw you, you were only a little boy in short pants, he said.

His voice was frail but there was fire in his eyes.

— Will ya come in for a cup of something?

He sniffled a drop that was about to drip from his nose and wiped the sleeve of his coat across his face.

It's amazing the effect that two Solpadeine down on top of a feed of drink can have. It's a cocktail that sorts out the head but destroys the brain. Because at that moment, a very profound thought occurred to me, but for the life of me I can't remember exactly what it was. But it ran along the lines of – If I was a child when Jojo Duggan last saw me, well, back then, he must have been a young, fit man in his prime, and I must have been the small, vulnerable one. And somewhere along the line, through the twists of time – I am now the strong fit one in my prime and he is now the small, vulnerable one …

His eyes steadied under twitching brow.

— Sur' any son of this man here, he said and pointed to my dad, – has no right to pass Jojo Duggan's house without calling in for a cup of something.

— Well, if I've no right to pass, I'd better come in! I heard what you did to the guard! I said and winked toward my dad.

He left a roar of a laugh out of him and wheezed and coughed and spluttered and coughed and laughed,

— Ah, Jesus! You can't be listening to him and his aul' stories, Jojo said, and he nudged my dad.

⁓

The cough bottle was taken from the shelf and placed on the table.

— Cough bottle? I questioned.

Three crystal-clear cups were poured.

— Down the coarse cut! That'll soften your cough! Jojo laughed.

— All the way from the hills of Iveleary, my dad said. – 'Tis the
 best you'll get!
The feeling was warm, and we drank to the dead. The cups were
refilled, again and again.

～

They never made it to the funeral that day, and I never made it to
work. It was one of those spontaneous and unplanned encounters.
Spending time in the company of the living seemed more important
than paying respects to the dead. The stories continued late into the
afternoon.
 — … and if there's one thing I've learned, he said. – When yer
 outnumbered, and the odds are stacked against you, you stand
 back-to-back and hold your ground against all-comers. Isn't
 that right, Jojo?
 — True, true, true for you …

We raised our cups to the health of the dead over and over again. With
each passing year, my dad and Jojo Duggan had witnessed the scythe
swing low and cut the ground from under their generation. And yet
there was something unstoppable about these two old men. They had
no fear of death. Back-to-back they held their ground and lived to tell
the tale. And maybe the final countdown would not be far away – but
my dad and Jojo Duggan continued to seize the day and they just
laughed in the face of death anyway …

He Ain't Heavy

Hairs stiffening to a ridge along the back of my neck like a trapped animal, teeth grinding, and knuckles whitened, frightened.

> I'll kill him.
> Maybe he hasn't seen me?
> Bastard!
> I'll kill him.
> Maybe he won't recognise me.

~

It was a sleepy Saturday morning on Half Moon Street, and just around the corner – Christmas. I was walking off a bit of self-inflicted pain. You know how sometimes, after a skinful, the hangover can be pleasurable, if you've the time or the inclination to go with the flow. Well, that's how it was.

Three days on the rip, a bit burned out, nerve endings frayed, throat and nose blocked with the fags, but all in all I was feeling fine and enjoying my stroll through the streets until the pubs opened, and then back in for the cure.

I found myself on Paul Street, when fate took a hand to my feet and turned them into French Church Street. My head was bells and seagulls and pigeons and footsteps and a kango hammer right between my eyes.

> Footsteps?
> Faint footsteps?
> On French Church Street?
> Far, far from me.
> And me?
> Far, far from home.

And that's when I saw him in the distance in black, the bastard of a man who tormented me and my brothers when we were too young to defend ourselves. Brother Keenan. I couldn't see his face. It was his walk I recognised.

He shuffled along French Church Street in my direction. I was trapped, no way out. My only escape was an about-face. But I had lost face to that man once too often in the past. So a course was set for a head-on collision.

The shine of his Brylcreem, swish of his soutane, smell of the chalk dust were the sights, sounds and scents that haunted my life. Even after all these years, I still wake up some mornings in fear. It wasn't so much the pain from the leather, it was in the anticipation that the terror lay.

I'll kill him.

I'll fuckin' well kill him …

I knew there and then that the score just had to be settled that very morning if I was to ever move on with my life. What I would do to that fucker if I ever met him had echoed from bar stool to home and back. I had often vowed publicly, usually in a public house in a bout of drunken bravado, that I would level him flat to the ground if I ever came face to face with him, and here I was, trapped – trapped by my own pride.

In a surge of painful memories, my pocketed fist clenched tightly. The wind-whistling leather, sometimes systematic, sometimes sporadic, and like a wolf with a herd of sheep he'd swoop, pick the most vulnerable and destroy. The sheep huddled closer in silence.

Seanie Cronin.

His dad hadn't worked in years, I suppose for the best part of young Seanie's life. Ma Cronin's nerves were bad, she had taken to the bed. And probably because he had so much time on his hands, Da Cronin took to porter. Anyway, the upshot of the whole shebang was that Seanie was always late for school, well, half of the time anyway.

— The clock was stopped, Brother.

It was a good excuse for a 10-year-old, but a feeble excuse for a Christian Brother.

— 'Twas stopped then, was it, Seánín?

Brother Keenan smiled as he grabbed Seanie by the ears, lifted him clean off the floor and swung him in the direction of the window.

— Can ya see the clock on Shandon, Seánín?

Seanie squealed, Brother Keenan smiled and the sheep, giggling nervously, huddled.

⁓

My pace was slow, his face out of focus. One quick clatter into his ear, my plan was made.

⁓

Jimmy Murphy. Murph …

Murph's mam and dad fought like cat and dog, we all knew it, but there was no shame in it. They loved each other, that was how they got on. Murph would be up half the night listening to this carry-on down in the kitchen, there was no real harm in it, but it must have been hard to sleep through. So it was no wonder that one Monday morning, small Murph was keeled over head down on the desk, asleep.

Like a soaring vulture, Brother Keenan's hand cast a shadow over the back of Murph's bowl-cut poll. And with a roar of,

— Wake up, man!

His manly hand crushed a clatter across small Murph's ear. A clatter that lifted him out of his desk and up against the wall in a heap, under the shadow of the Virgin.

— You look more comfortable there, man! You can stay there.

The sheep closed ranks. And Murph remained where he was, kneeling by his desk for the rest of that day.

⁓

There he was, no more than a few feet from me. Still coming in my direction. My right hand slipped from my pocket in preparation for the retribution, his cold eyes pierced the bridge of my nose. Then, out of the blue, he stopped.

— Ó Murchú, he said.

His cheeks stretched to a smile. It was a smile I had learned to fear, but in a strange sort of way, I was flattered. Brother Keenan must have terrorised almost every young lad from across the northside at one time or another, and here on French Church Street, after twenty-five years, he recognised me.

— Cíarán Ó Murchú, nach ea?

He thought I was my older brother Kieron.

— Ní hea, a bhráthair, ach Seán, I explained.

— Ah, conas 'tá tú, a Sheáin?

How are ya, Seán! How are ya indeed. My name is fuckin' John. Why am I speaking Irish to this tyrant? It's the language he terrorised me with. His language.

My mind was travelling at a fierce rate. And without stopping to think, I raised my elbow, ready to shoot out one clean smack into his ear, just as he drew alongside. But once again, he out-manoeuvred me and stopped. Caught off-guard, I stopped too. And for some reason I'll never quite understand, I answered him.

— I'm fine, Brother. How's yourself?

And then he started.

— Ah sure, I'm retired now, he said. – I miss de old days, so I do. I
    miss de boys. The good old days.

— Goodolddays?

My mind was spinning. Goodolddays me hole. But without taking a breath, he continued talking.

— Yourself, Cíarán and Pádraig got on famously. God bless ye, I
    always knew ye would, he smiled.

My big fist tightened, so tight it burned. I remembered a time when that fist wasn't big enough to conceal a gobstopper. That little fist burned too, six of the best from the wind-whistling leather. The

Christian was teaching me a lesson. It was for my own good, I was assured. But for the life of me, I can't remember my crime, but fuck-it, I remember the punishment.

Brother Keenan stood there, rambling on about the, – Goodolddays, his eyes rolling between wrinkled lids. He talked of my brothers Kieron and Paddy, their wives, their children, their lives, the detail was frightening.

My eyes skimmed across the top of his brush-cut, a view I'd never seen before. Was he smaller than I remembered? Or maybe I had grown? Then again, a lot can change in twenty-five years. He didn't seem as terrifying. His collar was looser. His brush-cut was wispy, grey and less defined.

He rambled on, mentioning names of boys, names I couldn't remember. He talked of the hurling and football legends. Beaming with pride, a fatherly pride, his mind filed through the pages of the lives of high-level civil servants, politicians, sportsmen, businessmen, entertainers and statesmen.

— My boys, he called them.

He stood there smiling. And then he talked of the social changes, the modern world, the spate of joyriding, vandalism, crime and violence.

— Different days, ha! he said and cast his eyes to heaven. – No controllin' them these days. What these young gurriers need is a good clip in the ear, and that would sort 'em out.

Enough of this gibberish, the time for talking was over. But then I said something.

— Brother! Dere's a few fellas who wouldn't mind giving you a good clip into the ear, I said.

My fist knotted. Brother Keenan smiled. His eyes softened.

— Shur', what young lad didn't fall out with his teacher? I always had my lads' best interest at heart. Sur', you of all people know that. You see, he continued. – My calling was to help young lads. Poor young lads. Young lads like meself. Young lads that didn't have a hope. Young lads who would never be invited to pull their chair up to the table. And I did the best I could with what I had. Tough days. Tough days. But no regrets …

And once again he smiled.

— Did you know, I'm a …

He hesitated and stopped like he was struggling to find the correct word.

— I'm a …

I'm a, I'm a …

A bastard, he said. – What is it they call it these days? Illegitimate, is it? Ill-eg-it-imate, that's it. My father ran off before I was born. So I suppose the Brothers are my family.

And the boys? The boys? Well, the boys are my boys. And I think of you all every day, so I do …

He smiled again, and for the first time, I saw his terrorising smile was in fact a tortured look of pain. Brother Keenan's pain.

— Ye were all great lads, he said. – And I think of ye all the time. Tough days. Tough days. But no regrets …

The lads were my lads. And the boys were my boys. But I sometimes wonder what it might have been like to have been called, – Dad. You know, instead of, – Brother. But no regrets. They were good days and I think of all of you all the time, so I do …

Slán, Seán …

His lips tightened and he made to pass by. My fist contorted and just as he drew level,

— Brother Keenan?

My right elbow rose to shoulder height.

— Seán? he hesitated.

I stood there looking into his watery eyes, something changed. I couldn't attempt to untangle and explain the thoughts and emotions that surged inside my head at that moment. Far too complicated and fucked-up to put any rational understanding on it. But for whatever reason, good or bad, I just stood there, unable to say or do anything.

— Seán? he said it again.

My right hand dipped.

— Happy Christmas, Brother Keenan.

I reached out across the decades, and we shook hands.

— Nollaig fé mhaise duit! he smiled.

Eason's Hill School. Shandon Cork. Cónal Creedon front row, 3rd from left.

My grip relaxed on his soft, chalky fingers, and he shuffled off.

My hand gnarled into a knotted fist, and I crashed it down into my left palm. After a lifetime of emotional self-loathing and self-mutilation, there I was on French Church Street actually physically hitting myself. I was a mess. I had just missed my once-in-a-lifetime opportunity to set everything right. Even all the odds.

My mind screamed,

Let him off!
Go after him!
One flake into the head!
No!

I watched as his distinctive shuffle faded off into the loneliness, back to his own heaven or hell, I'd never know. I watched as Brother Keenan turned into Paul Street, and walked out of my life forever.

~

It was a sleepy Saturday morning on French Church Street and, just around the corner, Christmas. I was walking off a bit of self-inflicted pain, you know how it is? But fate took a hand to my feet, and I stopped. I didn't go for that drink.

The cure had set in. So I turned on my heels and I went home.

The Entomologist

His face was mangled. He was crossing the bridge by the Opera House and heading in our direction.

~

I was standing outside the gallery with a friend of a friend, being told how important it was to have a working knowledge of conversational French if I went for a job in Euro Disney.

— Oui, mon ami. Plenty of work there, sanitary and maintenance, that sort a' thing, he said. – But you'd need a smattering of French.

— Did you get to meet le Mickey Mouse?

Cool question, I thought.

— I'm sick to death of that crack since I came home from Disney! A cooler reply.

It was late Saturday afternoon, and the streets were thronged, bumper to bumper, nose to tail like ants. If you've ever lifted a stone off an ant hive, you'll know what I mean. People were walking over each other with a sort of ant-like, no-nonsense, head-long no stop, no chat, no nod, no wink, heads down and scurrying.

So there I was talking about Mickey Mouse to a guy I hardly knew, and him advising me to move to Paris and get a job as a rubbish collector in Disneyland. The town was crawling, but out of the corner of my eye I couldn't help but notice the lad with the mangled face over by the Opera House. He was lean and mean, still on course, heading in our direction. As he came closer, it suddenly struck me that beneath the scarred and battered skin-deep surface – his face was a face from my past. I couldn't actually put a name, time or place on his face, and then it came to me. His name was John. I think it was John? It was something like John? John something or other. We both went to

Eason's Hill School. We sat in the same desk in school, from babies to first class right up to First Holy Communion. John? Or whatever his name is – was my first friend. Coming face to mangled face with one of my earliest memories was unnerving and unsettling.

At this stage, my man is Disneyland, this francophone friend of a friend was talking about the cost of Parisian accommodation.

— Well, a garret flat, you couldn't swing a cat in, would cost you ... He stretched his hands out to show me an approximate size of the apartment.

— ... actually, it's difficult to give an exact cost, because obviously it depends on where the apartment is located ...

The man from Disneyland was talking utter scutter.

— But you can be sure it would cost a lot more than a flat here in Cork, he insisted.

— What you're trying to say is that an inexpensive flat in Paris would cost as much as an expensive flat in Cork?

— Eh? Yes, exactly!

— So, what would an expensive flat in Paris cost? I probed.

— Jesus! I don't know, but it would be a lot more expensive than an expensive flat here.

Enough said about the cost of Parisian accommodation, he was now talking about the nightlife around Euro Disney. It was all a bit vague. I had visions of hundreds of young Irish, educated, French-speaking, rubbish collectors, blowing referees' whistles with Mickey Mouse ears on their heads,

— ... Raving the night away on E, man, he said.

I was finding it difficult to keep eye contact with my europhile friend as my attention was drawn over his right shoulder, to the mashed face of John, my childhood friend.

John was no more than twenty yards from us. He was smiling. But as my eyes focused, it became clear that his smile was more of a permanent feature, a knife gash which ran from the corner of his lip to his right ear lobe. He was my partner in school. I can see the two of us now, lined up in pairs in the yard. September winds curling around our dirty, exposed knees. We'd stand there, feeling the cold and fearing the classroom. Me and my best friend, sitting in the corner of the shed furthest from the toilets, eating our lón. Jam sandwiches and a ponnie of milk, maybe a lemon bun or a chester from our teacher ... Miss? Miss? Miss Collins ...

Jesus, it was all coming back! The memories were irregular and inconsistent, probably due to the fact that I was only four or five years of age when those formative memories were being formed.

Miss Collins
An Clár Dubh
Short pant
Fr. Hart
Trixie the dog
Oh Angel of God, My Guardian Dear

Me and my best friend were inseparable. And it occurred to me as odd that back then we talked all the time yet, for some reason I couldn't remember the detail of any conversations we ever had. But then again, what do kids of that age talk about? I remembered a navy blue balaclava that Johnny's granny knitted for him. It buttoned under his chin. It looked so snug inside the hood of his duffel coat.

Johnny? Johnny?
Of course, Johnny was his name ...
Johnny not John.
Johnny.

I wanted a balaclava the same as Johnny's, but my granny was dead. Funny but like all kids, even at that young age, there was always a conflict of competition between me and my best friend Johnny. But we were almost evenly matched, except for the minor detail that my dad was a bus driver, Johnny's dad was only a bus conductor. The last time I had seen Johnny, the both of us were wearing white bánín suits. Our First Holy Communion. We were parading around the North Cathedral, me and my partner, on our way to becoming strong and perfect Christians. He had grown up strong alright, but he was far from perfect.

So there I was, Saturday morning outside the gallery with my educated Euro-Rubbish Collector just back from Disney, he was talking about the traffic in Paris.

    — Cata-fuckin-strophic! Pardon my French, he said, – But it's the only word for it. They drive like lunatics.

Once again, his hands in the air, speaking in a very demonstrative, continental fashion. He was making a point and making it forcefully, so forcefully that the shoppers who didn't duck, bounced.

    — Pardonnez moi, he said, to the woman with the shopping as he accidentally elbowed her against the railings of the gallery.

She just snarled and glared and continued on her way.

    — So, says I. – What kind of car were you driving? Citroën? Renault?

    — Car? his voice raised in pitch. – I've no car. It's top of my list, now that I'm home and have a few euro in my pocket to apply for the driving test.

And I'm thinking, – *Is this fuckin' eejit for real?*

Here he is talking about the traffic in Paris, and he can't even drive.

    — I'm just telling you how the French drive, he continued. – Bloody looneys, the whole lot of them. It's a wild and crazy place, man! But there's loads of work in Disneyland, you'd want to get there soon before the place is built. They were on Thunder Mountain before I came home …

He talked and talked, babbling on about the cost of car insurance, road tax, the price of a litre of petrol …

    — 'Tis all litres they have in Paris. They don't do gallons at all.

And the price of the pint.

    — Of course, the French don't drink pints. 'Tis all wine they drink, he said. – They adore Le Piat d'Or.

And I'm thinking, – *What the fuck?*

Johnny was now only a few feet away, and as his notched face came into focus, it became clear that there was layer upon layer of nicks and splits well concealed beneath a more recent bruising. It was this latest damage that made his face look so hideous. His eye was badly swollen, the white was blood red, and his cheek and forehead were scraped, bruised and battered, his lower lip was split. And yet, he walked with confidence, chin out on hunched shoulders as if he owned the street – not a care in the world. By his side, keeping pace, his shorter and less bruised sidekick. Johnny wore his battle scars with pride as he strode along with a gatch of authority. And though their presence did not go unnoticed by every single person on the street that day. The seemingly oblivious masses automatically parted and made way for Johnny and his buddy – they passed by, unhindered, unacknowledged as if unseen.

It was clear to me that Johnny was aware of my gaze ever since I clapped eyes on him crossing the bridge. But I wondered if he remembered those cold schoolyard days in short pants, I wondered if he remembered me. Maybe he didn't carry memories, or maybe it wasn't as I remembered, or maybe …

Hands were flying in the air as my man from Euro Disney chuntered on about women, money and the price of drink, not necessarily in that order, sometimes all jumbled together in one nonsensical sentence. My attention strayed.

Just as Johnny came level, I raised an eyebrow and threw a faint nod of recognition towards him. He turned his head in my direction and winked his good eye. And that was it, in a knowing wink of an eye, our past was bridged, a life and friendship was fully acknowledged and copper-fastened to be picked up if we so wished at a later date. Without missing a beat of the pavement or upsetting the swaying of shoulders, or interrupting their stride, Johnny and his side-kick paced by.

    – Man! Oh man! Did ya see the state of your man's face? Dodgy
    boy! observed my man from Disneyland.

I just nodded in agreement, or acceptance, I'm not sure. But one thing is for sure, I didn't fear Johnny's scarred face, if anything, it was the man who put the scars there I feared. In fact, something inside me wanted to reach out to Johnny. But to what end? Sometimes there is no future in the past. I've heard it said that life is a train journey. Well me and Johnny got on at the same station but by the twists and turns of life we ended up in two totally different places. Johnny and his buddy were men on a mission – like Pancho and Lefty, two rough diamonds just riding into town from the wastelands. It was enough for me to know that at one time in my life, a long time ago, I was that boy's partner.

> – Well, I'm just going in here for a croissant and coffee. Will ya join me? I'll fill ya in on Disney!

An invitation from the Marco Polo of Euro Disney labourers. I looked at the perfect, sallow complexion of my educated friend of a friend, his healthy hair, bright eyes and sparkling teeth. He smiled. Through his smile, I saw confusion, disillusion, maybe neglect. He looked at me. In that moment I saw my own reflection in his eyes.

It occurred to me that we all carried scars, some conceal their scars, some don't. Johnny carried his scars like medals of honour, worn with pride for all to see, earned at the Battle of Life along the banks of the River Lee. And I suppose it's true to say that most scars heal with time, while others are best covered up and forgotten.

I watched as the rhythmical bobbing of Johnny's head faded off into the distance, into the haze of scurrying, aimless shoppers, like a grasshopper on an ant hive.

⁓

Incidentally, the coffee was delicious, a good Nicaraguan, organic, freshly ground. The croissant? Well, it was so-so, or so I was informed.

> – Not quite as good as one would get in a patisserie, on a side street of Paris, he said. – But all in all, not bad for Cork.

So we sat there for the afternoon, talking about this and that and nothing at all, because we had nothing at all better to do. A most pleasant way to spend an afternoon, just me and my well-travelled, Franco-phone friend of a friend, chewing the fat and shooting the breeze. And it crossed my mind that there were a few grasshoppers on the ant hive that day.

Penny For Your Thoughts

With only an ear and a tooth-ribbed jawbone left on the plate, I suck the last trace of salted grease from the crubeen. Wiping my hands along my trousers, I spit the gristle out on top of what was once a smiling pig's head. Raising the glass to my lips, the bitter-sweet stout cuts through and washes down the salt bacon.

— Ah, heaven ...

Through the bottom of the frothy porter-stained glass I can see the rows of bottles, optics and assorted bar implements on different shelves lined up behind the counter. These shapes, when seen through the haze of cigarette smoke that just hangs there, lit up by the odd shaft of cold shining sunlight, spark a memory. It's a fleeting memory. A memory of the rows of houses perched on the headland as the good ship *Innisfallen* came close to shore ...

∼

The homes on the headland slept peacefully, and the early-morning sun cut sharp shadows along the deck. The holy ground seemed within arm's reach, but yet was so far away. We glided along the rippled surface of Cork Harbour. And it crossed my mind that for many generations of refugees who had taken the coffin ships to the free world, the spire of St Colman's Cathedral was the last sight and memory of home they would carry with them – and there she was, standing proud above the town, welcoming us home.

I wondered if that bellyful of Macardles from the night before would lurch overboard or stay uneasily on the right side of the portside, swishing from side to side with every gentle roll of the keel. Big heads with red faces, hairy noses and ears, and mad, blood-shot eyes surfaced onto the deck. Voices, rough from cigarette smoke, and coarse laughter from drink broke the numb silence. There we were, lined up along the deck, the men who had built London and other English cities. The subways, motorways and flyovers were monuments to our sweat. We were the generation alienated by a culture so similar to our own – yet strangers on our own doorstep. We were Paddies. We were McAlpine's. We were Molly Maguires. We were shovels for hire and treated like shit. We had spent our youth mixing muck and following the river of concrete that flowed from the City of London all the way to the M25. For us, home would always be another place – a place we talked about, cried and lied about. We were no longer Irish, and we would never be British. The lives we lived, hard work, sentimental, pissing our wages against a wall in the pubs around Kilburn and other places like it, we became your typical Irishmen. No Blacks. No Dogs. No Irish. Call it racist. Call it whatever the fuck you like. But it is what it is, and we were what we were – a type that you will only find in immigrant bars between here and Cricklewood, but never back home on the aul' sod.

Beer bottles, bodies and cigarette butts littered between the decks. I made my way below for a cup of tea to settle the stomach and fill those stretched and unending minutes until docking time. But I was feeling good among my own, going home.

Half past nine in the morning, and I found myself on the curved platform of Kent Station in Cork. Mick, a young wiry lad, by my side. I met him in the queue for the duty-free on the boat and just like that we became drinking buddies on the Irish Sea. I suppose you could say we cut the travel time in half by sharing the journey. He was a man with a plan, a bit younger than me. And maybe his plan was vague and scattered, ranging from opening a pub to buying and doing up old houses, but this lad Mick was still young enough, with the enthusiasm and the ambition and strength of youth to turn a plan into action. Intending to say,

 – Goodbye and good luck!

When I opened my mouth the words I heard were,

 – Have you time for a pint?

 – I'll have a straightener before I strike west, he said.

Mick smiled and we crossed the road to the Park View. Tapping on the window, I shouted in a whispered voice through the letterbox.

– Bridie! Bridie! Come down and let us in.

With a nod and a wink we shuffled from foot to foot to the sound of bolts sliding, keys and chains rattling from the far side of the door. As the door opened, we could hear John cursing under his breath. His sleepy, grumpy head pivoted upwards until his eyes came level with my chin, his lips broadened.

– Well, Christ, come in, come in. If it isn't yourself now. Come in, come in …

He locked the door behind us and poured two creamy pints of Murphy's. The conversation flowed as the pints poured. There was so much news to catch up on. I was sad to hear of Bridie's death, but I was home and I was feeling too good to fully sympathise with John's loss and bereavement.

With a nod and a wave, John made his way out from behind the bar and up the lonely stairs. Mick and myself retreated from our bar stools to the sanctuary table in the corner. There was talk of this and that and broad strokes of gossip. There as a bit of, who's doing what and who's doing nothing at all. The one thing we both agreed was that there was nothing glorious about the bitter-sweet memories of lonely, drunken nights in Kilburn. At about midday, Mick said he had to catch a bus home to Beara. So he picked up his bag and with a shout of,

– Up the Republic!

… he was gone.

Like something out of one of those Saturday matinee westerns, Mick was a shovel-slinger heading out to the wild west of Ireland to return to the city at a future date, shovel for hire.

I found myself alone. And Jesus, it was good to be home, drinking Murphy's, smoking Major. And there's something about the jingle of Irish money in your pocket, something about the harp on the back of a coin instead of the queen's head that connects deeply with the soul. The shops and pubs across the water throw it back at you.

– We don't take that Irish junk, they say.

Irish junk, that's what they called it. And it was said with insult intended. But we had the last laugh – slip a fist full of Irish junk into a slot machine in the pub for a few packets of cigarettes. We got our cigarettes and they got our Irish junk, seemed like a fair deal and fuck 'em if they can't take a joke?

A few pints in, I was steamed, and my thoughts were pleasant and varied. I took a handful of coppers from my pocket. They fell from my hardened hands to the table. I lined them up, harps up. I pushed the coins around the Formica top, making shapes and trains and snakes. One of the pennies had the queen's head on it.

Maybe it was the drink? Or maybe it was the solitude? Or maybe I was just happy to be home and feeling a little emotional? Whatever the reason, my mind was drawn to the coins. I turned them over, studied every stroke of Celtic craftsmanship. I caressed them between thumb and finger.

On the ha'penny, the sow with her bonhams reminded me of a picture I once saw in an old English magazine. It was a cartoon of a bloated Irishman with a big red head and tufts of hair sticking out from his hat, nose and ears. He had a rope tied around a pig's leg and printed along the bottom were the words,

A PIG GOING TO MARKET.

The memory insulted me. In a fit of drunken nationalism, I shouted across the empty bar,

— Animals!

Do ya hear me? Dey treat us like fuckin' animals. We're like the dirt we dig.

Never again! You mark my words. Never a-fuckin-gain …

I suppose talking to myself is an acceptable pursuit when there's no one else around to notice. So, muttering and cursing, I continued to turn the coins over, one after the other. There in front of me lay the whole menagerie of Irish L.S.D. in pounds, shillings and pence. The hen with her chickens on the penny. The rabbit on the thru'penny bit. The sixpence had the greyhound. The bull on the shilling. The two-shilling piece with the salmon and the half-crown with the horse. Then I came to the penny with the queen's head. I flipped the coin …

— A kangaroo? A bloody kangaroo, I laughed.

An Australian penny. This penny from the land down under had been in my pocket for months. I had noticed it every time I reached for a handful of change. It was slipped to me in my change one of the nights, and that useless piece of copper had followed me around from pocket to pocket, pub to pub, ever since.

And that's the interesting thing about foreign currency: it might be worthless in an over-the-counter cash transaction, shopkeepers and publicans will reject it as junk, but there's something deep inside the human mind that never lets us forget that money is money. And money is not something you throw away. So you hang on to it. And that's why every home up and down the country has a biscuit tin, or a drawer, or a jar packed with worthless foreign coins. It's just not natural for humans to throw out money, no matter how worthless it is.

I supped, sat back and smiled. This kangaroo, an animal and a culture totally alien to me, yet it seemed to shine a new light on the pig of our ha'penny. For some reason, I was no longer insulted by the sight of the pig, after all, there are two sides to every coin. I remembered hearing somewhere that the pig was one of the most intelligent of all animals. And without doubt, in the darker days of Irish history, it was always the pig that kept the wolf from the door.

My attention was drawn to the other coins laid out on the table. And maybe it was the drink, or maybe it was the low-lying light of the afternoon sun streaming in beneath the blinds, but the imagery of the embossed beasts seemed to take on a significance that I had never noticed before. It was like, one after the other, they all came alive there in front of my eyes to tell their story.

The hen with her chicks on the penny was Mother Ireland, nurturing, protecting and feeding the weakest. The thru'penny bit with the rabbit, a symbol of fertility and the large families of the predominantly Catholic nation of Celts that lived on this island. The greyhound on the tanner conjured up visions of Cú Chullainn and the mythical Fianna of ancient times and how they preserved and protected our nation, our culture. The strength and temper and determination of the bull on the shilling, an animal to be feared when provoked, like the Irish over the centuries. The elusive, maybe mythical Irish Salmon

THE NEW DECIMAL CURRENCY

½p or £0-00½

1p or £0-01

2p or £0-02

5p or £0-05

10p or £0-10

50p or £0-50

"DECIMAL DAY"

15 February, 1971, will be "Decimal Day". On that day our present system of £ s d will end and we will begin to use a system where £1 = 100 new pence [100p].

NEW COINS

Before "Decimal Day" three new coins will be in circulation. These are: 5p [=1s.]; 10p [=2s.]; 50p [=10s.]. The new ½p, 1p, and 2p coins will come into circulation on "Decimal Day". (These three coins have no exact equivalents in £ s d.)

THE CHANGE-OVER PERIOD

The change-over period will last from 1 to 2 years from "Decimal Day". During this period the present 1d., 3d., and 6d. coins will remain in circulation side by side with the new decimal coinage. On Decimal Day the new 50p coin will replace entirely the 10s. note which will be withdrawn from circulation on that day.

Half-crowns will be withdrawn on 1 January, 1970.

WRITING DECIMAL MONEY

Pounds are still written using the pound sign [£]. New pence are written using the sign p, or as decimals of a pound. Remember £1 = 100p. Examples: 40p or £0·40; 12½p or £0·12½; 5½p or £0·05½; £3·27½.

In writing amounts over a pound the pound sign [£] alone is used with the decimal point. Example: £6·12½; £6·37½; £8·02½.

The pound and new pence signs [£] [p] are *never* used together.

CONVERSION

During the change-over period it will be necessary to be able to convert from £ s d to decimal currency and vice versa. Here is the table which will be used for these conversions.

CONVERSION TABLE

Old Pence [d.]	New Pence [p]	Old Pence [d.]	New Pence [p]
1	½	7	3
2	1	8	3½
3	1	9	4
4	1½	10	4
5	2	11	4½
6	2½	1s.	5

EXAMPLES OF CONVERSIONS

3s. 2d. = 16p or £0·16   12s. 11d. = 64½p or £0·64½
4s. 6d. = 22½p or £0·22½   £3 17s. 6d. = £3·87½

of Knowledge there on the two-shilling piece. While the horse on the half-crown conjured up the force and endurance of a people that had survived eight hundred years of oppression. A nation that had persevered through successive famines, rebellions and persecutions. And maybe it was the diffused light of the declining sun streaming in through the slit in the blinds, but I did find peace of mind. The anxiety that had been spiralling up from deep inside seemed to dissipate and disappear.

Eventually, John came back down from upstairs. He asked if I was alright. So I called another pint.

~

But all that was an old memory of a long time ago.

Time flies when nothing changes. Fifteen or twenty years sitting here in the Park View supping pints, living the good life. My once-hardened hand lowers the near-empty glass from my face. With the obscurity of the frothy glass removed from in front of my eyes, the bottles and optics behind the counter no longer have the appearance of houses on a headland. The *Innisfallen* and St. Colman's Cathedral welcoming me home are faint memories from a long time ago. With a gentle thud on the beer mat, a pint of stout is placed in front of me by a familiar old hand.

— How was the pig's head and crubeens? John asks.
— Pig's head? I mumble.
He looks down at the devoured mass of grease, gristle and bone on the plate.
— Are ya finished? Will I take it away?
— You can, take it out a' that, John.
I point to my money on the table.

He raises his leg, places his foot on the stool next to me, he leans over and begins counting the coins into his hand.
— 10, 20, 30, 40, and 5 and 3. That will be one pound and 48 new pence.
John turns his head sideways and says,

— You never went back to England that time? Did ya?

I look up at his old face and don't reply.

— You must be back now, ten years?

— Seventeen and a half, says I.

— Time flies when yer having fun.

— You said it, John. You said it …

And maybe it's an echo from my past, or maybe it's the reality of my present, but I notice there on the table a ha'penny, one of them new decimal coins. What is it they call them? A half new pence or something? It's small and shiny. I pick it up and turn it, feels as worthless as toy-money.

There on the flip side is a Celtic design of a bird. Something from the Book of Kells, I suppose. But it doesn't look anything like any bird I had ever seen with its neck all twisted and contorted. Decimalisation was here and here to stay. And we were all too busy fiddling with our metric conversion tables to heed the announcements of the changes yet to come. These flimsy new sparkling coins like trinkets given to the red man by the colonisers before they wiped them from the face of the planet.

And I ask myself, is this how we view ourselves? Transformed by the stroke of a civil servant's pen into a flock of skittish birds, all weak-necked and gangly. Is this what Europe offers us? What was wrong with what we had?

Pleasantly steamed, my mind held down the conversation. It was a conversation of questions. I questioned the civilisation of a people who had left mainland Europe thousands of years ago and moved to this western-most island in search of a new beginning, this land of milk and honey seeking a peaceful existence – a people who had dared call ourselves a nation and had spent centuries fighting for the right to establish that nation. And after centuries of slavery, oppression and bloodlust genocide, we had finally burst in twain the galling chain, and taken back what was rightfully ours. Our freedom. But was it freedom or was it just a transfer of ownership?

The poor are still living in fear of eviction, traders and shopkeepers taxed out of existence, small businesses living in fear of the city sheriff, river bailiffs catching and intimidating the unemployed young lads as they strokehaul the odd salmon from the river – not a lot had changed from medieval times.

And it crosses my mind that maybe we had all been victims of a sleight of hand, concealed in the confusion during the transition of power. As we celebrated our newfound freedom, our own self-proclaimed elite had deviously stepped into the hand-made shoes, tailor-made shirts and the grand houses of the lords and ladies of London. What freedom, only a reshuffling at the top of the deck. And I wonder if anything has changed at all in this new, free Ireland.

I can hear the hum of John chatting away in the background. He's talking about modernisation, spouting out a few buzzwords.

– I might have to get into, what do they call it? The lunch-time trade and pub grub, he says.

He's talking baloney. John can't even cope with me and the few auld cronies he calls his regulars, and he knows it. But my brain is too steeped and I'm in too deep with my thoughts to answer, so I give him the odd nod, just to let him know I'm listening.

As if teasing out the pieces of a scrambled jigsaw, my brain throws up images of an Ireland, new and old. I struggle to make sense of it all. I see famine and food mountain. I see Viking and tourist. I see Maebh, Gráinne, Constance and Mary. I see Éamon, Seán and Charlie. I see leaders elected to deliver this new Ireland. And it seems to me that our leaders have a direct line to the men who had lost the civil war. And it's not healthy when the losers wear laurels. Could this be the problem of the solution to the Irish problem, that our leaders were losers? I see the crosier and a people crucified. I see abortion and freedom without choice. I see freedom, or is it a mere transfer of ownership? The *spailpín fánach*, cottier or unemployed blue-collar worker, men like me, don't get a look-in in this new Ireland, this free Ireland. And it's a sad state of affairs when the working class have no work at all. It seems to me that our liberators, having failed to grab the bull by the horns, are now in the horns of a dilemma. Our leaders have decided to wash their hands of all responsibility, and hand over the ownership of this free Irish nation, land, culture and traditions to the greater power – the United States of Europe. My mind is a mess, and I'm struggling.

John's conversation comes in more clearly.

— Remember yer man?

— Which man? says I.

— Yer man that arrived in here with you.

— Arrived in here with me? Nobody arrived in here with me.

— Ah you do! Remember yer man. Remember he arrived in here with you when you came back from England that time?

— Who? When?

— When you arrived home that time. Fresh off the Innisfallen. Remember you knocked me up at the crack of dawn, and I left ye in for a drink …

— The lad I met on the boat home?

— The very man, says John.

— Mick? Was Mick his name? I think it was, says I.

— Mick. I think Mick was his name.

— Ah, sur', Jesus, I only met him on the boat home …

— Ah? Right, says he.

On the table, a heap of new, small, glossy decimal coins, and there in the middle a big old brown ha'penny with the pig. It must have slipped through the net of decimalisation and was still with me.

— Do ya ever see him now? John continued.

— Who? Do I ever see who? says I, a bit dazed from drink.

— Mick! Yer buttie, Mick.

— Jesus, I only met him on the boat. Sur' I told you that. Christ, 'tis like the Spanish Inquisition with you …

— Jesus, tetchy! Tetchy! Just wondering, that's all, says John. – You know, just wonderin' how's he getting on? Did he ever go back to England that time?

I stop to gather my thoughts.

— The last I heard, he was working as a brickie.

— A brickie, John repeats.

— Jesus, is there an echo in here or something? I heard he'd emigrated to Australia …

– A brickie, you say. Well, b'the hokey. Off in Australia. A brickie
...
And for some reason I'm reminded of that old Australian penny with the kangaroo from years back.
– That's right. A fuckin' brickie. Would ya believe that? A brickie, and him a labourer. Must be a mighty country, all the same, to have a labourer workin' as a brickie. An' over here the brickies are workin' as labourers.
I pause to take a breath.
– Say la vee! says John.
– Say what? says I.
– La vee! Say la vee! says he. – French, like.
– Oh, right, says I.
– Thank God we'll all be saved by the Common Market ...
– C'est la shaggin' vie! says I.
I look at John, his big, broad smile with not a tooth in sight, his head bent unevenly between his hunched shoulders. It seems to me that John had also noticed the change in this new Ireland. But the truth of the matter is, that me and John aren't exactly sure what has changed or what the consequences of this change will be. All we know is that the rug has been pulled out from under us, and we are where we are. It's a case of the less said, the better. Me and John are a little long in the tooth or hardened in the gums. Manning the barricades is a young man's game. He reaches deep into his pocket, pulls out a shining new twenty-pence coin, and like a card player with a winning hand, he crashes it down on top of the dirty old pig.
– Beat dat in two darts! John shouts.
And it strikes me as odd that this new twenty-pence coin, with the horse embossed, is a replica of the old half-crown, the old 2/6. But twenty new-pence is the same as four old shillings – forty-eight old pence. And my mind struggles with the contradiction in the basic sums. I mean Jesus, the financial experts put it up on the wall in black and white for all to see: two-new pence equals one old penny yet, twenty-new pence equals forty eight old pennies. You don't have to be a mathematical genius to figure that one out. And in a jumble of

thoughts it seems to me that someone somewhere pulled a fast one, and something happened and I'm not exactly sure what.

John says something about inflation and the vanishing paper money.

— You mark my words, he says. – The day will come when there'll be no money at all.

— No money?

— There was one of them young yuppie reps in from the brewery during the week, all talk about merchandising and marketing, and standing here at this very counter he told me that the way of the future will be credit. We'll all be living on credit. No cash at all.

— Like a slate behind a bar?

— Something like that, says he.

— Really?

— Well, that's what the rep said.

— And how would that work?

— Well, as he explained it, in the future folk won't even see their wage-packet.

— No wage packets at the end of the week?

— No. Yer wages will go straight to the bank to pay off the debts you run up the previous week.

— To pay off your bar tab?

— Not just your bar tab. Everything!

— Everything?

— Everything, says John. – Yer groceries, yer clothes, yer electricity even yer bus fare – everything will be paid for by credit. You won't even see your wages. It'll go straight into the bank to pay off last week's slate ...

— For fuck's sake! Was he on drugs or what?

— Far from it. This fella went to college, UCC...

— College? Well Jesus, UCC mustn't be much of a college if he can only get a job in the fuckin' brewery. And did this genius say anything about what would happen if your wages don't cover the tab you run up during the week?

— I asked him that, says John. – And he said that's how the bank make their money.

— What! How could the bank make money by me not paying my bar slate. For fuck's sake! T'is too much education they has and not enough common sense.

— Well, as he explained it to me, the future will all be about *institutionalised credit*. *Institutionalised credit*, that's what he called it. Everybody will be given a line of credit, even poor people, students, the unemployed on the dole even people with sweet fuckall to their name will have credit. Everyone will be given a line of credit and allowed live beyond their means, not enough to put them into debtor's prison, but just enough to have them working for the banks. There's be no more fifty-pence for the gas meter, no more press button A, or press button B for the phone – even the phones will be paid by credit. The banks will have all our wages before we spend it. Do you see what I'm getting' at?

— That's a load of aul' bollocks …

— Well, that's what he said. There'll be no money in the future, everything will be on the slate.

— That'll never catch on, says I. – Neither a borrower nor a lender be I.

— Well that's what the rep said …

— Fuck's sake …

John mutters something about Lady Lavery on the old pound notes and how Michael Collins was riding her, when it would have been more in his line to keep his hands out of Lady Lavery's knickers and keep his eyes on the prize of the Republic.

— Ah, but sur' that's the Brits for you. Every dirty trick in the book.

John straightens his head as best he can between his shoulders. He then raises his shoulders uncomfortably onto his hunched back and turns towards the bar. Again he says something about pub grub being the next big thing,

— … the days of pig's head and crubeens are numbered.

— I suppose next you'll be gettin' one of them, espresso coffee makers? says I, and I leave a big dirty old laugh out of me.

I pick some gristle lodged between my teeth with the corner of my cigarette box. John limps back behind the bar, and as he drops down the flip-lid of the counter he says,

> — Espresso? I tell you this much, if there's one thing I know, it's that here in Ireland, coffee will never replace the good old pot of Barry's best. Espresso? Espresso me ass-oh!

John cackles a laugh. He throws two more crubeens out on top of the white paper and lays off two more pints. He sits down behind the bar – just the top of his baldy head showing. With a flick of his wrists, he goes back to reading his newspaper.

The clock ticks and then tocks. Steam rises from the boiled pig and the dying sun cuts rays of godliness through the dust and smoke. The feeling is warm and safe. This is the life. And I think to myself that some might say that life has slipped through my fingers, but you don't get much better than this: stout, cigarettes, with a bellyful of pig – enjoying the present is the pleasure and leisure of royalty.

I sit back and sup. Through the bottom of the frothy porter-stained glass I can see the rows of bottles, optics and assorted bar implements on different shelves lined up behind the counter like the rows of houses perched on a headland. My mind weighs anchor and sets sail through the foam and mist on a voyage through time. Tacking into the wind, I set a course through the past or the future depending on the way the tide flows and wind blows …

The Pigeon With No Hole

— So, you're a bar manager? I asked, it was a leading question.
If I played my cards right, this encounter could very well lead to a few
free drinks.
— Yep! he smiled smugly. – Fully trained. How about yourself?
— Me? I'm a teacher. Eh, fully qualified.
— What do you teach?
I found myself struggling to explain that I was a teacher, but I was a
teacher without students, without a school, without a job. The country
caught up in that cursed cycle of recession and unemployment, he
gave me that patronising, knowing look.
— Cutbacks …
I offer an excuse for my idleness. But with my job description well
beyond its best-before date and with no let-up in this recession, I was
an unknown variable. I was a pigeon without a pigeonhole.
The bar manager viewed me with suspicion. He was unsettled by
my unemployment. Different things to different people, like abstract
art. I was a painting without a picture, difficult to define. But I was me.
I was free, and the drink was not. I quickly reorganised my thoughts
and turned the conversation.
— So, what bar do you manage? I probed.
Backfooted by my question, he shuffled uneasily left to right.
— Well, eh, well, I'm actually between jobs at the moment, he said.
– I'll probably get a few nights during the Jazz Festival.
And like everyone else in this crumbling port town I understood the
curse of recession and unemployment, so I spared him the sympathy
and gave him a knowing look. In that moment, I saw him for what he
was. The manager became man. We talked.
But there's a certain freedom in having nothing – nothing to lose
and everything to gain. Like a pigeon without a pigeonhole, we had
left the flock, left the loft, flown the coop. We spread our wings and
rose into our colourful world, out of reach of the masses. The teacher
and the bar manager soared skywards, way above their heads.

Out of Limbo

Today was a big day for me, it was Eddie's Confirmation. I had things to do, and I was running a bit late.

I didn't bother with a shower. You know the way that sometimes you couldn't be bothered with a shower. Well, that's how it was. I didn't have a shave either. I suppose I'd seen enough of the shower and shave routine in the old days before I found myself. Anyway, I didn't have that much time. It was now nine o'clock and I had to get over to Crosse's Green to sign-on, and then make my way back up to the North Chapel by eleven o'clock for Eddie's Confirmation. One quick look around the bedsit – everything was off.

– I'll clean up this mess when I get back,

I promised myself again. And then I stopped.

– No, the new me begins here and now!

A quick run around the room, scent-checking socks, underpants, and armpits of garments. Into a black plastic rubbish bag with everything going to the launderette. This way, I could kill a few birds with the one stone.

I mapped out my morning. Drop my laundry into the launderette for around 9.30. Cut across by the Opera House, up French Church Street, through the English Market, maybe even have a cup of coffee in Iago's. Give myself until a quarter past ten. Then down Tobin Street, past Triskel, over to Hanover Street and sign-on. I should be out by a quarter to eleven. Then it would be just a simple matter of cutting across Washington Street, up the Marsh, back into the North Main Street, up the North Main Street, across the North Gate Bridge, up Shandon Street to the North Chapel. I'd be there in plenty of time for the Confirmation. And when all that fuss was over, I'd have the rest of the day to myself. Seemed like a fairly full morning for an idle man. I threw the black plastic bag over my shoulder, took one more look around the room.

— I'll sort this place out when I get back.

I promised myself again.

I stepped out into the fanlight-lit hallway. In the darkness stood Herman, measuring tape in hand, measuring his uncut sculpture.

— Ah, Pluto! So, zat was your daughter, yes?

He was incapable of concealing his nosiness.

> — Well actually, Herman, she's not really my daughter, she's my ex-girlfriend's daughter. I only fed and clothed her for a year or two.

Herman looked confused but, to be honest, I didn't have the time or energy to even try to explain to him.

— More rubbish, Pluto?

He pointed at my bag of laundry.

— Laundry!

I gave a short reply.

— You are going downtown, yes?

I explained my plan of laundry, coffee, dole and Confirmation.

— Wait just one moment, I go with you. I get my laundry, yes?

Ah Jesus! This was all I needed. So I stepped out onto Waterloo Terrace, dropped my laundry bag to my ankles. I slumped there on the wall waiting for Herman the German.

— Come on, Herman, will ya? Jesus, I'm mad late!

I looked down onto the geometry of Kent Station.

— Kent Station, Kent Station, Kent Station …

Kent! Kent! Kent!

Always interested in sounds and rhythm, I mouthed the words again and again until they lost all meaning and became just a pulse of sound. I remembered a time on the Cork to Dublin train, somewhere up around the midlands, and the clickety-clack of the train on the track was like a backbeat to the ticket collector calling,

Port-Laois-eh, Port-Laois-eh, Port-Laois-eh …

To my mind it sounded just like Pete Seeger singing *The Lion Sleeps Tonight*. You know the part that goes,

A-wim-away, a-wim-away, a-wim-away …

Well, it was just like that. And I remember at the time, sitting on the train, thinking that it must have been similar to the way Strauss composed *Tales from the Vienna Woods*. I saw in a book, or a film, or a magazine, or something that, Strauss was riding in an open-top horse drawn carriage through the woods on the outskirts of Vienna, and just like that the music came to him. It was the orchestration of nature's sounds coming together to create music in his head. Isn't it magical the way creativity works? The only difference between me and Strauss is that the song created in my head had already been composed by somebody else. Still, though, it was interesting?

   — Herman, will ya come on, I haven't all day!

Spring had sprung and the warm, life-giving sun massaged the back of my hands. My eyes drifted across the calm of the city beyond the two rivers to the silos on the quays, right over to the grassy rolling hills on the southside out beyond Togher and Ballyphehane, all the way to the airport.

   — Hermaaaannnn!

Standing there stamping my feet, getting the blood to my toes, and the second-floor window shot open.

   — Pluto, will you ever shut fucking up! There's people 'round here trying to sleep!

Brenda the Brasser was obviously still awake.

   — Eh? Sorry, Brenda. Sorry. Just waiting for Herman. Go back to sleep. Sorry.

Her window slammed shut. Again, I stamped my feet.

   Ah yes, Kent Station down below me. The curved parallel lines of Kent Station. Now that's another odd one. I always thought the principle of the railway was straight lines. You know, maximum efficiency, maximum acceleration, shortest distance between two points, that kind of thing. It sort of makes sense. But it would make ya wonder, why in the name of all that's good and holy did they build the platform at Kent Station the shape of a banana. Must be some good reason? It must be the only mainline station in Ireland, if not the world, that's built on a bend. Interesting?

   — Come on, Herman! Fuck's sake …

   — Coming, I coming!

Herman thundered down the stairs and out the hall door.

— Keep it down, Herman boy, will ya? You'll wake Brenda.

— I sorry, I sorry!

He stood there, two black plastic laundry bags, one for whites and one for colours. I suppose you'd expect that from a German.

— Come on, Herman, will-'a, will-'a. I'm mad late.

I threw my eyes towards town, and we strolled off out of Waterloo Terrace, the early-morning sun casting our shadows westward.

— Did ya ever wonder why the station was built on a bend? I mean, could you imagine if you were a Dublin train driver. It's your first day on the job. And you're arriving into Cork, and you come through the pitch darkness of the tunnel doing a hundred miles an hour. Next thing you shoot out of the tunnel, dazzled by the light, and into a fuckin' bend …

Do trains have steering wheels?

But it'd make you wonder why they built the platform at Cork station on a bend?

I looked to Herman.

— The Travisti Brothers, he replied matter-of-factly.

— Travisti Brothers?

— Yes, the Travisti Brothers. You Cork people, really! You do not know your own city! You mean to tell me you never heard of the Travisti Brothers? Yes? No?

— Eh? I might have heard of 'em like, says I, lying through me teeth.

— The famous terrazzo floor layers. Travisti Brothers. Italian, yes?

— Oh, them Travisti Brothers? Yeah sure, what about 'em?

I still hadn't a clue what or who he was talking about. Herman went on to explain how the Travisti Brothers, Gino and Mario arrived to Cork as passengers in old Papa Travisti's scrotum. In time they learned the age-old art of terrazzo-laying, passed down from mouth to hand over generations of Travistis since Roman times. I still couldn't make the link between the Travisti Brothers and the bend on Kent Station platform.

— You see, said Herman, bringing our procession of laundry bags to a sudden halt.

He pointed down, over the wall towards the train station.

— Gino Travisti ordered more terrazzo than ze job required, and to conceal his miscalculation, they laid the station platform in a semi-circle. Yes? A curve? Yes? Strange, nobody knows this, yes? And ever since that time, Gino and Mario have been laying Travisti terrazzo all over Cork.

Herman was a mine of information. It crossed my mind that if I had a hat, I'd take it off to him, but naw, he'd only be getting a big head. But it is amazing what you'd pick up in a day.

By the time we reached the launderette, it was about half past nine. I was running a bit late. And Herman? Well, he was driving me around the twist. You know the way that some people are so mean? And it's not so much meanness. Herman would half his heart with you, generous to a fault. But money? Herman just didn't have it in him to put his hand into his pocket to spend money. And I suppose that's what meanness is. Well, that's what Herman was like. He stood there fumbling from pocket to pocket, jacket to trousers. I knew he was planning something that would involve him not spending money.

— You got ein rollie, Pluto?

Right, he wanted a cigarette.

— No, eh, I try not to smoke 'til teatime.

— But you smoked one this morning.

You'd want to be up early to catch Herman. He was on to me, and he wasn't going to let me off the hook.

— And why wouldn't I? I was totally stressed out, I explained. – With bells ringing, tapping on the window, banging on the ceiling and knocking on the door. What a way to face the day. Did ya ever wake up with *Waterloo Sunset* on yer mind?

I stretched out my right arm and strummed the fingers of my left hand across the invisible fretboard of my imaginary sunburst-red Gibson, finger-picking the intro to *Waterloo Sunset*.

Dwang diddy dwang!
Diddy dwang!
Diddy dwang!
Diddy dwang! Diddy dwang!
Bab ba ba ba ba

Ba ba ba ba ba ba
Ba ba ba ba ba
Ba ba ba ba

You know how it goes.

Herman dropped his laundry bags to the footpath, tuned up his air-guitar and then we began.

Ba ba ba ba ba ba
Ba ba ba ba ba ba

Duelling banjos on air guitars. We banged out the instrumental version of *Waterloo Sunset* at least once. It passed the time, but then I realised that I had no time to spare.

— Eh, what time does this launderette open?

Herman shrugged his shoulders. I laid down my guitar gently on the footpath. It was now half past nine.

— So you have no rollies, Pluto?

— I thought I told you already, I snapped.

— Is okay. Is okay. I go get some. Do you want to go half on a pack?

Herman just never gives up.

— No!

And I gave him a pound coin. He turned and headed up the street towards the shop.

— You keep an eye on my laundry, yes?

I just grunted and waved and sat down on my laundry bag, comfortable but stressed. I sat there on the footpath, trying not to think of the Confirmation, trying not to think of the time, as it flew by. So I sat there thinking …

— John Player Blue? Is okay, yes?

Herman was back. He slumped down on the kerbside and drew in deep on his assembly line cigarette.

— Here, g's one of them! I threw an index finger in his direction.

— But you say you don't smoke this early in the day.

— Yeah, well, that was then. This is now. And I want one now, okay?

— I never understand you Irish, full of contradictions. This will be your second cigarette that I witness. Here you are.

He drew a cigarette from the box.

— All contradictions, you Irish. I remember …

Herman hesitated and took a drag.

— When I first came to this country …

And there the saga unfolded. The epic story of how Herman came to be in Ireland. I had heard it a thousand times before. It was as interesting as a dead bluebottle all dried up in the corner of an old window frame.

The story goes that he was working in insurance or something in Dusseldorf when he heard some music. It was either the Clancys, or The Dubliners, or Johnny Logan, or U2, or the Wolfe Tones, or maybe it was Foster and Allen. Anyway, it didn't matter. Well, it didn't matter to me, it certainly mattered to Herman because it changed his life. He chucked the job and found his way to beautiful Bundoran in Donegal. Slowly he drifted south along the western seaboard and found himself in Cork by the Lee. That was ten years ago.

I sat there, listening, not out of manners or interest but because I couldn't be arsed changing the subject. All I wanted was to ditch my laundry in the launderette, if the place would ever open, get over to sign-on and back up to the North Chapel for Eddie's Confirmation. So I sat there listening. Herman couldn't tell a story to save his life, but it didn't stop him trying. He rambled on and on and on – from near tears to loud guffaws of laughter with the twists and turns of his curly tale.

He relished the fact that all the crucial changes in his life were brought about by pure chance. Big swinging mickey! So what? There he was, sitting on the kerb, waiting for the fuckin' launderette to open. It wasn't as if he had reached the zenith of mankind with all these uncanny twists of fate. If anything, poor aul' Herman was on the scrap heap. And you know what? He didn't even know it. But then again, maybe there were things about Herman that I didn't know. Maybe Herman comes from an immensely wealthy family. Maybe his family was one of those Nazi dynasties that made a fortune during the war and were able to hold onto it. Maybe this was all a bit of fun for Herman and in ten years' time he'll be sipping his brandy in the lap of luxury of a hunting lodge in Bavaria and recounting his days in Cork and how pure chance had brought him back into the family fold, back to his senses, back to his fortune. A fortune in gold and art that had been squirrelled away and was waiting for him, concealed in hidden vaults, no doubt. Maybe his time here in Cork is all part of his own personal master plan.

Not intending to be rude, I stood up from the footpath.

— Listen, Herman, I don't think this launderette's gonna open today.

I reached for my black bag.

— It vill open, it vill open. He may be a bit late. He is always late. But believe me when I say, it vill open ...

I didn't know if I was sick of waiting or worried about being late for Eddie's Confirmation. But I definitely knew I had to lose Herman. He was driving me absolutely insane.

— I'm gonna have to go, Herman. I must head over towards the dole. I really don't have the time to be hanging around here, well not today anyway.

— I go with you.

Herman moved to get up.

— What? You will in your hole! You're gonna come to the dole with me? Sure, you're not signing on, you're on a FÁS scheme.

I threw my eyes to heaven.

— I have things to do in town, Herman smiled.

What could I say? So, our little parade of black plastic bags struck off, down Devonshire Street, up Pine Street, towards town.

By the time we reached Christy Ring Bridge I was up to my eyeballs with Herman. A nice guy, I'm sure, but enough is enough is enough.

— Halt! Halt! Look zere!

Herman dropped his laundry bags and pointed into the river.

— What? Where?

I really wasn't interested.

— Zere, Herman shrieked. – Zere!

— Where?

— Zere! Zere in der river!

His eyes were popping out of his head.

I dropped my bag to the pavement. It was one of the most tragic sights I had ever seen. There, in the middle of the river, was a pigeon. He was floating backwards on a turned tide, out to sea. What was most distressing was the pigeon's lack of distress. He sat there, floating backwards, looking quite content. He seemed resigned to his situation. God only knew how he got into the river, or how long his unwebbed claws battled the inevitability of the turning tide. But there he was, floating downstream, to his almost certain doom, happy as Larry, looking around, enjoying the free ride and view.

    – Ve must do something! Herman shouted.

    – Do something? Ya mean like jump in after him or something?

    – Nein! Nein!

Herman always resorted to speaking German when under pressure.

    – Vot we need is ein rope or ein piece of wood.

    – A rope? Piece of wood? Are you off your chuck!

But before I could raise an eyebrow or lift a hand, he was gone at a gallop, running up Lavitt's Quay to the nearest lifebuoy.

    – Gone! Gone! he shouts, slapping his forehead. – Ze life belt is gone! Typical! You Irish! Phaaa!

But he didn't stop there. He kept running. And running must be contagious, because I ran after him, around the block to the stage door of the Opera House. Herman stood there flaking the door. The door shot open.

    – What d'ya want?

    – Ein bird! In ze river!

Herman explained the plight of the pigeon in his best pidgin English. I can only guess that the stagehand in the Opera House understood him perfectly. Because before I knew it, Herman was off again, running up Lavitt's Quay, but this time he had a 12-foot 3×2 under his arm. Like a knight in shining armour he charged towards the river. I followed on, carrying the bags of laundry.

By the time I caught up with Herman, he was at Patrick's Bridge – pointing frantically into the river towards the pigeon.

    – Ah no! You must be joking, Herman!

- No joke, Pluto. Now, hold onto my jacket.

And he climbed over the railings of Patrick's Bridge.

- Now, he grunted. – I vill guide zat poor pigeon over to ze quayside with this stick and ve can save him at ze steps, yes?
- Eh, I dunno, Herman, I dunno.
- Alright! Alright! Here he comes.

Herman stretched towards the pigeon, and I held on to his coat, knuckles whitened.

- Now! Now! He lunged forward. – Now!

A valiant effort, but he missed the pigeon by a mile. I grappled to hold on to Herman. He rotated the full 180 degrees, dropped his 3×2 to the footpath and climbed back over the railings of the bridge to safety. And like someone possessed, he took off running to the far side of the bridge, dodging traffic. By the time Herman took up his position inside the far railings, the pigeon had floated out of reach. We stood there watching as the pigeon bobbed up and down, not a care in the world. I understood what the bird was feeling, it's the freedom experienced when one accepts the inevitability of destiny. But Herman was not so philosophical.

- Der Animals Home!

He pointed in the direction of the bus office.

- Zey may have a net or something, yes?

And once again he ran. At this stage, I was wrecked from all the running and finding it difficult to keep up. Anyway, it was getting late, busy day, things to do.

I could see Herman up ahead; he was beating down the door of The Animals Home.

- 'Tis useless, Herman. This place don't open for another ten minutes. By then the pigeon will be halfway to the Atlantic.
- Quick! To the docks! Ve vill get something there for sure. Come on, quick. Ve vill catch that pigeon at ze next bridge.

And once again, he was off, running like a lunatic down past the Sextant and Carey's Tool Hire, down beyond the Idle Hour, down among the hoppers and silos, and I, like a bigger lunatic, still running after him with the laundry bags hanging off me.

He wasn't very tall, but he was built like a brick. It looked like he had just fallen out of one of the early-morning houses. He stood there in his donkey jacket and hobnail boots, swaying from side to side. Herman made a beeline for him.

— Say wha'? says he. – A pigeon?

The docker scratched his head.

— Yes! He ist drownink!

Herman was relieved at last to be understood.

— Drowning?

The docker's words were slurred.

— Yes, Herman gasped. – Zere in ze river!

Gasping for breath, holes burnt in my lungs from the fags, I stood there awe-filled as Herman the artist explained the plight of the pigeon to this drunken docker. The docker swayed and nodded and shook hands with Herman.

— So, ve get some rope, yes?

Herman waved his hands in the air.

— Rope? said the docker. – Rope for what?

— For ze pigeon!

— The pigeon?

— Yes, ze pigeon!

— Sur' Jesus, the place is polluted with pigeons! said the docker. – Like what's another fuckin' pigeon?

The docker threw his arms in the air and staggered off in the direction of the Marina Bar.

I was inclined to agree with the docker. What is another fuckin' pigeon? So I walked away. And that's where I left Herman and his two bags of laundry, pleading with the drunken docker. Anyway, today was a big day for me, it was Eddie's Confirmation. I had things to do, and I was running a bit late.

Come Out Now, Hacker Hanley!

Christmas? A funny old time of the year is Christmas.

It's a time that puts the head spinning and the mind doing somersaults. It's a time when grannies and granddas become mammies and daddies, and mammies and daddies become children again. A time when old friendships are rekindled with a trinket or a card, a time when those dead and gone are remembered. It's a time when the magic of belief is restored. And I suppose that's it, Christmas is a time of belief.

Christmas comes and Christmas goes, but there's always the one that stands head and shoulders above all the rest. It must have been twenty, thirty or forty years ago – or so. It was a long time ago, a time when people were buttoned up, in the days before Velcro.

Christmas week, and Hacker Hanley was spreading it around the street that there was no Santy Claus. He was making his case and putting up a good argument. He was saying that even his own Uncle Jerry, a man who had lived on the northside all his life, would often get lost on his way from the pub. Sometimes Uncle Jerry wouldn't get home 'til the following day.

> – So, how could Santy Claus with only a handful of reindeer find his way around the world without getting lost!

There was a certain logic to what Hacker was saying, and before we could fully digest his reasoning he struck with a killer blow.

> – And don't start me on how Santy gets around the whole world to all the boys and girls in the one night! One night! Impossible! It's a scam! he roared. – The whole thing is nothing but a scam.

And maybe Hacker had a point, but it still didn't explain how every single Christmas morning without fail, Santy Claus would always leave a nice, neat bundle of presents at the foot of my bed. Now, that was the reality, a reality that could not be denied. But doubt was creeping in. I had heard the whisperings of the big boys, but my belief in Santy Claus was still strong, strong but maybe questionable.

I mean, the facts spoke for themselves. Santy Claus came to my house every Christmas. He left presents at the end of my bed. It all made perfect sense to me. When Hacker's theory was raised up to the light I could see right through it, there were more holes in it than a sieve. And the big hole in Hacker's argument was,

— Why? Why would anyone in their right mind put presents at the end of my bed, and then give the credit to Santy Claus?

So, without due consideration for my own health or safety, I jumped to defend Santy Claus's honour. Within three minutes I had a black eye, a split lip and my mam was frog-marching me up the street by the scruff of the neck. She was reading me the riot act every step of the way.

— Go on! Get in there ya little scut! Fightin' in the street, ya, ya little caffler ya! Fightin' on the street, like a gurrier, on the very eve that the baby Jesus was born! Go on! Get in there! Ya, ya little scut!

Then straight up the stairs to bed without even as much as a sausage.

— Now! Get up them stairs and say yer prayers, ya little scut! You'll be lucky if Santy Claus calls at all to ya this year!

— Santy might not call to me this year, Mam?

— Oh, he'll call alright, she said. – You can be sure of that! But with all your tormenting of your mother, I wouldn't be surprised if he has you on The Bad Boys Blacklist! The Lump a' Coal Brigade!

— Bad Boys Blacklist? Lump a' Coal Brigade?

— Too right you might! Santy has a Bad Boys Blacklist for little scuts like you and Hacker Hanley. And once your name gets on that blacklist, the only present he'll be bringing you will be a lump of coal …

— Lump of coal, Mam?

— Nothing but a lump of coal! D'ya hear me! Lump of coal!
And it'd be good enough for ya, fighting on the street like a little
caffler!
Now! Not a peep outa ya! Go on! Get up them stairs and go to
bed and go to sleep!
You'll be lucky if he comes at all …

∼

It never snows down our street, but Christmas spirit was thick on the
ground. Outside I could hear the men from The Devonshire Arms
murdering *Good King Wenceslas* with a devilish chorus of howling
and roaring. There I was, tucked up in bed listening to Santy Claus
on the radio.

— Ho, ho, ho, boys and girls. This is Father Christmas signing off
from the North Pole. I hope you were all good children this
year, and you'll all be sound asleep when I visit your home later
tonight with my bag of presents …

And with one more,

— Ho! Ho! Ho!

He was on his way.

My mind was tortured as my head filled with my mam's threats of
the Bad Boys Blacklist and the Lump a' Coal Brigade. My brain was
churning and turning with the seeds of doubt that had been planted
by Hacker Hanley. What if there is no Santy Claus? Then again, there
had to be a Santy Claus. If there was no Santy, who was that on the
radio? But maybe there is no Santy? Or worse? What about the Bad
Boys Blacklist? What if there is a Santy and he puts me on the Lump
a' Coal Brigade? To the lonesome sounds of Christmas cheer down on
the street, my thoughts slipped and slided with this and that, until my
eyes gently closed, and I drifted to timelessness …

Well, I was snapped back to reality with a jolt, by the sound of
someone fumbling outside my bedroom door. Then the creaking of
hinges as the door eased open. If it was my mam and she found me

awake, I was in trouble. But if it was Santy Claus, I was in big trouble. I clenched my eyes tightly shut, pretending to be asleep. I could hear the shuffling around the room. My heart thumping like a hammer on an anvil inside my chest, I peeped out through flickering eyelashes. And there he was, the man himself, Father Christmas …

- Fa- fa- fa- Father Christmas? Is that you, Father Christmas? I stumbled over the words.
- Faddur Christmus? he said in a flat Cork accent. – Don't mind yer Faddur Christmus. My name is Santy, boy!
- Santy Boy?
- No, no. Not Santy Boy! Santy Claus, boy!
- Oh! Santy Claus Boy!
- Das right, boy! says he. – Santy Claus!

Now, looking back on it, Santy Claus Boy didn't look anything like I had expected. He was nothing like the Father Christmas I'd seen on telly or Christmas cards. Well, for one thing, he was only slightly overweight. And for another, he had no flowing white beard, just the grey stubble of two days' growth on his chin. No red suit. He wore a brownish-orange-coloured duffel coat that was grim and dusty from the road, and a red beanie on his head. On his feet, a well-worn pair of black steel-capped work boots. And his world-renowned joyful personality and seasonal cheer was sadly lacking. Santy Claus Boy was not a particularly jolly character. Not as much as a, – Ho! Ho! Ho! out of him. In fact, grumpy is a word that springs to mind. He was grumpy.

- What are ya gawkin' at? says he. – I haven't all night, boy. I'm havin' fierce trouble with me goory, 'tis up on the flat roof. Me back axle is seized up, me bridle is banjaxed … And you're the only man I could turn to.
- Me, Santy Claus Boy?
- Dat's right, says he. – I saw how you stood up to Hacker Hanley! You're the man I want in my corner!

Well, let me tell you, I was out of my bed and into my dressing gown and up the stairs to the flat roof in two shakes of a reindeer's tail.

Our flat roof glistened with a dusting of soft white snow. It was magical. And there, harnessed to a sleigh carrying more toys than Kilgrews Toyshop window, were the reindeer lined up in pairs. I mouthed their names

— Rudolph, Prancer, Dancer, Donner, Blitzen …

— What're ya mumbling about, boy!?

Santy Claus Boy stopped mid-sentence.

— The reindeer, I said, pointing to the sleigh.

— De reindeer? says he. – Do they look like reindeer to you?

And sure enough, on closer investigation, there in front of my eyes was the strangest array of beasts I had ever seen in my life.

> — Rudolph's for real, says he. – Rudolph is the only reindeer in the pack. And this Rudolph here? Well, she's not the original Rudolph, do you know what I mean? This is the great, great, great, great granddaughter of the first Rudolph. But the rest are all Hollywood. Pure Hollywood!
>
> This team pulling my sleigh are a selection of hand-picked beasts from the eight corners of the globe. Hand-picked for their fitness, intelligence, skill, intuition and experience in traversing their own particular terrain …

Then Santy Claus Boy guided me along the line and introduced me to each, one after the other.

He had a moose from Newfoundland in Canada called Clyde.

A Chinese yak called Peihua.

A sika deer from Tokushima in Japan by the name of Akio.

From Africa a gazelle named Naboa.

A camel from the Sudan called Midhad.

Rodriguez a llama from Peru.

From the Italian Alps, Salvatore, a mountain goat.

And finally, out in front, leading the pack, Finbarr an Irish red deer.

— Finbarr? From Ireland? says I.

— Chalk it down, boy. Hand-picked! All hand-picked, says he. –

Anyway, enough of this gibberish, what about me harness and me back axle?
- Tell ya the truth, Santy Claus Boy, I know nothing about fixing a harness! But d'ya know, O' Connors' Funeral Home next door used to have horses years ago and maybe they might have an old bit of a harness hangin' up in there somewhere, like ...
An' Dalys' Garage, down Pine Street, they're bound to have a jar of grease for your back axle.
- Me Dazza! he smiled and clicked his fingers. - Your head wasn't made for a hat!
Santy Claus Boy handed me a list, a mile long.
- You organise the presents for the boys and girls, he said. - I'll be back in a jiffy!

He was running late and had no time for small talk, so I got busy organising the bundles of toys for all the girls and boys. And with a hop, skip and most almighty jump he launched himself into the air and glided across the lane that separated our house from O'Connors' Funeral Home, a spray of snowflakes falling from his boots like star dust. Santy Claus Boy vanished down O'Connors' chimney.

I examined the list.

     Sean Carr – Believer

     Christy Lane – Believer

     Deirdre Lane – Believer

     Conor O'Brien – Believer

     Angela O'Connell – Believer

     Frank McAuliffe – Believer

     Denis Griffin – On A Need-To-Know Basis

     Michael O'Connell – Believer

And before I knew it, he arrived back across the roof, with a bridle from O'Connors' under his oxter.
- The wrong colour, says he. - But what Finbarr don't know won't bother him.
He handed it to me, and I swapped it for the broken harness. And

Cónal with Santy Claus Boy.

Santy Claus Boy was off over the rooftops and down to Dalys' Garage to see if he could find a pot of axle grease.

Mar Coughlan – Believer
Alma Dowling – Believer
Barry Johnson – Believer
The Bourke Twins – Two Believers
Brendan Kenneally – Believer
Claire Galvin – Believer

Santy Claus Boy, dropped off the pot of axle grease, and set about delivering the toys, returning regularly to refill his sack.

Patsy McAuliffe – Believer
Alma Dowling – Believer

Alma was on the list twice, so I crossed her off.

Jer Lyons – Believer
Geraldine McAuliffe – Believer

The bridle repaired, a dollop of grease onto the back axle and Santy Claus Boy was sliding down the slates, back from his final delivery. By the look on his face I could tell that something was not quite right.

— Come here to me, says he. – What's the story with Hacker Hanley's presents!
— Hacker Hanley, Santy Claus Boy?
— Yes! Hacker Hanley. Where are his presents?
— Sur' Hacker's a Non-Believer, Santy Claus Boy. So I put him on the Bad Boys Blacklist!
— The what?
— The Bad Boys Blacklist, Santa Claus Boy? The Lump a' Coal Brigade!

The look of confusion on Santy Claus Boy's face turned to disillusion.

— Bad Boys Blacklist? Dere's no Bad Boys Blacklist, he whispered. – There's no Lump a' Coal Brigade!
— But Tragic Ted don't believe in you, Santy Claus Boy!
— Look, says he. – Sit down there 'til I talk to you.

Me and Santy Claus Boy sat on the side of the roof. He talked and I listened.

> — How do I put this now? he said. – See, most of the trouble in this world is caused by one man questioning another man beliefs. But I tell ya straight now, says he. – You must always, always question yer own beliefs. But never, never question another man's beliefs. See, there's two types of people in this world. Them that believes and them that don't believe …

Santy Claus Boy paused for just enough time for me to take in all that he had just said.

> — Now, I has enough to be doing Christmas mornin' to be trying to please the believers than to be bothered me barney bringin' lumps a' coal to the non-believers. Do y'know what I'm sayin'? Now get up there like a good young lad and give us a hand puttin' together a few things for Hacker.

Me and Santy Claus Boy made up a most special bundle of toys for Hacker and I threw in a box of Lego for good measure. Santy Claus Boy was off over the roof tops with his final delivery.

His work in Cork done, he gave one last check to his harness and back axle. Then climbed up onto the sleigh.

> — Before ya go, Santy Claus Boy?
> — Yes?
> — Meself and me brothers have a slice a' cake and a bottle a' stout laid out for ya down the kitchen.
> — A bottle a' stout?

Santy Claus Boy looked at me as if I had two heads.

> — A bottle a' stout, he said it again. – I only works one day of the year and it's the one day that I gets a rake a free drink. I don't know what people be thinking. Sur' I can't drink on Christmas Eve. I couldn't be locked outa' me skull and flyin' around the sky.
>
> I'd be a danger to meself, not to mind everyone else!
> — But ya must get hungry, Santy Claus Boy?
> — Hungry? A glint came to his eye. – Hungry me? Ah now, there's

no fear of me. Sur', I'd often take a slug of a bottle of milk or tear a leg off a freshly cooked turkey.

I tell ya, dere's many a cat got no Christmas dinner because of a turkey leg I was after eating.

But speaking of food I must call over to Noreen Griffin in An Stad Café.

— Noreen Griffin? Sur' Noreen's too old for Santy!

— Excuse me? Noreen's a believer, he snapped. – And what's more, Noreen Griffin makes the best apple tarts in Cork! In Cork? His lips broadened to a smile. – In Cork? In the world!

And off he went scuttling across the rooftops towards An Stad Café. Eventually, he arrived back with tell-tale apple tart crumbs all down his duffle coat.

Santy Claus Boy made ready for the next leg of his journey. He was heading west to Allihies on the Beara Peninsula. There Finbarr the Irish Red Deer would be switched with Clyde the Moose and then on to Newfoundland in Canada.

With Hacker Hanley's argument still playing on my mind, I decided to put a straight question to Santy Claus Boy, afterall, we were on first name terms …

— Eh-hem? Before you go?

— Yes? says he.

— Do ya mind if I ask ya a question?

— Fire away, says he. – Fire away …

— Well it's been on my mind for some time now. How do you manage to get around the whole world to all the boys and girls in one night?

— Simple, says he. – You must keep goin' west! Always keep the settin' sun in sight. Keep goin' west! Because as long as you have the settin' sun in sight, the dawn of the next mornin' will never creep up behind ya …

Of course, the aul' International date line comes in handy too like. Well that was that. Problem solved. I needed no more convincing.

Truth be told, I was a little teary-eyed, I was sad to see him go. But there was a job to be done and Santy Claus Boy was the man to do it! Struggling to hold back my tears I asked,

- Will you call to me again, Santy Claus Boy?
- That depends, he said.
- Depends?
- Yes, says he. – It depends on you.
- Depends on me, Santy Claus Boy?
- I'll put it this way, he said. – The day you stop believing in me, that's the day I'll stop believing in you.

- Right! says he. – Give me a hand turning this thing around …
We pushed the sleigh so that it stretched diagonally across the roof, making room for the take-off. Santy Claus Boy climbed aboard.

They had lightning in their eyes and fire in their breath as their hooves thundered off across the roof. And up, up and away, the sleigh lifted to the sky, knocking sparks off the gutter as they reached for the stars. They circled above my head …

- Give something nice to me Aunty Kit and Uncle Jack in Adrigole, I shouted.
- You're a sound man! he roared from the circling sleigh. – One of our own!

Santy Claus Boy circled the sleigh one more time, he raised the whip above his head and laughed as it cracked over Finbarr's antlers.

- Are ya right there, Finbarr!
And with a roar of,
- Come out now, Hacker Hanley!
He was gone, shooting across the southern sky, westward!

≈

So there you have it.

I still believe in Santy Claus Boy, and Santy Claus Boy still believes in me. Each and every Christmas, without fail, he finds his way down into the belly of Cork city – across the rooftops, past slate-clad, buckled beams and chimney pots and all the way to my house. He stopped bringing me presents years ago. But every Christmas morning I know in my heart and soul that Santy Claus Boy has been – spreading Christmas cheer and sprinkling Christmas spirit and restoring the magic of belief.

> As I say now, it was a long time ago.
> Ten, twenty, thirty years ago or so.
> It was a time when people were buttoned up,
> in the days before Velcro.

PANCHO AND LEFTY RIDE AGAIN

RIDE AGAIN

A COLLECTION OF SHORT FICTION

1995

ELEVEN
BONUS
TRACKS

2021

Dockets And Dowels

Dedicated to the memory of Paddy Daly – John Street

Like my grandda and my grandda's da, my da was a cabinetmaker, a master craftsman. The lads up in Mulla's Yard said he was a genius – he could make a full piece of furniture, no nails or screws used.

I swear to God, you can never really know what goes on in another man's head, but it's hard to believe that something as simple as a wooden dowel could turn my dad away from cabinet-making. It was like, up until then, his whole life swung around Mulla's Yard. But one day, snap! No more. The day of the dowel dawned.

> – Sure any half-wit could throw a cabinet together these days, he'd say.

Maybe it had to do with the fact that Mulla died, and his son, the Graduate took over the running of the yard, or that the Graduate ran the yard from the office, and he didn't know one end of a hammer from the other. Maybe it was because there was no respect for the wood joint, nor the men who knew how to make them. Whatever the reason, there was no doubt but that dowels had destroyed the detail of the craft, and enough was enough, and my dad's head was turned.

> – Sure that's not furniture!

He'd throw de mallet down.

> – Look! Either you make it or someone out foreign will make it! Take yer pick, the Graduate would say and walk away.
> – Dockets an' dowels, my dad would say and throw the eyes to heaven. – 'Tis all dockets an' dowels these days.

It was like my dad saw his craft die in front of his eyes and with its death he caught a glimpse of his own mortality. Somewhere along the line it dawned on him that he couldn't face eternity in some thrown-together plywood box fastened with a few dowels. He was a cabinetmaker and only a casket fitting of a master craftsman would do. That's why at the age of fifty-eight he decided to make his own coffin in the kitchen at home.

He drew together boards from trees grown on different continents. Boards hand-picked from shipments as they arrived into Mulla's Yard, boards brought together, planked and hobbled away home. It took over a year, but he was in no rush. He wanted the finest collection of grains to be found either side of the hardwood jungles of Burma and the Amazon Basin for his masterpiece.

No nails, screws or dowels used, but perfected joints, handed down from generation to generation, grains married so tightly together that no man could pull asunder.

> — Look a' this, son, he'd say. – That's a dovetail. And that? That's a T-joint. An' see that one there in the corner, that's me own secret F-joint. And I'll show you how to make one a' them one a' these days.

My sister Kathleen lined his coffin with quilted yellow, green and black silk, the colours of Glen Rovers. And in the true tradition of quilters she stitched in a square that didn't match the pattern, a planned mistake so as not to challenge God's pride by creating perfection; split down the middle half red and half white for Cork.

They say that you'd know a shoemaker's wife by the holes in the soles of her shoes, and there's a grain a' truth in that. Because with all my dad's skill we didn't have a stick of furniture. I mean we had beds, the odd chair and all that but no shelves, no presses, no sideboards nothing special, not if you don't count the coffin. It stood there in the middle of the kitchen on two carpenter's trestles, a sheet thrown over it protecting my dad's handiwork and a few wads of white paper to save the sheet. It was our table, and we'd gather around …

Kippers of a Friday, roast of a Sunday, one of the days between

Monday and Wednesday it'd be bacon and cabbage and with payday on Friday it was usually fried bread of a Thursday. Same old ding-dong dinner time, same old ping-pong chit chat, like mass night after night, every day of the week except that is for Saturday. Saturday was my dad's day. It always began with his excuse for the weekly feast of entrails, off-cuts and offal.

> — The pig, he'd say. – The pig is the one animal that you can ate every bit of. And d'you know why? I'll tell you why! 'Cause we're Christians that's why. 'Tis the one thing that the Catlicks an' the Prosidents has in common. We all ates the pig. Now the Hindoos, an' the Muslins, an' the Buddas, an' the Jewman, an' all that shower don't eat no pig. They has no God. And that's why we eats de pig. Because here in Cork we show our devotion to the one an' only true Jesus Christ Our Lord by not wastin' one mouthful of de God-given flesh of de boar, de sow or de banbh …

He'd bless himself to hammer home his point.

> — Not only is it religious, he'd say. – It's part of our culture. The people a' Cork were eatin' pigs' heads long before St. Finbarr found us.

And he was right, because where we came from, the head of the pig often kept the wolf from the door. Never the fur-lined devilish faces of the cow or the sheep, always the pig, whose human-like fleshy jowls, for some reason, tasted easier on the conscience. Still, there's something evil when two eyes stare out at you from a pot. Maybe that's why he cooked them half-head at a time, split skull and jaw with hammer and axe, slit with carving knife down between the eyes, along the centre line of the snout, right through the palate of the mouth, all the way home to the jawbone.

I'd sit there, watching. His sleeves rolled up beyond his elbows and him tearing into and devouring the pig's head. Held firmly by the ear in the one hand and the snout in the other, scraps falling from his mouth to the white-paper-covered coffin. He'd bate into the prime cut of the cheek muscle just above the tooth-ribbed jawbone, gristle and grease seeping down over his hard hands all the way to his elbows, and the fat from the pig's eye socket, forehead and lock being smeared all over my dad's face as he'd battle with the jaws of the beast.

◇

At the age of seventy-two he tried the coffin for size, found it a mite tight, must have put on a bit of weight. Kathleen blamed it on the pig's head,
— All fat an' bone, she said.
So he took to training, walking and things, getting fit for the coffin. But as she got older, and he got feeble, the pot-boiling came to an end when my dad's pride gave way to his age and Kathleen took a tighter hold on the household. He was lost for a while, just hanging around like someone waiting for God.

Then one day he pulled the sheets off the coffin. He rubbed his fingers along the grain, no knots, not at all. And it all began simply enough. A little bit of inlay here and there, a simple scroll along the side. He then carved the full forty-nine lines of St Patrick's Breastplate,
Christ be before me,
Christ be behind me,
Christ be about me …
Right down the length of the lid. And then with oak, walnut, ash and cherry veneer he inlaid the symbols of his craft: the mallet and chisel, the tenon saw and plane, the pencil and pot of glue and the square and dividers, one at each corner. It was medazza, but he just didn't know when to stop.

Somebody mentioned that the square and dividers was a Freemasons symbol and suggested that St Patrick might have been a Protestant.
— St. Patrick spent too much time up North with de unionists to be a real Catholic.
So my dad carved the Virgin Mary on the end panel up by his head, draped around her feet he inlaid the tricolour in mahogany, ash and pine.

– Let there be no mistake about it, he said. – Not only am I an Irish Catlick, but I'm an Irish republican Catlick.

But he didn't stop there. Glen Rovers were remembered by a set of crossed hurleys and sliotar. Then right above St Patrick's Breastplate he carved the top section of Shandon steeple with a big golden fish inlaid in beech. He said that the fish on top of Shandon looked down on him in life, so it may as well look down on him in death. Of course he knew Shandon was a Protestant church, that's why he put St Mary's, pillars and all, on the left panel.

When my dad's brother, Uncle Miah, saw St Mary's, he said it was a nice touch,

– Remembering the 1916 Rising ...

– 1916 Rising? my dad questioned.

– You know like, the GPO?

Uncle Miah pointed to the coffin.

– The GPO?

– That's it there, isn't it?

– The GPO? Ah, Jesus no. That's not the GPO, Miah boy! That's St Mary's Pope's Quay.

– Really? It looks like the GPO to me. But now that you mention it, St Mary's Pope's Quay looks like the GPO, don't it?

Enough said. My dad chiselled the words *St. Mary's, Pope's Quay*, under the carving, and so as not to offend the rebels of the 1916 Rising, he put the names of the leaders down the right-hand panel. And that wasn't the end of it ...

Ronnie Delaney was commemorated by a pair of running shoes and the words *Ronnie Delaney Olympic Gold, For Ireland and for Glory*. On went Sonia O'Sullivan, *No Drugs Here*. Daniel O'Connell, Michael Collins, St Finbarr, Terence MacSwiney, Tomás MacCurtain, Christy Ring, Blackrock Castle, Patrick's Bridge, he even had a Síle na Gig at his feet, and the work went on until every inch of the coffin was overlaid, inlay on inlay, sort of like a beautiful body mutilated with tattoos.

– ... and not a dowel in it, he'd say proudly.

And that's the way it was, day in day out, tapping away at the coffin whenever he took the notion, right up until the day he died.

~

His funeral was a grand affair, lying in state, wrapped in silk, in a casket that would do any master craftsman proud. A smug smile on his face, they all came to pay respect, even the Graduate and the crowd from Mulla's were there, most too young to remember my dad, all carpenters, not a cabinetmaker between them. They all stood around the coffin admiring my dad's handiwork, pointing out the inlay saying and things like,
   — *Look, there's Sonia O'Sullivan.*
   — *Look at that, the GPO.*

And I'm there telling them that no nails, screws, or dowels were used, only handcrafted joints handed down from generation to generation. The women of the street, *oouing* and *aahing* over Kathleen's silk lining; never the best at taking compliments, she just vanished into the kitchen and rattled a few cups and saucers.
   But it was a happy occasion, people telling stories, that sort of thing. The priest said that in all his day's burying people he'd never seen a coffin like my dad's. And after the prayers, myself, Uncle Miah and a few of the lads shouldered the coffin from the kitchen. It's a strange feeling, carrying your father in a box.

   — Hoi! Hold it, lads! Hold it!
Uncle Miah brought the procession to a halt.
   — Back it up! Back it up! Here, look, try it this way. No! No! Turn
     it 'round! Try it that way! Try it on its side …
We tried it sideways. We tried it lengthwise, we even tried it upright, but it wouldn't turn in the hall. One into one just wouldn't go. The crowd who had piled out onto the street waiting, were back in the kitchen again standing around the coffin, advice flying, but nothing else moving. The sound of bottles being cracked open, big roars of

laughter from the back. The Graduate was telling me that the furniture trade had changed since the recession ended.

— It's all quality furniture they want these days, he said. – If they're going to buy, they'll only buy quality. They'll pay top dollar for it. Leave the old dab n' dowel for the cheap imported stuff. But Jesus, these days you can't get a craftsman for love nor money …

And he was off talking about something else.

Uncle Miah cleared the house and closed the front door behind them. We lifted my dad's board-like body from the coffin and lay him on the floor. And then with the big rusty saw from under the stairs, he cut the coffin in two, right down between,

Christ be behind me,
Christ be before me …

Twenty-eight dowels to put it together again, six top and bottom, eight on each side and we tacked a sheet of plywood to the base, just in case. We placed my dad back into his masterpiece.

— Com'on! Hurrup! said Uncle Miah. – Wha' he don't know, he won't know.

Our front door opened out. And my dad, the master craftsman, was carried shoulder-high, by the tradesmen through the streets of Cork.

A-Rat-at-at-at

Did I ever tell you about yer Great Grand Aunt Julia?

    — My Great Grand Aunt Julia, Grandda?

Your Great Grand Aunt Julia was no sloucher.
She stood shoulder to shoulder with
Terence MacSwiney and Tomás Mac Curtain, so she did.
And what about your Great Grand Uncle Liam?

    — My Great, Grand Uncle Liam, Grandda?

Well, he fought in the trenches durin' the Great War.
No word of a lie, Mossie boy.
Your Great, Great, Grand Uncle Liam, give or take a few Greats like,
enlisted in the British army to go and fight in the trenches, so he did.
On me mother's soul, Mossie boy.
A corporal. A corporal in The Great War.
Out there in the trenches on the edge of no-man's land, fightin'!
Fightin' in the Battle of the Somme.
The bravest of 'em all.

    — And did he get a medal, Grandda?

Did he get a what!
Ah, ya gotta' picture the scene, Mossie boy.
Trenches.
Trenches, knee-deep in blood, death and gore.
Vermin, squirmin' around their feet.
Grown men crying out in pain, in fear, clutching crucifixes.
Praying to gods they didn't even believe in.

Bodies?
Bodies and limbs.
Limbs of comrades scattered left and right of 'em.
Thunder of cannon and rattle a' gun.
An' then?
Then?
Then?
Then there was none.
Nothin'.
Not a sound.
Nothin' in the wide earthly world.
Not a sound – 'til the smoke cleared.
Then all you'd hear was the odd cry of pain –
from the dying and the wounded in the distance.
The lost souls in no-man's land.
And after a while, you mark my words, Mossie boy,
that stopped too.
Silence!
Not a sound!
Nothin'.
It was then that your Great, Great, Great, Grand Uncle Liam,
give or take a few Greats like,
heard it for the first time.
A-Rat-at-at-at! A-Rat-at-at-at! A-Rat-at-at-at!
First, he thought it was a woodpecker, in the distance.
A-Rat-at-at-at!
A-Rat-at-at-at!
A-Rat-at-at-at!
You'll never guess what it was?

— Machine gun fire, Grandda?

No, not machine gun fire, Mossie boy.
A-Rat-at-at-at!
A-Rat-at-at-at!

It took my Great, Great, Great Grand Uncle Liam a few minutes to figure it out.
A-Rat-at-at-at!
A-Rat-at-at-at!
An' do ya know what it was, Mossie boy?
I'll tell ya what it was.
It was the sad and lonely sound of the little drummer boy.
He was lying wounded, dying,
out in the middle a' no-man's land.
He was bleeding to death in a shell hole.
And I tell, Mossie boy.
No-man's land is no place for a boy.
There he was rattling out a futile tattoo on his little drum.
A-Rat-at-at-at!
A-Rat-at-at-at!
A-Rat-at-at-at!
As if to say:

Save me! Please, I'm dying. God almighty, will someone save me ...

— And did he die, Grandda?

Will you hold yer whisht now, Mossie boy.
I'm getting to it. I'm getting to it.
Now there were German snipers lined up along the far side a' no-man's land.
And that little drummer boy was like bait.
The Germans, sittin' there like a cat on a mouse-hole.
Just waiting for one heroic eejit to stick his head above the sandbags.
And they'd have shot it clean offa' his fuckin' shoulders.
Pardon my French, Mossie boy.
But your Great Grand Uncle Liam,

— Give or take a few Greats, Grandda?

You said it, Mossie boy!
He couldn't take no more of it.
A-Rat-at-at-at!
A-Rat-at-at-at!
A-Rat-at-at-at!
So, what does he do?
I'll tell you what he did!
He climbs up out of his trench.
All his comrades shoutin' and roarin'
and draggin' at him to stay down!
But your Great, Great, Grand Uncle Liam,

    — Give or take a few Greats, Grandda?

You better believe it, Mossie boy.
He struggled to break free.
He climbs out onta' the top of his trench.
And all he could hear was:
Click-click!
Click-click!
Click-click!

    — Click-click, Grandda?

Right along the German line.
German snipers cocking their firin' pins.
And your Great Grand Uncle Liam plum straight between the cross
wires.
In that split of a second, your Great, Great, Great, Grand Uncle Liam
saw his life flash before his eyes.
He knew his destiny was in the hands of the gods.

    — And did they shoot him, Grandda?

They thought about it. They thought about it.

But all your Great, Great, Grand Uncle Liam could hear was:
A-Rat-at-at-at!
A-Rat-at-at-at!
A-Rat-at-at-at! … in the distance.
So, what does your Great, Great, Grand Uncle Liam do?
I'll tell you what he did!
Your Great Grand Uncle Liam stretched out his arms,
like Christ on the cross,
ready to give up his life that another man –
albeit a drummer boy – should live.
He sucked in a lung full,
the taste of death and blood and gore.
Then slowly,
slowly with uncertainty,
he started off across the bombed-out barbed wire of no-man's land.
Singin'…

> Come on boys an' you'll see lads an' lassies full of glee.
> Famous for all they would make yer heart thrill.
> The boy's they won't har-um you.
> The girls they will char-um you.
> Here's up 'em all says the Boys of Fairhill.

> Come on boys and have a day with our bowling club so gay
> The loft of the bowl it would make your heart thrill.
> When you hear the Shea boy say:
> Timmy Delaney has won the day.
> We beat 'em all says the Boys of Fairhill.

Sing up, Mossie! Sing up!

> Oh, the Blackpool girls are very rude,
> They go swimming in the nude.
> Here's up 'em all says the Boys of Fairhill.

Go on, sing up, Mossie boy!

Oh, the smell off Patrick's Bridge is wick-ed.
How do Father Mathew stick it.
Here's up 'em all says the Boys of Fairhill!

An' your Great, Great, Grand Uncle Liam walked out,
out over the blood and the guts,
and the death, of no-man's land.
Out to where that little drummer boy was lyin'.
An' didn't he reach down,
pick him up,
sling him over his shoulder
and carry him home to the safety of his comrades.
An' one by one the Germans raised their heads above their trenches.
They knew that my Great, Great Grand Uncle Liam,
give or take a few greats, like.
Was either the bravest man they had ever seen,
or else, he was totally off his fuckin' chuck.
Pardon my French, Mossie boy.
But didn't they join in singin' *The Boys of Fairhill* – in German,
An' then the British,
they came up outa their trenches and they started singin' too.

Oh, the Sunbeam girls are very tall,
Up against the Sunbeam wall.
Here's up 'em all, says the Boys of Fairhill.

Come on, Mossie boy, sing up! Sing up!

Cathy Barry sells drisheen,
Fairly bursting at the seams.
Here's up 'em all, says the Boys of Fairhill.

Shandon Steeple stands up straight,
and the River Lee flows underneath.
Here's up 'em all, says the Boys of Fairhill.

Come on Mossie boy! Sing up! Sing up!

Oh, the Blarney hens don't lay at all.
And when they lays they lays 'em small.
Here's up 'em all, says the Boys of Fairhill.

An' then didn't some fella funt a ball up into the air.
Right into the middle of no man's land.
And they all came out for a kick around.
An' if the old people from around here are to be believed,
your Great, Great, Grand Uncle Liam played a blinder.
But the Germans won fair and square.
2-14 to 3 points.
They had a corner-forward from Na Piarsaigh playing for them that day.
So that was it.
That was the day your Great, Great, Great Grand Uncle Liam,

    — *Give or take a few Greats, Grandda?*

Oh, chalk it down, Mossie boy.
That was the day he saved the little drummer boy
from a fate worse than death.

    — *Did my Great, Great Grand Uncle Liam get a medal, Grandda?*

Did he what!
Your Great Grand Uncle Liam got four medals, Mossie boy!

    — *Four medals, Grandda?*

That I may be struck dead!
Eh? He got one from the British – for bravery.
One from the Red Cross – for saving a man's life.
And, one from the German High Command – for usin' his noggin'!

Because whatever you might say about the aul' Germans,
they always respects a man who uses his noggin'.

— *But I thought you said he got four medals, Grandda?*

Four medals?
Oh, right? Eh?
Right? The fourth medal?
Ah, yes!
Your Great, Great, Great, Grand Uncle Liam, give or take a few greats,
like.
Well, – he got a medal for *Man of the Match* as well.

Bethlehem

— Right lads! Put away the books!
We're going to carry on, from where we left off yesterday.
And where did we leave off yesterday?
Brother Scully's eyes trawled the classroom. From the horn-rimmed corner of his glasses he could see the Parrot fluttering and spluttering on the edge of his desk.

— Brudder! Brudder! Brudder! Brudder! Brudder!
Timmy Perrott was the Parrot, not because his name sounded like parrot, but because he was a parrot. He was Brother Scully's parrot. I can see him now, the little beak on him, and he up and down, and out of his desk, with his hand flapping in the air, crowing out, repeating Brother Scully word-for-word and finishing Brother Scully's sentences with a squawk.

— Brudder! Brudder! Brudder! Brudder! Brudder!
— Well, Mr Perrott?
— The birth of Jesus, Brother, squawked the Parrot.
— The birth of our Saviour Jesus Christ. Dead right, Mr Perrott!
So, why? Why did Mary and Joseph go to-oooo?
— Bethlehem, Brother? chirped the Parrot.
— Right again, Mr Perrott.
So, why? Why did Mary and Joseph go to Bethlehem?
Brother Scully could smell the fear of weakness. He could sense weakness in a raised eyebrow, the twiddle of a pencil or the shifting of a shoe. Again he eyeballed the classroom, desk by desk, row-by-row, bowl cut by ring-wormed bowl cut, eventually stopping at Nicky Flynn.

— Well, Mr Flynn, maybe you'd enlighten us as to why Mary and Joseph went to Bethlehem all those years ago?
— Ehm? Mary and Josuff went to Bethlehem, to ehm?

— Come on, Mr Flynn, we did all this last week!
— Ehm? Mary and Josuff went to Bethlehem for the?
For the Christmas, Brother?
— The what!?
— Home for the Christmas, Brother?
— Home for the Christmas! Sur' Jesus Christ and his holy mother, there was no Christmas back then, man! That was the first Christmas!

But there was a truth in what Nicky Flynn was saying, because every year from early November, the only talk on our street would be of Nicky's dad coming home for the Christmas. Nicky's dad was a Dagenham Yank, and like hundreds of other men from across the northside, he spent fifty weeks of the year over in London down Dagenham way, up to his balls in axle grease, keeping the wheels of industry turning for Henry Ford Motor Factory. Living in a kip, eating out of tins and sending what money he didn't drink home to feed his wife and child. But every year for two weeks at Christmas time Nicky's dad and a ship-load of men would come home from Dagenham. And when the men from Dagenham hit the town, they hit the place running. Two weeks of drinking, singing, bawling and brawling. Two weeks of slicked-back hair, crisp white shirts and clean fingernails. Two weeks of being the big shot, two weeks of spending sterling hand over fist like Yanks.

I can see the women of our street in clusters on doorsteps and they whispering,
— Would you look at the big shot, and he back from Dagenham with his wads of dosh, and the gatch of him, like lord of the manor. And he over there in Dagenham living in a kip, and he eating out of tins. And he back here like cock of the walk. He only sends home what he don't drink ...
The women of our street didn't like Nicky's dad. No. The women of our street did not like Nicky's dad at all.

I can see him now, all scrubbed-up, hair cut to the bone, short back and sides topped off with a slick greased quiff, looking sharp in his shop-bought new blue serge suit, brown shoes polished to glass and a crisp white shirt with collar and cuffs as keen as razors.

And year after year for those two weeks at Christmas time Nicky Flynn would look on as his mam and dad played a game of happy families. Himself lording it about like some retired gent, with the braces down and the newspaper under the elbow, and he up and down wearing the well-worn track between the bookies and Hoskins pub. Strutting around like cock-of-the-walk and he handing out coppers to the dirty-faced kids around the street.

The women of our street didn't like the cut of him. They didn't like the walk of him. No by Christ, they didn't like him at all. They were still whispering about what happened the previous Christmas, that time he dragged Nicky's mam out of the house by the hair and kicked her arse up and down the street.

— Like a wild animal bellowing, they whispered. – Could hear him roaring from inside the house. And he after spending all his money on Beamish and slow Boxing-Day horses. Christmas done and all his money was spent. Poured good money after bad, down his throat then pissed it up against the wall of Hoskins pub, so he did. The bastard, God have mercy on my soul. Dragged her out of the house by the hair and booted her arse up and down the street, and he roaring,

– *Where's all the money I sent home, ya bitch!*

And she's the bigger fool to be putting up with him. But sur' Jesus, later that night then she's over in Hoskins with him. The two of 'em like as if nothing happened. The two of 'em like love birds cuddling and canoodling and flooring pints. On me mother's soul, over in Hoskins they were. No one at home looking after the child.

– *My little panda,* he called her. – *with the two black eyes.*

And they giggling like young lovers. The gall of him.

And maybe the whispering women knew best, and maybe they were right, but one thing is for sure, in the weeks leading up to the Christmas of my ninth birthday, Nicky's mam was like a blue-arsed fly scrubbing the doorstep, polishing the knocker and letterbox, beating the rugs, cleaning the windows, painting the walls. Make no mistake about it, she wanted Nicky's dad to know that every penny of his hard-earned money sent home over the previous twelve months had been put to good and proper use, because as sure as night follows day, Nicky's dad would be coming home for the Christmas.

— Home for the Christmas? Home for the Christmas!
Brother Scully shook Nicky Flynn by the ears.

— Sur' Jesus Christ and his Holy Mother, there was no Christmas back then, man.
That was the first Christmas.
We did all this last week! Why did Mary and Joseph go to?
— Bethlehem, Brother! chirped the Parrot.
— Spell Bethlehem?
— B-e-t-h-l-e-h-e-m, Brother.
— Good man, Mr. Perrott. Good man.
So why, Mr. Flynn? Why! Come on, man! Come on!
Why did Mary and Joseph go to Bethlehem? Why, man! Why!
Nicky Flynn's eyebrows knotted as his brain battled with the question, – *Why did Mary and Joseph go to Bethlehem?* Brother Scully still prodding, poking and pucking,
— Why, man! Why!

But the big question in Nicky's mind was, why every Christmas, just when everything was settling down and they were beginning to be like a real family, his dad packed his bags and headed back across the Irish Sea to England.

Year after year it was always the same. Come the first Sunday of January, the singing and the drinking and the spending and the brawling and the bawling would come to an end when his dad and a ship-load of the Dagenham Yanks headed for the docks and the boat back to England. They were heading back to their shabby digs and bedsits, leaving their wives and children behind them.

Every year Nicky would see his mam and the other women, standing on the quayside with streaming eyes, and their men folk up on deck, hung-over and penniless; waving, caffling and singing *The*

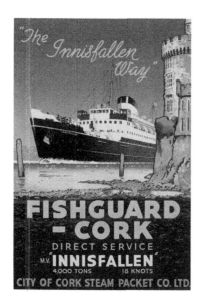

Banks. Nicky would stand there on Horgan's Warf with the bitter January winds swirling around his schoolboy knees cutting him to the bone. He'd stand there looking on as the Innisfallen sailed down river, past the boat club and the fine houses of Tivoli, past the Marina and Blackrock Castle, around the back of Spike, out between the forts of Camden and Carlisle, and all the way to Roches Point lighthouse. Then setting course for the narrows of the harbour and straight out into the wild Atlantic where they would turn sharp to starboard and it would be full steam ahead all the way for England. And as the sound of the men singing faded, the women and children would peel off in twos and threes and head home to the lonely hills of Gurranabraher, Churchfield and Farranree. How many times did Nicky Flynn hear his mother say,

— Maybe next year yer dad will get a job closer to home.

Brother Scully still flaking wildly, his eyes bulging and he roaring,

— Why, man! Why! We did all this last week, Mr Flynn!
  Why did Joseph and Mary go to Bethlehem!

— Joseph was, eh? Joseph was lookin' for a job closer to home, Brother?

— A job? A job, is it! Why would Joseph be lookin' for a job, and he a fully qualified, self-employed car-pen-ter! Why, man! Why!

Then Brother Scully turned on me, the big red head on him,

— Christy Buckley! Maybe you can shine some light on the situation?
  Why Buckley! Why! Come on, man, we haven't all day! We haven't all day! Come on, man! Come on, man! Why!

— Why what, Brother?

A clatter lifted me clean out of my desk.

— Don't you why-what-Brother me, Buckley me bucko!
Yer asleep, man! Yer asleep!

Brother Scully still roaring like a lunatic,

— When they're offerin' you the offer of a day's work, ya won't hear
that either, Buckley! And why won't Christy Buckley hear the
offer of a day's work!?

— Brudder! Brudder! Brudder! Brudder!

— Well, Mr. Perrott!

— 'Cause he'll be asleep, Brother!

— Dead right, Mr. Perrott! Christy Buckley will be asleep. Now,
repeat the question for the benefit of Mr. Buckley!

— Why did Mary and Joseph go to Bethlehem? squawked the
Parrot out the side of his beak and slid back onto his perch.

Brother Scully fixed his gaze on me.

— Well, Buckley, you've heard the question.
Why? Why from your vast knowledge of theology and all
matters biblical, do you think, in the wide earthly world, did
Joseph and Mary happened to venture to the little town of
Bethlehem, all those years ago?

— Ehm?

— Come on, Buckley! Come on! We did all this last week!

— Mary and Josuff, eh, went to, eh?

— Now think about what you're sayin', Buckley. We're not dealing
with any old village or cross-roads here, ya know. We're talking
about the town, the town where the Saviour, the Saviour Jesus
Christ, was born. The birth of civilisation. Right, Buckley! So
why? Why did Joseph and Mary go to Bethlehem?!

— Ehm? F-f-for the Christmas, Brother?!

— Ah, for cryin' out loud, man!

Another flake into the head followed a jab to the ribs.

— Didn't Mr. Flynn just say that a minute ago, and didn't I tell him
he was wrong. Yer asleep, man! Yer asleep!
Get out b'the wall, Buckley! Out b'the wall!

And by Christ, I'll deal with you in a minute …

Right lads! I'll say it one more time and one time only.

Mary and Joseph went to Bethlehem to fill in a census for-um!

Why did they go!?

And a room full of dirty-faced bowl cuts sang out the reply.

— Mary and Joseph went to Bethlehem to fill in a census for-um!

— Why did they go?

— To fill in a census for-um!

— One more time for Mr Flynn, why did they go?

— To fill in a census for-um!

— A census for-um!

— A census for-um!

— A census for-um!

— A census for-um! – A census for-um! – A census for-um!

Leaning against the radiator, Brother Scully looked out across the city. He smiled at the insanity of it all, and wondered why any man in his right mind would head off across the desert with a pregnant young girl on the back of a donkey just to fill in a census form. He smiled when the thought crossed his mind that the baby she was carrying wasn't even Joseph's.

— Jesus, some census form that turned out to be? he whispered.

Father's Name: God Almighty.

Father's Occupation: Creator of Heaven and Earth.

Wiping the tears from his eyes, Brother Scully held his hand to his mouth, restraining his guffaws of laughter.

— A census for-um!

— A census for-um!

— A census for-um!

— A census for-um! – A census for-um! – A census for-um!

The Market

Dedicated to Kay and Rebecca Harte

Jesus, I'm late.
I'm late, but I hesitate.

At Princes Street corner –
a lone troubadour treats *The Land I Love the Best* with care.
I cut through the Mutton Lane into the Market –
a shortcut, scenic route to the Grand Parade.

The Market is glowing.
A bit like *The Wizard Of Oz* when it turns to colour.
Vegetables freshly dug from green and leafy country gardens
tumbling from stalls.
Chickens, rabbits, wood pigeons, pheasants and ducks strung up in clusters.
Trays of eggs from every caste of farmyard, and waterfowl
stacked to the canopy.

Art students straddling the fountain sketching moving still-life.
The knobbly knees of café society
poke through the railings of the ceiling slung Farm Gate.
The air is thick with sound and scent.
The most beautiful aroma of exotic herbs and spices
from Mr Bell's Spice Emporium.

Hot breads from the Yukon Bakery.
Pesto, chorizo, bitter balsamic vinegar,
sweet olive oil, freshly sizzling crepes,
fish and all creatures of the Atlantic Ocean.
And meat? More meat than you could shake a stick at.
And all this blending beautifully with
the sing-song sound of people talking.

Jesus, I'm late.
I'm late, but I hesitate.
Ah well,
May as well be hung for a sheep as for a lamb.

Pana Done Wrong

Dedicated to John Breen

Patrick Street was mad. It was pouring out of the heavens. A gale-force wind had the Christmas lights thrashing around above our heads. Carol singers, shopkeepers, hawkers, everybody looking for money. I got the job of relief postman, doing double shifts. Only three weeks seasonal work, but it was worth it, you need money for the Christmas.

Anyway there I was, two hundred quid in my arse pocket, Christmas Eve and not a present bought. So, I knocked off early and headed into town. I knew exactly what I was looking for.

A cap for my dad for bingo, to stop him getting soaked waiting for the bus to the Glen Hall. He'd love that. For my sister Kathleen and her husband I was getting a big box of biscuits. See, they'd have loads of people calling around, the biscuits would be handy. And for the niece and nephew: two Cadbury Deluxe selection boxes. Of course, I had to get something special for my beautiful Yvette.

This was our first Christmas together as man and wife. Her first Christmas in Ireland. Her first Christmas away from home, and it wasn't going too well. She had all these fairy tale memories of French Christmases: Yule-logs, sleigh rides, eggnog, port and brandy. I was worked to the bone, getting the post out. She was spending most of her time hanging around the flat, so I decided I'd make it up to her by getting her something special, something nice, something romantic. A bottle of perfume and some sexy underwear. The French love that kind of thing.

So, there I was Christmas Eve, two hundred quid in my pocket, outside Roches Stores, and who did I meet only Tragic Ted.

— Ah, Ted! Long time no see.

— Pluto, man, how're things?

— Good! Good! Workin' like a dog, though. Christmas postman, double shift. Just snatchin' a bit a' time to do a bit a' last-minute shoppin'. How's yerself, Ted?

— Strugglin', you know yerself, just back from England for the Christmas.

— How's England?

— England? England's a kip. Have ya time for a pint?

— God, I'd love to, Ted – but to be honest, I really has to get me shoppin' done.

— Sur' look, I'll come along with ya, we can go for de one after.

Now, this wasn't exactly the plan, but what could I say? Anyway I was delighted to see Tragic, hadn't talked to him in years.

First stop the Men's Department Roches Stores for my dad's present. One blue peaked cap. Perfect. No delays. We queued at the cash till.

— So, eh! What do ya think, Ted? I held up the cap.

— Not bad, not bad, but eh, what size is it? he asked.

— Size?

— You know like, is it 7, 7¼, 7½, 7¾, 8, 8¼ …

— Size?

— Like, what size is yer dad's head, Pluto?

— What size is me dad's head? Jesus, Ted, I don't even know the size a' me own head! Tell you the truth, I didn't even know that heads had sizes.

— Well, you'd want to know his head size before you go gettin' him a hat, he said.

I explained I had no time to be measuring my dad's head. All I wanted was a cap to keep him dry for bingo.

— For bingo? Why don't ya get him somethin' like a book, you know, like a book on bingo.

— Do they have books on bingo, Ted?

— They has books on everything.

— A book on bingo, it was settled; we could get it later. I left the cap on the counter and walked out of the shop.

There I was, standing in a checkout line, a mile long in Dunnes Stores, one big box of biscuits and two Cadbury Deluxe selection boxes in my arms.

— So, eh, who are these for anyway, Pluto?

— Me sister Kathleen an' her kids, I said.

Ted gave me one of those looks.

— Somethin' wrong, Ted?

— No, no, not at all. I'm sure your sister'll be delighted.

— But?

— No buts. But eh? I don't think too many mothers would want all that sugar an' sweets comin' into the house, ya know like.

And he was right.

— So eh, what do ya suggest, Ted?

— I suppose you could always get 'em a few books.

He wasn't joking.

I explained that we weren't really a book family. I mean my favourite book is *The Commitments*, but I still haven't read the book, if ya know what I mean. But Ted was making sense. So before we went to the bookshop, I had to get Yvette's present.

Now, I wasn't too happy having Tragic Ted traipsing after me around Brown Thomas's perfumery and Women's Underwear Department. Not the easiest thing for me to be doing on me own, not to mind having Tragic Ted and a langer load a' store detectives in tow.

He talked me out of the perfume, saying that you can't just buy a scent for a woman, it was something more personal than that. Anyway he had me convinced that the biggest insult you could give to a woman, especially a French woman, was to buy her the wrong perfume.

— It's as personal as dogs' piss to a bitch, he said.

So we scrapped the perfume plan and headed off up to the ladies' underwear.

I was glad Ted was with me. I mean like I'm the sort of fella who's too embarrassed to buy condoms, not to mind fingering me way through rows of lace, silk and satin suspender belts, stockings, corsets, bustiers, basques, bras, boob-tubes, seamless, strapless, crotch-less, thongs, G-strings, French-cut, low-cut, half-cup, cotton, camisoles, baby-dolls and teddies – and that was only the first three racks. At the back of the shop I could see the leather, rubber and the odd ostrich feather.

    – And they say men are sex mad!

I looked to Ted. He was busy burrowing his way through the stock.

    – Eh, can I help you, gentlemen?

Her head popped up from behind a rack of bras.

    – No, no we're fine, said I.

    – Don't mind him, said Ted. – We're lookin' for something nice for his girlfriend for Christmas?

    – Does anything catch yer eye? she asked.

    – I push my eyeballs back into their sockets, – Look, anything at all, said I.

    – So, eh, what size would you like?

    – About the same as yerself, maybe a bit fuller in de chest area and keener in de waist. I said

She gave me one of those, – *Men!* looks, and she lifted up a bit of a lacy thing.

    – What about this? she said.

    – That's perfect! said I. – Just, put it in a bag.

    – Hoi, hold it! Hold it! says Ted. – Ya can't just take de first thing that's waved under yer nose, Pluto man. Ye gotta check out de merchandise.

    – Ah, come on, Ted. I just wanna get outa here.

    – Chill out man, now that we're here we may as well do it right. Eh, excuse me Miss? You might show us that one there, like a good girl. Do you have it in red?

. . . and off they went down through the shop. I stood there like an expectant father in a maternity ward. Eventually, my choice was made for me. A nice silk French-cut knickers, with matching lacy brassiere and suspender belt, pink in colour,

    – Nothing smutty like black or red, said Ted. – And two pairs of stockings. One black and one white. Perfect, Yvette would love this.

— So gentlemen, will I gift-wrap it for you?

— Not at all, said Ted. – We'll eat 'em here.

He laughed, she wrapped. And then Ted turned to me.

— Are ya sure 32B is her bra size?

— Well, that's the size of the bra she has at home.

— Yeah! But not all bras are the same.

— How'd ya mean not all bras are de same? A 32B is a 32B, isn't it?

— Ah! For God's, sake! A bra isn't like a sock, Pluto. It's not like one size fits all.

— Look, this is a 32B, and she's a 32B, and no more about it!

I was beginning to get sick of Ted and his advice at this stage.

— 32B or not 32B, that is the question, said Ted. – But have it your own way, and he stepped back.

But he had planted the seeds of doubt in my brain.

— What exactly do ya mean, Ted?

— I'll put it this way, he said. – A 32B, is a 32B, is a 32B, but there's no guarantee it will fit her. Different cuts, fabrics, structures and suspension, 'tis like buying a cover for a two-seater couch, you has to try it on.

— So what are ya sayin', Ted?

— I'm sayin' put 'em back on the rack, and save yerself a bellyful a' heartache, 'cause believe you me, if it's too small, she'll think that you think she's gettin' fat, and if it's too big, she'll think her *Bob-a-lou-ees* are too small.

— Her *Bob-a-whaties*?

— Look! I'd say you'd save yerself a bellyful of grief if ya bought her a good book.

That solved everything, all I had to do was get a few books. So I went to the Hi-B for a pint with Ted. I called a pint. Ted called a pint. Then it was my call again. And that's the way it went for the afternoon.

At twenty to five Christmas Eve, meself and Ted made a mad, staggering dash to Waterstones to pick up a few books, stopping off on the way at Elbow Lane to roll a one skinner.

So that was it, that was the Christmas I bought my dad *The World Book of Anthropology*, Waterstones were clean out of books on bingo. I got my sister and her family an atlas, they'd never been outside Cork in their life. And I got Yvette a book on French cookery. What can I say, Tragic Ted is one right tulip to go shoppin' with …

It was my first Christmas with the beautiful Yvette, and my last …

Plenty More Fish In The Sea

Dedicated to Doireann Ní Bhriain and Andy Pollak
(Ennis Book Club Festival 2016)

D'you know, Sis love,
I just don't know what to say to ya.
I'm not gonna tell ya there's plenty more fish in the sea,
because that's the last thing you want to hear.

But there is though.
There's more fish in that sea than you could shake a stick at.
But no, I'm not going to tell you that.
See, from where you're standing there's only one fish for you.
But out there, out there is a vast ocean, Sis love.
I'm tellin' ya, Sis love.
Swimmin' around in that ocean, ya has every class a' warm-
     blooded, cold-blooded, scaly and slimy article that you could
     think of.

There's flat-fish, blow-fish, jelly-fish, fish with thick shells and fish
     with no backbone.
You got your sharks and your sea snakes and your mullets.
And of course you'll always have the odd octopus
and they stretching out their slimy tentacles pawing at anything
     that passes.

But you mark my word, Sis love.
D'ya hear me?
Any fella,
Any fella that'd leave my sister,
my beautiful Sis, standing there waiting on the side of the street,
Is nothin'.
Nothin' but a fuckin' pollock!

Changing God

Dedicated to the memory of Jimmy O'Sullivan

Historians will swear blind that back around the sixth Century St Finbarr founded Cork, and maybe he did. But the old people on our street tell it differently.

Seemingly, Finbarr set out from Dublin in the footsteps of Patrick. He was heading south to Cork, but along the way, or so they say, he lost his way. He spent six months wandering around the Bog of Allen, living on wild mushrooms and berries. He fought off feral hedgehogs, rabbits and hares. He was eaten alive by midges, stung by wazzies and scarred and blistered from head to toe by gorse, nettle and blackthorn. As my dad put it,

— What that man went through made an eternity in St Patrick's Purgatory seem like a week in Butlin's.

Starving, delirious, and just at that point when Finbarr thought God had forsaken him, didn't he poke his head through a gap in a bush at a place known locally as Finbarr's view. There laid out before him was the majestic, beautiful Lee Valley. His fading eyes focused on a bustling little market town on an island centred in a crystal-clear stream. Finbarr had found Cork.

Or as my dad put it,

— 'Twas a few lads from our street found Finbarr, and he was a lucky man that they did.

Legend has it that the saint spent his first night across the street, where now stands the Ashley Hotel. Next morning, after a good night's sleep in a feather bed and a fine feed of pig's head, they brought the saint up to the top of our street where my friend Jimmy O'Sullivan's great, great, grandfather gave him a cut and a shave.

Because as my dad put it,

- When you're tryin' to persuade people to change something as fundamental as their gods, presentation is half the battle.

Anyway, what I'm getting at is, generations of Creedons have been getting our hair cut by generations of O'Sullivans. As a young boy in short pants I'd arrive into Jimmy's dad, Tommy, with a note from my mam and the strict instructions,

- Let the bone be your guide.

Tommy would bridge the armrests with a plank and invite me to sit up. There is something very comforting knowing that long before I was born my grandfather sat on the very same board.

An intimacy develops between men in a barber shop. It's a place where we congregate without a smoke screen or a glass to hide behind. It's a place where great sporting moments become greater with every re-telling and also-rans are still running. It's a place where heads meet. It's a place where boys become old men and old men become boys again. But above all the barbershop is a place where men talk, and talk is free when treated with the confidentiality of a confessional. And every milestone of my life be it my first day at school, first Communion, first date, first job – has always been marked by a visit to O'Sullivan's barber's chair. It's a bit like a recurring rite of passage.

There is a magic to a relationship that develops over generations, yet ours is a relationship that is seldom explored beyond the confines of the barber's chair. For the most part, Creedons and O'Sullivans only ever see eye to eye in a mirror. Although there was that time, ten, fifteen years ago or so, when totally out of the blue, me and my dad went for a day's fishing with my friend Jimmy and his dad Tommy O'Sullivan. I could ramble on about fishy-tales and the ones that got away. But suffice to say, it was a magical day. One of those you just file away.

And when all was said and done, it was just me and my dad driving home into the setting sun. He was glowing, in full flight. He was telling me all about the day St Finbarr was found in Cork by the lads from our street way back in the sixth Century.

He said that Finbarr came to Cork with a mission: One nation, One people, One God. But back then, we Corkonians had a god for every change in the weather, so Finbarr compromised and offered the Trinity Package.

There was a blissful lull in the conversation as me and my dad just wallowed in the warmth of our company. Then I broke the silence. I asked my him if he thought it had been difficult for Finbarr to convince the people of Cork to change their gods?

— Not at all, says he. – Not at all!

We Corkonians did not change our gods.

We only changed their names.

Follow Your Nose

A sleepy Saturday mornin' on Half Moon Street
and just around the corner? Christmas.
I'm walkin' off a bit of self-inflicted pain,
you know how it is?

Three days on the ran-tan.
Three whole days – drinkin' me seasonal bonus.
You know how it is – when the belly's had a skinful,
the mind is willing – but the body isn't able.
Well, that's how it is.
Just out for a scove – meself on me own,
no particular place to go
Just followin' me nose.

Just follow yer nose?
That's what me grandda used to do.
A great man for followin' his nose was me grandda.
On me mother's soul – he could find his way to work blindfolded.
All the way from his front-door step up on Dublin Hill,
down into the belly of the city – just …
Just followin' his nose.

The first thing that would hit my grandda and he leaving the house
would be the thick country smell of cattle,
from the dealers' fields beyond the grotto in Blackpool.
Led on like a …
Like a bull by the ring, he'd close his eyes and follow his nose.
Past the stale stench of last night's stout and cigarette smoke
from the string of pubs along Dublin Street.
Past the Glen Hall – the full length of Thomas Davis Street.

And with the first hint of crusty bread
coming from the ovens of Healy's bakery
over on Great William O'Brien Street,
he'd know he was at Blackpool Church.

Then that sweet smell of molten sugar …
The shawlies making toffee apples up on Gerald Griffin Street,
would carry him past the oak casks of the distillery

and onto the Watercourse Road.
Ahhh, pleasure …

A pleasure – cut short by the piercing, deathly, toxic,
foul cloud coming from the slaughterhouse off Denny's Lane.
But then, just for a whiff of a second the subtle scent of sherbet,

drifting down from Linehan's Sweet Factory,
would carry him past the putrid pelts of the tannery
and on to the first taste of human waste at Poulraddy.

Turnin' right onto Leitrim Street there'd be no mistaking the warmth
of the moist malt of brewing stout – billowing from Murphy's stack.
He knew then he was on the right track.
So he'd put the hands into the pockets – and whistle.

Whistle all the way from Poulraddy Harbour,
to the Home Farm Stores.
Eyes wide shut.

And though still out of sight – at the corner of Pine Street,
the River Lee and Carroll's Quay would come into scent.
High at low tide.
Low at high tide.

Wouldn't turn left nor right,
but keep on straight to Three Points Corner –
where Devonshire Street, Leitrim Street and Coburg Street melt into one.

He'd stay right on track,
being passed from scent to scent like the baton in a relay race.
Spurred on by the aromatic blending of –
Moore's vegetables, Griffin's shoemakers, Noreen's apple tarts.
Must be Friday 'cause there's kippers in Creedons'.
O'Connell's butchered beef and O'Sullivan's cured bacon.
At Falvey's Corner, he'd stop. Stop dead.
Struck by a tidal wave of fishy smells from the Baltimore Stores,
enough to knock a horse.

And for the first time on his scove, my granddad open his eyes.
Look back at the eastern face of Shandon.
Where half-past seven means twenty-five to eight.
Then turnin' right onto Bridge Street,
the fine wines and exotic spices of Madden's,
would carry him 'cross Patrick's Bridge.
Through the gateway of the city.
All the way to work.
Just …
Just by following his nose.

Cónal with Finbarr on Devonshire Street. Photo: Michael MacSweeney.

Pine Street

It's a city of steps and steeples, more steps and steep hills. And there above the heads of the merchant princes and paupers, the golden fish on Shandon casts a knowing eye over the fish bowl that I call home.

We wake to a dawn chorus; the men of Blackpool and the Red City of Gurranabraher walking and whistling their way up our street and all the way down to the docks and to the Motown of Fords and Dunlops. It's no word of a lie, but Cork is like living in a musical, don't ask me why. Maybe it's the sing-song sound of people talking, or the way we engage in a such an animated way about nothing at all. But sometimes, sometimes it seems as if the whole town might just break out into song without a moment's notice.

Two channels of the River Lee insulate the beating heart of the old city from generations of northside : southside rivalry. Two factions claiming superiority in sport and in song – holding up mirrors to each other, reflecting carbon-copy monasteries, breweries, cathedrals, towers and bridges.

We don't call it the inner city, it's just plain downtown. Home for me is a spaghetti bowl of streets centring on Three Points Corner, where Devonshire Street, Leitrim Street and Coburg Street meld into one. My family have lived and traded here since the Vikings. A busy little shop more social than commercial and bivouacked in various nooks and crannies – my parents, twelve siblings, a clatter of pets and a string of guests who came to dinner and stayed.

Outside the streets were bustling too, with families talking and taking air. Shawl wrapped Mary selling apples on Pope's Quay, Connie the Donkey hawking sawdust for soakage to publicans and to those who butchered beef or cured bacon.

Without a blade of grass downtown, street soccer evolved into a sport all of its own. You'd find us there every day after school, droves of downtown dirty-faces, red faced and roaring, funting a ball up and down Pine Street – every boy, girl, cat and dog chasing an inflated pig-skin like coursing greyhounds. Toddlers tackled teenagers, and the dogs of the street always waiting on the wing to score on the re-bound.

Shep Dorney, a bow-legged black and tan terrier from number-seven, will always be remembered for her sensational equalizer with a diving header. Her snout drove the ball home past the corner of the post, into the back of the goal rattling a clatter of steel shuttering across Smyth's Stores' enough to leave Roy Keane in the shade. And with no set time limit, a game once lasted from June right through to September. The final tally on the score sheet recording the decisive victory: 674 to 453.

But with the death of a child the people of downtown surrendered sovereignty of our streets. Flesh and bone gave way to rubber and steel when blood soaked into concrete and asphalt – a schoolboy's bones were crushed beneath the wheels of a truck. The families moved out soon after that, out to the reservations in the wastelands. Ironically, where once the downtown dirty faces played, now stands a multi-story car park, keeping the car safe from people...

And yet, this morning and I heading down towards the Skeety Bars Steps, I paused awhile at the corner of Pine Street.

In my mind's inner ear, I swore I could still hear the shrieks of downtown dirty faced delight as quarter irons knocked sparks off the road – set a pig skin squealing: rip, roaring, like a rocket, rattling the back of the onion sack, sending shuddering waves along Smyth's Stores' gate.

Soul Of The Savoy

Dedicated to the memory of Fred Bridgeman

Rise up! Rise up!
Fred Bridgeman fingers his organ,
getting a handle on *the Messiah*.
The Legion of the Lost, he will lead the way.
Two thousand souls will go, raise rafters,
sing-songing along at the Saturday matinée.

Raids on ice-cream lady under cover of dark.
Sweet wrappers and chewing gum thicken the air,
like a screen of black snow.
And that's why we go – to the flicks, y'know.

And I'll be dere, if you'll be dere.
But will you be dere dough?

Fred Bridgeman was organist at the Savoy Cinema.
A two-thousand seater cinema situated on Patrick's Street, Cork city.

Pluto's Vision Of Heaven

for Hugh Quillinan

I take Yvette by the hand, and on and on we make our way to the brow of Patrick's Hill. There we stop and look back down into the goldfish bowl. We don't turn to salt.

Yvette tugs my hand and leads the way. We climb the wall at Bell's Field. There before us is a world framed by the salt and pepper cellars of the belfries of St. Anne's and the North Cathedral. My eyes embrace the beautiful northside laid out before us like a kitchen table at Christmas time, crammed packed with dainties and delights, stretching as far as the eye can see and vanishing over the hill at Blarney Street and Knocknaheeny.

— Breathe it in, I say.
We walk through the knee-high meadow and nestle down into a sheltered hollow. We're sprawled there barefoot on a grassy ridge above the city, saying nothing. Bolts of pleasure and pain as my memories travel across Brewery Valley, stopping off along the way at the North Monastery, Eason's Hill, Murphy's stack and land-locked Poulraddy Harbour; past each laneway, step and steeple, from the Bishop's Palace right over to the dome of City Hall. Then all the way back to Redemption Road and over the city to the spiked towers of Holy Trinity, St Finbarr's and the green tops of St Francis.

In the distance the County Hall scrapes clouds, picking up the gold of a dying sun. I gaze out westward, out along the beautiful Lee Valley to the Carrigrohane Straight. There, like a last grasp at life, a setting sun sends flames of red and orange and yellow licking high up into the sky.

View from Bell's Field – painting by Josef Keys.

— Looks like Ballincollig's burning.

My city is a royal town, dressed up in crimsons and gold. In the distance, through the mists of time and coal smoke I hear the cry of an Echo boy, the sound of men walking and whistling their way home from work to the Red City of Gurranabraher, the chimes of an ice-cream van across on Spangle Hill, the bells of some cathedral or other, the yelps of children from Roche's Buildings playing ball along the road.

And as I say good-bye to this city of pain, it occurs to me that there is a harmony of movement and colour and sound. Everything is as one: the aromatic blending of Murphy's brewery, Linehan's sweet factory and Donnelly's bakery ...
Yvette snuggles into me.
     — Dis could be heaven, I whisper.
     — Could be, she smiles. – Could be ...

Photo: John Minihan

Biography

Cónal Creedon is a novelist, playwright and documentary film maker. Appointed Adjunct Professor of Creative Writing at University College Cork.

His novel, *Begotten Not Made* (2018), has achieved literary award recognition: the Eric Hoffer Award USA 2020, the Bronze Award New Generation Book Award USA 2020, Finalist in the Montaigne [Most Thought-Provoking Book] Award USA 2020, Nominated for the Dublin International Book Award 2020. Book of the Year Irish Examiner. Top Books of the Year – Liveline RTÉ Irish National Radio. Other books by Cónal Creedon include, *Cornerstone* (2017), *The Immortal Deed of Michael O'Leary* (2015), *Second City Trilogy* (2007), *Passion Play* (1999) cited as Book of the Year BBC Radio 4, *Pancho & Lefty Ride Out* (1995), *Pancho & Lefty Ride Again* (2021)

Cónal's award-winning plays include; *The Trial of Jesus* (2000), which featured as part of the Irish National Millennium celebrations, received two Business to Arts Awards by President of Ireland, Mary McAleese and was nominated for an Irish Times Special Judges Theatre Award 2000. *Glory Be to the Father* (2001), produced by Red Kettle Theatre Company, Waterford. Cónal's *Second City Trilogy* of stage plays achieved high acclaim from theatre critics in Shanghai, New York and Ireland. *The Second City Trilogy* picked up a number of awards at the 1st Irish Theatre Awards New York, including Best Actor, Best Director and nominated Best Playwright. *When I Was God*, a production from the Second City Trilogy was also awarded Best Actor and Best Supporting Actor at ICA Federation Awards 2014. In 2021 it was awarded Best Production, Best Actor and Best Director at the Irish National Play Awards.

Cónal's film documentaries achieved high critical acclaim, including being shortlisted for the Focal International Documentary Awards UK and numerous broadcasts by RTÉ [Irish National Television] with international screening at Féile an Phobail West Belfast Festival, World Expo Shanghai, China, Origin Theatre Festival New York, USA, the Irish National Centenary Commemorations and at NYU New York University, USA.

Cónal has written and produced more than 60 hours of original radio drama broadcast by RTÉ, BBC, CBC, ABC. Cited as Best Radio by Irish Times radio critics 1996 and 1998.

Recognition for Contribution to the Arts

- Appointed Adjunct Professor of Creative Writing UCC
- Appointed (Covid-Pandemic) Goodwill Literary Ambassador for Cork City 2020
- Awarded Lord Mayor's Culture Award 2020
- Awarded Lord Mayor's Culture Award 1999
- Invited Scholarship Forum, Fudan University, Shanghai, China 2008
- Speaker at James Joyce Foundation/Centre Irish Studies, Zurich, Switzerland 2019
- Speaker 7-City Reading Tour, Irish American Cultural Institute, USA 2008
- Invited Guest of Honour, 10th Anniversary Shanghai Writers' China 2018
- Keynote Speaker Merriman Summer School, Glór, Ennis, Ireland 2015
- Keynote Speaker Daniel Corkery Summer School, Inchigeela, Ireland 2016
- Keynote Speaker Launch Cork Europa Erlesen, Irish Embassy Berlin, Germany 2014
- Appointed Heritage Ambassador for Cork City 2017
- Appointed Culture Ambassador for Cork City 2020
- Nominated Cork Person of the Year 2001
- Nominated Cork Person of the Year 2018

Theatre

1999   *When I Was God* – Red Kettle Theatre Company

2000   *The Trial Of Jesus* – Corcadorca Theatre Company Featured as part of the National Millennium Celebrations. Awarded two National Business to Arts Awards.Nominated for Irish Times Theatre Awards.

2001   *Glory Be To The Father* – Red Kettle Theatre Company National Tour: Waterford, Kilkenny, Cork, Galway, Sligo.

2001   *When I Was God* – Everyman Palace Theatre, Cork, Ireland.

2001   *When I Was God* – Bewley's Theatre, Dublin, Ireland.

2002   *When I Was God* – Madder Market, 3 Cities Festival, Norwich, UK.

2005   *The Cure* – Cork Opera House/ Blood in the Alley Theatre Co.

2005   *After Luke* – Cork Opera House/Blood in the Alley Theatre Co.

2005   *The Second City Trilogy* – Comm European Capital of Culture.

2008   *When I Was God* – USA Premiere [Green Room New York)

2009   *When I Was God* & *After Luke* – (Irish Rep Theatre New York) Awarded Best Director 1st Irish Theatre Awards New York.
Nominated Best Actor 1st Irish Theatre Awards New York.
Nominated Best Production 1st Irish Theatre Awards New York.

2010   *When I Was God* & *After Luke*
Chinese Premiere, Shanghai World Expo.

2010   *When I Was God* & *After Luke* – Cork Arts Theatre. Ireland.

2011   *The Cure* – JUE International Arts Festival, Shanghai. China.

2011   *The Cure* – Halfmoon Theatre. Cork Opera House. Ireland.

2013   *The Cure* – USA Premiere. Green Room Theatre New York.
Awarded Best Actor. 1st Irish Theatre Awards New York.
Nominated Best Playwright. 1st Irish Theatre Awards New York.

2014   *When I Was God* – Fletcher and Camross Drama. ICI Drama Festival.
Awarded Best Actor. ICI Federation Drama Festival Awards.
Awarded Best Supporting Actor. ICI Federation Drama Festival Awards.

2016   *The Cure* – Irish Arts Centre Queens, New York.

2019   *The Cure* – Arlene's Grocery, New York.

Books

2018 *Begotten Not Made* – a novel published by Irishtown Press Ltd.
   – Awarded the Eric Hoffer Award for commercial fiction 2020, USA.
   – Bronze Award in NGBA Book Awards 2019, USA.
   – Finalist the Montaigne Award 'Most Thought-Provoking Book' 2020, USA
   – Listed for the Dublin International Book Award 2020 (to be announced)
   – Shortlisted for Readers Favourite Book Awards 2018, USA.
   – Cited as Best Book of the Year – Irish Examiner.
   – Listed as Books to Read for 2020 – Liveline RTÉ.

2017 *Cornerstone* – Editor of anthology of UCC student writing.
   Published by UCC & Cork City Libraries.

2015 *Immortal Deed Of Michael O'leary* – pub. by Cork City Libraries.

2007 *Second City Trilogy* – a trilogy of internationally award-winning stage plays, published by Irishtown Press ltd. Commissioned by European Capital of Culture 2005. Productions in China, USA and Ireland.
   Awarded Best Director. 1st Irish Theatre Awards New York, 2009.
   Nominated Best Production. 1st Irish Theatre Awards New York, 2009.
   Awarded Best Actor. 1st Irish Theatre Awards New York, 2013.
   Nominated Best Playwright. 1st Irish Theatre Awards New York, 2013.
   Awarded Best Actor. ICI Federation Drama Festival Awards, 2014.
   Awarded Best Supporting Actor. ICI Federation Drama Festival Awards, 2014.

1999 *Passion Play* – a novel cited as,
   – Book of the Year (BBC Radio 4)
   – Book of the Week (The Irish Examiner)
   – Book on One (RTÉ 1 – Irish National Radio)
   – Book of the Week (RAI – Italian National Radio)
   Translated into Italian, Bulgarian with extracts published in Germany, China.

1995 *Pancho And Lefty Ride Out* – a collection of short stories. pub. The Collins Press. Short stories have been adapted for stage, film and radio.
   Short stories have been published and broadcast extensively in newspapers, magazines, literary periodicals and collections.

With translation into German, and China – Cónal's short fiction gained recognition in

– Life Extra Short Story Awards,
– Francis Mac Manus Short Story Awards,
– George A. Birmingham Short Story Awards,
– One-Voice Monologue Awards BBC
– The PJ O'Connor Awards.

Radio Drama

Cónal has penned over 60 hours of original fiction, short stories and plays, for radio. His work has represented Ireland in the World Play International Radio Drama Festival 2000 and was subsequently broadcast on participating networks: BBC Radio 4, ABC (Australia), RTHK (Hong Kong), LATW (USA), CBC (Canada), BBC World Service, RNZ (New Zealand), RTÉ.

1993   *Come Out Now, Hacker Hanley!* (RTÉ Radio)
1994   *After the Ball* (Francis MacManus Awards)
1994   *Every Picture Tells a Story* (RTÉ Radio 1)
1994   *Caught in a Trap* (C.L.R Drama Competition RTÉ)
1994–98
   Under the Goldie Fish (85 half-hour episodes – RTÉ)
   Listed one of Best Radio Programmes in 1996 & 1998 – The Irish Times.
2000   *This Old Man, He Played One* (World Play International Fest.)
2001   *1601 The March of O'Sullivan Beara* (Docu/drama Battle of Kinsale)
2002   *The Cure* (Monologue – RTÉ)
2003   *The Prodigal Maneen* (Awarded the C of I Bursary RTÉ)
2003   Adaptation – *Guests of the Nation* (Frank O' Connor Centenary – RTÉ)
2004   Adaptation – *Tailor and Ansty* (RTÉ Drama)
2004   *Passion Play* – Book on One. (RTÉ Radio)
2005   *Adventure of the Downtown Dirty Faces.* (5 short stories – RTÉ Radio)
2005   *No. 1, Devonshire Street* (BBC Radio 4 & BBC World Service)

TV Documentary/ Film

2010   *Flynnie, The Man Who Walked Like Shakespeare* (Producer/writer/director).
Nominated Focal Documentary Awards. London, UK.

2007   *The Boys Of Fairhill* (Producer/writer/director) Screened RTÉ.

2006   *If It's Spiced Beef* (Producer/writer/director) Screened RTÉ.

2006   *Why The Guns Remained Silent In Rebel Cork* (Writer/director) Screened
RTÉ.

2005   *The Burning of Cork* (Writer/director)
Screened RTE. Cork Archives. Cork City Hall & World Expo Shanghai 2010.
NYU (New York University) USA, West Belfast Festival, Origin Theatre New
York USA.
Public screening as part of the official Irish Government Centenary
Celebrations.

2001   *A Man of Few Words* (Short film produced by Indie Films)
Screened on RTÉ & various film festivals.

1995   *The Changing Faces of Ireland. RTÉ* (co-scripted six-part series)
Screened on RTÉ.

Other

·   Radio presenter for RTÉ & columnist with The Irish Times. 1999–2001
·   Writer-in-Residence Cork Prison 1997
·   Writer-in-Residence Cork County Council. 1998
·   Writer-in-Residence Cork Everyman Palace. 1999–2001
·   Writer-in-Residence Shanghai Writers' Association 2008
·   Writer-in-Residence University College Cork. 2016

Special – Covid Online-Streaming Presentation/Productions

June 2020	Green Room – concert Cónal Creedon and John Spillane – Cork Opera House.
July 2020	Filmed discussion: Story of portrait by Eileen Healy – Crawford Gallery Cork.
July 2020	Féile an Phobail, documentary streamed and interview – Belfast.
Sept 2020	Online film – Flavours of Cork – European Association – SPD – EU.
Nov 2020	The Cure – Online streaming, Everyman Palace Theatre.
Nov 2020	When I Was God – Online streaming, Everyman Palace Theatre.
Nov 2020	After Luke – Online streaming, Everyman Palace Theatre.
Dec 2020	Public Reading commemoration of Burning of Cork – Cork City Hall.
Dec 2020	Screening of documentary – Burning of Cork – Cork City Hall.
Dec 2020	Concert with John Spillane – Everyman Palace Theatre.
Feb 2021	Screening – Burning of Cork – 1st Irish Theatre Festival New York.
Feb 2021	Yan Ge, Museum of Literature Ireland, Dublin. Chinese New Year.
March 2021	The Cure – Online streaming [Covid-19] Everyman Palace Theatre.
March 2021	When I Was God – Online streaming – Everyman Palace Theatre.
March 2021	After Luke – Online streaming – Everyman Palace Theatre.
March 2021	St. Patrick's Day – The Traditions of St Patrick. The Crawford Gallery.
April 2021	World Book Day, with Tina Pisco and Sara Baume. World Book Day.
May 2021	LITREAL: The New Standard. Interviewed by Dr Shasikala Palsamy, India.
June 2021 a.	Cork City Hall, conference: Senior Chinese officials Program 2021, China.
June 2021 b.	Cork City Hall, conference: Senior Chinese officials Program 2021, China.
July 2021	The Writer's Mindset – with Yvonne Reddin. Dublin Ireland.

Reading Tours include

Switzerland	James Joyce Foundation Zurich 2020.
	Centre for Irish Studies Zurich University 2020
Italy	4 city Reading tour Italy – 2001.
	Rome, Florence, Venice, Perugia.
UK	Various reading tours.
	Dylan Thomas Centre – Swansea. 2000.
	Filthy Mcnasty's – London. 2001.
	Madder Market Theatre – 3 Cities Festival – Norwich. 2002.
China	Presented a number of reading tours to Shanghai, China.
	Shanghai International Literary Festival. 2008.
	Fudan Uni. Shanghai, People's Uni. Shanghai, Le Ceile Shanghai.
	2009.
	Shanghai World Expo. 2010.
	Shanghai Jue International Arts Festival. 2010.
	M on the Bund & Shanghai Writer's Association. 2013.
	Guest of Honour – 10th Anniversary – Shanghai Writers' Association 2017.
USA	Irish American Cultural Institute, 7 city coast-to-coast reading tour USA. 2007.
	New York, Albany, Rochester, Omaha, Montana, San Francisco, New Jersey.
	NYU – New York University 2019.
Austria	Sprachsalz Literary Festival. Tyrol Austria. 2014.
Berlin	Launch of Cork Europa Erlesen – Translated by Jurgen Schnieder. 2016.
	The Literaturwerkstatt Berlin festival 2011
Ireland	Numerous readings at literary festivals – Including,
	Keynote Speaker at Daniel Corkery Summer School. 2019.
	Speaker at Merriman Summer School. 2014.

Selection of Reviews

The novel's interior is much indebted to Joyce. The way Creedon combines the child-centred perspective of *Paddy Clarke Ha! Ha! Ha!* with the tough teenage world of *The Commitments* and the domestic cruelty of *The Woman Who Walked into Doors* is ambitious and effective. His exposition of his characters' thought processes owes much to Flann O' Brien's skewed sophistication and Patrick McCabe's scabrous vision as to an earlier prototype of Seán O' Casey's Joxer. Creedon has found a form all of his own.

 C.L. Dallat, Times Literary Review [TLS]

Fathers and sons and the damage done: this is the theme, with variations, of the Cork writer Cónal Creedon's fine plays *After Luke* and *When I Was God*, which can be seen in a nearly pitch-perfect production. Mr Creedon's words are enough to create a world that is at once comic and dramatic, poetic and musical.

 Rachel Saltz, New York Times.

The highlight of last year's theatre in Shanghai came all the way from Cork in Irish playwright's Cónal Creedon's double-header of short plays – powerful, yet punctuated with humour, lyrical and richly colloquial. They were terrific!

 That's Shanghai Magazine [China].

Irish playwrights (from Yeats and Wilde and Synge and Shaw on down to now) are always good going on great, and the latest in that endless chain is all but unknown in America, Cónal Creedon. Unknown no longer, Creedon's short, idiosyncratic *After Luke*, and even shorter, punchier *When I Was God*, comprise a disturbing two-hour double-bill. Idiosyncratic? Bite off any hunk of either work; it's all as chewy as leather yet weirdly digestible. None of this would be unfamiliar to, let's say, D. H. Lawrence, or, for that matter, George Orwell. What hasn't been heard before is the thorny voice of 48-year-old Cónal Creedon of County Cork, Ireland, who, from all reports, is a lot gentler in the flesh than on paper.

 Jerry Tallmer, New York Villager.

They were discussing what should go into the Irish Millennium Time-Capsule. If they are looking for something to represent Ireland, how about Cónal Creedon's *Under the Goldie Fish*? It's so off the wall, that it shouldn't ring true, but the most frightening fact is that it does...

Eilís O'Hanlon, The Sunday Independent.

This is contemporary theatre that plays like the works of a past master. The work of Irish playwright Cónal Creedon, are quite simply a delight, [but] not in an all-sunshine and light way. On a sparse stage on which the characters can only live or die, it lives. Underlying all is a love of language and a keen observance of detail – Creedon is lyrical, and uses rhyme and rhythm, without being showy, and enriches with the Cork colloquial without alienating – Come back soon, you are always welcome on the Shanghai stage.

Talk Shanghai. China. Arts Editor.

As written by Cónal Creedon, such moments resound with wince-inducing authenticity before they are eclipsed by an inspirational twist – words, inflected with the faintly Scandinavian accent of Munster, soar like a bracing breeze off the River Lee.

Andy Webster, New York Times.

Under the Goldie Fish would make Gabriel García Márquez turn puce in a pique of jealousy... Gold card radio with plums on.

Tom Widger, The Sunday Tribune.

I don't know why Cónal Creedon hasn't been produced on Broadway yet. Certainly his plays are as deserving as any recent work from Ireland that has made that cut. In fact, he has more to say, more concisely, than just about any of his dramatic contemporaries.

Cahir O'Doherty, Irish Central New York.

Everyone loves the Irish. It's just a fact. Creedon's script is a rich fusion of melancholy poetry and affable banter. Aidan O'Hare and *The Cure* are a match made in monologue heaven. Its potency lies in the profound ability of the playwright and the actor to connect directly with people. *The Cure* is a truly fine piece of theatre, one that is Irish to its core but anything but provincial in its scope. You couldn't ask for anything more than this.

Smart Shanghai Magazine.

Vigorously sustained by stylish performances and an ingenious script, which marries comedy and pathos with a sure hand. They'll love it. It's impossible not to.

The Irish Times.

Cónal Creedon's *Second City Trilogy* is a significant dramatic achievement. Creedon constructs predicaments for his characters that ring true universally. In three companion pieces that play logically together, the playwright puts a marginal view of society centre-stage, and, with warmth and humour, offers a view of life from the side lines. What ensues is a solid replaying of a classic and timeless family conflict. Taken altogether, the *Second City Trilogy* is an important a landmark in drama, its achievement is to find a theatrical language that can accommodate the poor and depressed Ireland that we have come from, and the new, confusing, complex reality we now find ourselves in. Creedon, director Geoff Gould, and the cast deserve credit not only for offering up an entertaining night of theatre, but for contributing to our understanding of where we have come from and where we are going. Any drama that can do both is indeed worthy of praise.

The Irish Examiner.

Creedon's rootedness in Cork qualifies him to chronicle the transformations that not just Cork City, but all of Ireland, caused by the economic boom of the 1990s – called the Celtic Tiger – and the aftermath. At times it feels Beckett-like, you might think the people are too unusual to exist, but they actually do.

New York City Arts.

It's one of those books where it often feels inappropriate to either laugh or cry, at times surreal, frequently hilarious, often poignant but never, ever dull – The reader enters the twilight zone.

U Magazine.

Creedon can create characters, not just mouthing amusing philosophical meanderings, not just cold abstractions, these are creations of Creedon's great humanity. It is essential that I tell you here that you must finish this book. A wonderful inventive comedy.

The Sunday Tribune.

I imagine there are few things harder to be than a contemporary Irish playwright. Given the theatrical history of the Emerald Isle, its lyric tradition, it must be either a very daring or very foolish individual indeed who steps up to be measured against the likes of the Irish literary pantheon. On the daring end falls Cónal Creedon, author of *After Luke* and *When I Was God*. The two plays are the latter parts of Creedon's seriocomic *Second City Trilogy*, focusing on life in present-day County Cork. Both plays are about the family dynamic, specifically the relationships between fathers and sons. In *After Luke*, two half-brothers, Maneen and Son, share a memory so terrible that it sets them at odds with each other all their lives. In the centre is Dadda, Maneen's father, who does his best to keep the peace but can only do so much. As he sagely says "…when two elephants go to war, 'tis the grass gets trampled."

In *When I Was God*, Dino lives in the shadow of his father's regrets, and under the pressure of his expectations. It's a classic plot, the father using the son to live the life he wished he could have had. To tell the rest would rob the reader of one of the funniest moments of the evening. Creedon's main device in these pieces is repetition. I found myself laughing uproariously as the words stayed the same, but the meaning was in constant shift, each repetition raising the stakes to a beautifully bittersweet conclusion – driving the action and the comedy. Creedon's show holds up very well against the pantheon of Irish theatre, taking chances with some very risky devices. It's a fun night out, and I'd be interested to see the trilogy in its entirety; if the first act is as entertaining as the last two, it would be well worth it.

Peter Schuyler, NY Theatre Review.

The Cure is a dramatic creation that straddles what we once were and what we have become. It examines closely the fracture at the heart of our contemporary experience – scavenging the thesaurus for sufficient superlatives for this fine piece of writing – yes, we liked it. We liked it a lot.

The Irish Examiner.

A one-man show at the Ke Center proves that you don't need a huge cast to produce a hit – their recent collaboration with Irishtown Productions proves that they are on top of their game. Cork playwright Cónal Creedon's gritty soliloquy *The Cure* saw Irish actor Aidan O'Hare command the stage as a man left behind by a racing economy and changing city. Creedon's use of language is dizzyingly attractive. He manipulates repetition to great effect, bringing the opening lines back several times in chilling sonata form. As for the staging, the Ke Centre's stark space was the perfect backdrop for a bleak but redemptive piece of drama.

    Asia City Network, Shanghai, China.

A pair of tenderly drawn plays by Cónal Creedon, set in Creedon's native Cork, probe the tough love and tough hurt – exchanged by men in Irish Families. Both plays – are intimately conceived and performed, tracing in chiaroscuro, the intersection between kinship and machismo.

    New Yorker Magazine.

The Cure is the bittersweet tale of a man who has emotionally lost his way. As with the previous two plays, Creedon explores the frustrations of average lives, to the backdrop of historical happenings in the playwright's hometown. And as with the previous two, the script is lyrical and rich with colloquialism, the melancholy lifted with moments of delightful amusement. ("When the chemistry goes in a relationship, he reflects on marriage and drink, "There's nothing for it but to take more chemicals) – A fine piece of theatre ...

    That's Shanghai Magazine, Urbanatomy Shanghai.

A complex enthralling piece of theatre that boasts the dual achievement of entertaining and educating – a testament to Creedon's shrewd writing skill.

    The Irish Independent.

I got to see *The Cure* at the Half Moon Theatre last night. It is terrific. It's great fun. It's just fantastic. Just so well done by Mikel Murfi. It's a credit to Cónal Creedon. Don't miss this play, you need to go and see it – the cultural highlight of Cork 2005.

    Opinion Line 96fm.

Creedon's great gift seems to be observation, 45 tense, funny and pointed minutes, convincing and memorably skilful. *When I Was God*, is both a treat and a treasure.

    The Irish Times.

This play operated on two levels; it was hilarious but poignant. Creedon's gift is his ability to distil the very essence of his environment. It is this sense of place and people and his gently anarchic view of life which makes his works so deliciously attractive.
The Irish Examiner.

Creedon's play shifts easily between the past and the present, revealing a sharp ear for dialogue, keen eye for observation and a deep affection for his characters as Creedon brings a deft pathos and humour to the tragicomedy of a peculiar father son relationship, a delight that demands to be savoured.
The Sunday Tribune.

BOOK OF YEAR – Highlights of the Year.
Cónal Creedon's recently published novel *Begotten Not Made* is a beguiling tale of tragic Christian Brother who forsook a potential love affair for the cloth having met a young nun on the night Dana won the Eurovision Song Contest.
Collette Sheridan – Highlights of the Year – Irish Examiner.

Selection of – BEST BOOKS OF THE YEAR.
It's a delight to read. Cónal Creedon's *Begotten Not Made*. One of the most peculiar books I have read this year.
Theo Dorgan, Liveline. RTÉ Radio 1.

READERS' FAVORITE BOOK AWARDS USA.
★ ★ ★ ★ ★
This is a work of quirky and conceptual literary fiction. For readers who enjoy fully realized, unusual lead characters, look no further – Cónal Creedon has created what feels like a real person, on whose shoulders we sit as the narration takes us deep into his life and work, his philosophy and his sense of love in moments which are both moving, bizarre and very amusing at times. The harsh backdrop of Irish life clashes beautifully with concepts of heavenly and mortal love, miracles and strange appearances, painting a world which is ethereal in its fairy tale moments yet painfully recognizable and relatable too. I particularly enjoyed the dynamic dialogue, as its pacing really moves scenes along. Overall, *Begotten Not Made* is a highly recommended read for literary fiction fans searching for truly unusual books that keep you thinking long after the last page is turned.
KC Flynn, Readers' Favourite Book Awards.

US REVIEW OF BOOKS.

This book spins a delicious yarn that tips nearly every sacred cow of Christianity– a timely sport in this era of diminished participation in monastic life and the laity's scathing criticism of the Church's sins and shortcomings – all the while spotlighting the archetypal unrequited romance made fresh in the monastic setting. In the backdrop is the soul of devout Irish Catholic culture and the lives of the working-class men and women of Cork who lend a down-to-earth stability to the tale as well as zest and colour. As a bonus, the author includes his fanciful pen-and-ink drawings and tasty stories within the story, such as Sister Claire's retelling of a saga about Mossie the Gardener and his war hero pigeon, Dowcha-boy. This is a plot thread sure to tickle even the most obstinate funny bone, and it specifically lends a magical yet realistic aura to what could have been a far more level, self-conscious story.

Creedon's well-honed, multidimensional cast of characters, his vividly portrayed settings and interiors of 1970s and contemporary Cork, and his measured but lyrical prose nail every nuance of the story arc. The author has ripped open his Irish heart to spill this marvellous pastiche, a real-life creed that must be absorbed with one's heart open wide to the pathos and poignancy of love lost and found, life lived and unlived, and spirituality bound to blind faith or soaring on the wings of perception. Ultimately, Creedon's tour de force pays tribute to an end-of-life journey that paradoxically celebrates the winter of regret and the eye-opening gift of having nothing left to lose.

Kate Robinson, US Review of Books.

I thoroughly enjoyed reading *Begotten Not Made* by Cónal Creedon – it maintains a Joycean flavour throughout the story. The writer's perspective in introducing the reverend brother's intellectual interpretation of authentic Biblical facts is so brilliant that it encourages you to fact check.

Ronald Clifford, Irish American Examiner. New York.

Cónal Creedon's new novel puts a magic-realist twist on the tale of a cleric's unrequited love for a nun. Brother Scully delves back through his analysis of scripture, which has led him to a unique and highly plausible theory regarding the true paternity of Jesus Christ. Inside the covers of *Begotten Not Made*, there unfolds a tale that's part poignant love story and part meditation on the phenomenon of faith, a uniquely Corkonian take on magical realism served up with Creedon's customary flair for colourful dialogue and tall tales – a fairy tale for the 21st Century.

Ellie O'Byrne, ARTS, Irish Examiner.

Begotten Not Made is rewarding, straddling a fine line between pathos and comedy. We see the disintegration of Brother Scully – between the torment of his unrealised love and his unique take on Catholicism, he doesn't believe in the divinity of Jesus and has a theory as to his real paternity. This is a troubled man, literally crumbling into a despairing heap as an elderly man. Brother Scully elicits sympathy despite his obnoxiousness – a hard man to like but Creedon's talent is to draw out the humanity of this demented individual. There is a lot more to this novel than sexual and spiritual frustration – It is funny, and it has real charm. There are elements of magic realism here which give the novel an air of fairy-tale. *Begotten Not Made* is well written, strong on highly amusing dialogue and has a twist that is satisfying, well worth the wait. Like all good art, the local becomes universal with its truths and its understanding of human nature.

Colette Sheridan, Weekend

Last night I finished Cónal Creedon's *Begotten Not Made*. It is multi-layered, funny and touching, at times madcap or magic realist, quintessential storytelling, and has a wonderful and satisfying ending. It's about the unrequited love between Brother Scully and Sister Claire, a novitiate in the convent across the valley from his monastery in Cork city. That spiritual affair began on the night in 1970 that Dana won the Eurovision Song Contest, and it lasts for almost fifty years – their correspondence continues: Scully and Claire send a signal to each other every morning at dawn by quickly switching their bedroom light off and on. That one single act of devotion gives Scully the courage to live out his chaste life. But not all is how it seems. And there is a sting in this tail.

There are several poignant moments in the novel, the most moving of which is when towards the end of their hour or two together in 1970, in the garden, Scully and Claire are faced with a crucial decision. And that predicament, upon which their fates turned, reminded me of that great Cavafy poem, *Che fece... il gran rifiuto* (The Great Refusal)

Cónal has drawn a number of fine pen and ink illustrations to accompany the story which lends a charmingly quaint feeling to the rich reading experience.

Danny Morrison, Director of West Belfast Festival Féile an Phobail.

Begotten Not Made, a multi-faceted fairy-tale which gives a fresh twist to an ancient story – the life of Jesus. The book deftly presents an insight into human frailty:

through the complicated love that arose between Br. Scully and Sr. Claire on the night Dana won the Eurovision. Equal parts hilarious and poignant. The story unfolds as Br. Scully grapples with his existence and his sanity and his unique exploration of the nature of belief. The book is also resplendent with illustrations by the author.

Aisling Meath, The Southern Star.

It's all there in *Begotten Not Made*, alongside the mysteries of the scripture, the alchemy of love, the pathos of life and the legend of a war hero racing pigeon: a picaresque epic that at times dips into the surreal.

Donal O'Donoghue, Books. RTÉ Guide.

Begotten Not Made is incredibly nuanced in that sympathy. Brother Scully is developed far beyond the definitions of his profession, beyond the collar, he is intellectual, emotional, sensitive and troubled. Such nuance is explored intricately in Cónal's classic, conversational style, ranging from profound humour to tinges of sadness and airs of dark comedy. The humour of the novel is colourful in every sense of the word, which Cónal infuses to dramatize the life of Brother Scully's adolescence. These playful anecdotes are threaded throughout the novel giving the lives of the characters depth and sincerity. At the end, the book is really set in that one hour, a feature reminiscent of Joyce.

Liz Hession, Motley Magazine.

What a rollicking good read it is. I have to confess that the Dowcha Boy pigeon business remained my favourite since it is so hilarious. But there were many such laugh out loud moments to be met with exclamation points in the margins. That whole Eurovision conceit was just brilliant. And coming round again and again to the flashing of the dawn lights. Loved the surreal moment when Scully walks off on the beam of light. And the great switcheroo of the ending was terrific. Wonderfully enjoyable book. Thanks a mill', Cónal!

David Monagan, Jaywalking With The Irish.

If there has been a sense that some documentaries on the Hidden Histories series have struggled to fully fill out the one-hour slot available, this was not the case with *Hidden History: The Burning of Cork* (RTÉ 1, Tuesday, 10:15pm). Instead, there was a sense that Neil Jordan (or indeed its own superb director, Cónal Creedon) could

fruitfully be let loose on the story with a twenty-million-dollar budget. Creedon's documentary told far more than just the story of the night of December 11, 1920.
Village Magazine Dublin.

The Boys of Fairhill, Cónal Creedon's documentary which detailed the many accomplishments of 'the boys' in hurling, bowling and dog-racing and pigeon fancying, indeed all the recreations which make a man's life worth living. The previous week Creedon had another erudite and evocative documentary about Cork, *If It's Spiced Beef...*and RTÉ is lucky to have him."
The Sunday Independent.

The impossibly surreal, hilarious and often poignant series, *Under the Goldie Fish*
Evening Herald.

For distinctive flavour, free rein to the imagination and even the odd passionate belief, there may never be a match for *Under the Goldie Fish...*Cónal Creedon's mad, bad, wonderful-to-know daily sitcom-soap... If you like your metafictions, intertextuality and just plain messin' in daily doses – Creedon's yer only man!"
The Irish Times.

Reviews Of Readings by Cónal Creedon

Don't be fretting now about the past gone glories of Irish literary genius since we're lucky to have walking among us Cónal Creedon whom I not only had the personal pleasure of meeting as fellow author in the Sprachsalz festival [Austria] but heard the man read his work. The brilliance was self-evident and undeniable. The audience were in raptures over the beauty of his sentences and rapier-like wit. He writes about the human condition in ways that find you deep down where you just have to laugh and weep. Read this author and your faith will be restored in both literature and life.

Alan Kaufmann. – [Author of: Jew Boy, American Outlaw Book of Poetry].
Sprachsalz Festival Austria, 2016

The members of the Merriman Summer School were utterly enthralled by Cónal Creedon's presentation of a selection of his writings – a presentation that was warm, deeply insightful, and so humorous and entertaining about the human condition. He was by far one of the most able speakers at the school.

William J Smyth, Emeritus Professor UCC. Merriman Summer School, 2015

Cónal Creedon gave a tour de force reading of his work as it applies to the theme of 'love and marriage' at the 2015 Merriman Summer School in Ennis, Co. Clare. The audience reacted to Cónal's brilliant writing.

Professor Linda Connolly, Director Merriman Summer School, 2015

Cónal Creedon's presentation to Rochester in 2008 is still being spoken about. He established an easy and lasting rapport with the audience in his talk, Cork, the Center of the Universe as he shared slides that proved his point with humour and intelligence. It would be grand to have a return visit from this literary giant!

Elizabeth Osta – President of the Irish American Cultural Institute. (IACI) 7-city USA coast-to coast IACI Reading Tour

Cónal Creedon was a massive hit A festival highlight and I hope he will come back.

Pat McCabe – Flat Lake Festival, 2011

Cónal Creedon brought the house down at this year's Flat Lake Festival, any comic would envy the laughs he elicited from the audience.

Eoin Butler-Kennedy – The Irish Times – July 2011

A Humorous Reading Creedon reads from his work … Creedon is a skilful reader, managing to keep the crowd engaged, a challenging feat for many writers who are often able to captivate with the written word and less with the spoken. Creedon is able to capture the simple moments of people's lives with honesty and humour.

The crowd finds his work quite humorous as he speaks of "battling the beast" (a pig) and anecdotes of St. Patrick, Protestantism, Catholicism, Free Masons and other topics worthy of a laugh when written of skilfully. The passage relates the tale of the life, death and funeral of the character's father. "It's a strange thing to carry your father in a box," he reads as detailing the humorous ordeal of trying to carry the father to the funeral in a coffin he himself handcrafted.

Shanghai International Literary Festival. Shanghai City Weekend – Trista Marie
[Lit Review THAT'S Shanghai]

A mention, too, to Cónal Creedon. He is the A No. 1 writer of Cork, in my estimation, and absolutely should be known more broadly internationally; he has the ear for every corner conversation, every magnificent touch of endearing absurdity he encounters. He's known well enough in Ireland but should have longer stilts by far. Find him, try him. He went on for a half hour about his father's years' long construction of his own coffin and had every single mug laughing in stitches – about his father's intricately planned demise. Chalk this whole experience down to the category What I Love Best About Ireland. I mean – that you can dream about a man you never met

David Monaghan – Ireland Unhinged & Jaywalking With The Irish.

The Spring Literary festival [2010] was incredibly successful this year. Aside from the quality of the writers and some of the amazing performances (Cónal Creedon and Martin Espada especially wowed) audience figures were consistently large at each event. We were obliged to move to a bigger venue for the fourth day to avoid breaking fire regulations on overcrowding.

Pat Cotter – Artistic Director Munster Literature Centre, Éigse Literary festival 2010

Cónal Creedon at the Rock on The Fall's Road – stole the show and the hearts of everyone who heard him that afternoon. A highlight of the West Belfast Feile.

Danny Morrison, Director of West Belfast Festival Féile an Phobail

Original publication details and acknowledgements for
Pancho and Lefty Ride Out © 1995

Published by The Collins Press, The Huguenot Quarter, Carey's Lane, Cork.

Text © Cónal Creedon, 1995.

ISBN 189825606

All Rights reserved.

No part of this publication may be reproduced or transmitted in any form or by any means, electronic, mechanical, photocopying, recording or otherwise without written permission of the publishers, or else under the terms of any license permitting limited copying issued by The Irish Copyright Licensing Agency, The Writers' Centre, 19, Parnell Square, Dublin.

The Publisher wishes to acknowledge the financial assistance of The Arts Council/An Chomhairle Ealaíon, Ireland.

Printed in Ireland by Colour Books Ltd., Dublin.

Book Design by Upper Case Ltd., Cork. Typeset by Upper Case Ltd., Cork.

This book is dedicated to all the Lefties of the world, for their encouragement in the face of adversity, especially dearest Fiona.

I would like to thank Connie Pa, Blake, Ollie, Tom McCarthy, Sean Dunne, Austin and Moira, Gerry and Aidan (Fr. Matthew Street), Sylvia (Uppercase), Con Collins and too many others to mention here by name – without whose help and support this collection would not have seen the light of day.

Pancho raised his broken body from the burnt West Texas soil,

— Take my stetson, Lefty. Take my stetson and ride, he whispered.

A posse of thirty men were just beyond that horizon. But Lefty stood fast; he knew the time was near. Pancho slumped lifeless to the red clay with the words,

— Think of me, Lefty, on his lips.

Lefty, loyal to the last, blessed himself, removed Pancho's stetson and replaced it with his own battered sombrero. He mounted up, and with a cry of,

— Ride with me Pancho.

Ride like the wind!

He thundered off alone, across the flat lands towards the Morning Star.

Pancho and Lefty's Last Stand. 1995